Siste

"I just heard something i

"What?"

"Mother is going to look into enrolling us in Betsy Ross next semester and she said that was very soon."

"Good. I'm tired of only looking at your ugly face."

"It's your face, too," I said.

"You don't see it because you don't want to," she said, raising herself on her elbows, "but our faces are not really exactly alike. I'm prettier. When we go to school, you'll see I'm right. I'll have more friends, especially more boyfriends."

"Don't let Mother hear you say that. You'll be in the pantry for days, and I won't come to keep you company through the door."

She lay back again. I was so angry that I didn't think I could fall asleep.

"Don't worry about Mother," she said. "Someday she'll think I'm prettier and nicer, too."

I didn't think there was anything she could say that would hurt me more.

But we were still young.

She would have lots of opportunities to come up with worse ideas.

And she did.

V.C. Andrews® Books

The Dollanganger Family Series
Flowers in the Attic
Petals on the Wind
If There Be Thorns
Seeds of Yesterday
Garden of Shadows
Christopher's Diary: Secrets
    of Foxworth
Christopher's Diary: Echoes
    of Dollanganger
Secret Brother

The Audrina Series
My Sweet Audrina
Whitefern

The Casteel Family Series
Heaven
Dark Angel
Fallen Hearts
Gates of Paradise
Web of Dreams

The Cutler Family Series
Dawn
Secrets of the Morning
Twilight's Child
Midnight Whispers
Darkest Hour

The Landry Family Series
Ruby
Pearl in the Mist
All That Glitters
Hidden Jewel
Tarnished Gold

The Logan Family Series
Melody
Heart Song
Unfinished Symphony
Music in the Night
Olivia

The Orphans Miniseries
Butterfly
Crystal
Brooke
Raven
Runaways

The Wildflowers Miniseries
Misty
Star
Jade
Cat
Into the Garden

The Hudson Family Series
Rain
Lightning Strikes
Eye of the Storm
The End of the Rainbow

The Shooting Stars Series
Cinnamon
Ice
Rose
Honey
Falling Stars

The De Beers Family Series
"Dark Seed"
Willow
Wicked Forest
Twisted Roots
Into the Woods
Hidden Leaves

The Broken Wings Series
Broken Wings
Midnight Flight

The Gemini Series
Celeste
Black Cat
Child of Darkness

The Shadows Series
April Shadows
Girl in the Shadows

The Early Spring Series
Broken Flower
Scattered Leaves

The Secrets Series
Secrets in the Attic
Secrets in the Shadows

The Delia Series
Delia's Crossing
Delia's Heart
Delia's Gift

The Heavenstone Series
The Heavenstone Secrets
Secret Whispers

The March Family Series
Family Storms
Cloudburst

The Kindred Series
Daughter of Darkness
Daughter of Light

The Forbidden Series
The Forbidden Sister
"The Forbidden Heart"
Roxy's Story

Stand-alone Novels
Gods of Green Mountain
Into the Darkness
Capturing Angels
The Unwelcomed Child
Bittersweet Dreams
Sage's Eyes

V.C. ANDREWS®

THE Mirror SISTERS

POCKET BOOKS

New York London Toronto Sydney New Delhi

Pocket Books
An Imprint of Simon & Schuster, Inc.
1230 Avenue of the Americas
New York, NY 10020

Following the death of Virginia Andrews, the Andrews family worked with a carefully selected writer to organize and complete Virginia Andrews's stories and to create additional novels, of which this is one, inspired by her storytelling genius.

This book is a work of fiction. Any references to historical events, real people, or real places are used fictitiously. Other names, characters, places, and events are products of the author's imagination, and any resemblance to actual events or places or persons, living or dead, is entirely coincidental.

First Pocket Books paperback edition November 2016

V.C. ANDREWS® and VIRGINIA ANDREWS® are registered trademarks of Vanda Productions, LLC

POCKET and colophon are registered trademarks of Simon & Schuster, Inc.

For information about special discounts for bulk purchases, please contact Simon & Schuster Special Sales at 1-866-506-1949 or business@simonandschuster.com.

Manufactured in the United States of America

10 9 8 7 6 5 4 3 2 1

ISBN 978-1-4767-9236-1
ISBN 978-1-4767-9245-3 (ebook)

THE Mirror
SISTERS

Prologue

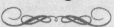

Haylee always blamed our mother for everything that happened to us and everything terrible that we had done to each other—or I should say, everything terrible that she had done to me. Many times as we were growing up, she would tell me to my face that whatever hurtful thing she had done wasn't her fault. It was because our mother wouldn't let her be her own person. I suppose I should have been a little grateful. At least she was recognizing that whatever it was she had done was wrong.

Don't misunderstand me. It wasn't that she was suffering the needle-prick pains of conscience. In fact, I now believe my twin sister might never have felt any despite the agonized look she could put on and take off like a mask. We were not a religious family. Mother never warned either of us that God was watching. She was watching, and she thought that was enough.

I knew in my heart that Haylee was just trying to escape her own responsibility by blaming Mother for things she did herself. No one could shed their guilt like a snake sheds its skin as well as my identical twin. And afterward, she could look as innocent as a rabbit that had just devoured most of the vegetable garden. But that sweetness could turn into a flash of lightning rage when only I was looking at her, even when we were just babies.

One time when we were eleven and our mother wasn't home and couldn't hear her, Haylee stood in front of me with her arms tight against her sides, her fingers curled like claws. She stamped her foot and screamed, "I am not you! I'll never be you! And you will never be me! Whatever you like, I will hate. If I have to, I'll scar my face just to be different. Or," she added, thinking more about it, "I'll attack you when you're sleeping and I'll scar yours."

The cruelty in her eyes stunned me so much I was speechless. She truly sounded as if she hated me enough to do just what she had said. Her threat kept me up nights, and it set the foundation for nightmares in which she would slink beside my bed with a razor between her fingers. To this day, I am certain she did stand by my bed, hovering over me and battling with the urge to act out her vicious promise.

To drive home her point this particular time, she seized the photo of us at our tenth birthday party, the party held in our backyard, where Mother had Daddy arrange for a party tent and had dressed us in identical pink chiffon dresses with pink saddle shoes. Haylee tore the picture into a dozen pieces, which she flushed down the toilet, screaming "Good riddance! If I never hear the word *twin* again, that will be too soon!" She stood there fuming. I could almost see steam coming out of her ears. My heart was pounding because in our house, saying something like that was like a nun declaring she never wanted to hear the word *Jesus*.

If I had any doubt that Haylee could get into a great rage without thinking of the consequences, her tearing up our picture should have convinced me, for how would we explain it not being there in our room, prominently displayed on our dresser? She knew I could never tell Mother what she had done. And she could never blame it on me. It was an unwritten rule, or rather, a rule Mother had carved into our very souls: we must never blame each other for anything, for that was like blaming ourselves.

Even if I did tell, it wouldn't help. Haylee was better than I was when it came to winning sympathy and compassion for herself and justification for any evil or mean act she would commit. I could easily picture her on the witness stand in a courtroom, wringing her hands, tears streaming down her face as she wailed about how much she hadn't wanted to do what she had done to me. She would look so distraught that she might even have me feeling sorry for her.

After she had calmed herself, she would quietly explain to the jury why our mother should be the one accused, certainly not her. She wasn't all wrong. Once I was older, I had no doubt that Haylee would be able to find a psychiatrist eager and willing to testify on her behalf. Even back then, I wasn't going to disagree with her about what our mother had done to us. I wanted to be my own person, too, but I didn't want to have to hate Haylee the way she felt she had to hate me.

Yes, I would blame our mother, too, for what eventually happened to me, just as Daddy would. And I have no doubt that anyone reading this would agree, but despite it all, I still loved our mother very much. I knew how hurt she would be over what Haylee had done and the things she had said. Her heart would suffer spidery cracks like the face of the porcelain doll her father had given her when she was five. I would hold her hand and I would put my arm around her. I would lean my head against her shoulder, and I would cry with her, almost tear for tear, as she moaned, "What have I done to my precious twins? What have I done?"

1

There was nothing Mother worked harder at than keeping us from differing from each other, even in the smallest ways. From the day we were born, she made sure that we owned the exact same things, whether it was clothes, shoes, toys, or books—we even had the same color toothbrushes. Everything had to be bought in twos. Even our names had to have an equal number of letters, and that went for our middle names, too, which were exactly the same: Blossom. I was Kaylee Blossom Fitzgerald, and my sister was Haylee Blossom Fitzgerald. That was something Mother had insisted on. Daddy told us he hadn't thought it was very significant at the time, so he'd put up little argument. I'm sure he regretted it later, as he came to regret so much he had failed to do.

Although neither of us had the courage to

complain about our names, we both wished they were different. By the time we were sixteen, Haylee had gone so far as to tell people she had no middle name. When anyone looked to me for confirmation, I agreed. That was one of those little ways Haylee gradually got me to oppose things Mother had done. I was the reluctantly rebellious twin practically dragged by my hair into the fiery ring of defiance.

Actually, when I think about it, we were lucky to have two different first names. We couldn't be Haylee One and Haylee Two or Kaylee One and Kaylee Two based on who was born first, either. Mother would never tell us who was first, and Daddy hadn't been in the delivery room. He'd been on a business trip. I don't know if he ever asked her which one of us was born first, but I doubt she would have told him anyway. She'd pretend not to know, or maybe she really believed we were born together, hugging and clinging to each other with our tiny pink hands and arms as we were cast out of her womb and into the world, both of us harmonizing in a cry of fear. Whenever Mother described our birth, she always said that the doctor practically had to pry us apart.

"I thought there was only one of you at first. That's how in sync your cries were. One voice," she would say, and she'd look starry-eyed, with that soft smile of wonder that fascinated both Haylee and me when we would sit on the floor in front of her and listen to the story of ourselves. As we grew older, she wove the magical fabric in which we would be dressed, wove it into a fantasy about the perfect twins. There was one rule that if broken would bring about disaster: we had to be loved equally, or some dragon monster would destroy our enchantment.

Daddy wasn't anywhere nearly as obsessed about treating us equally in every way. There was never a doubt in my mind that it was something he believed Mother would grow out of as we grew older. He humored her with his smiles and nods and especially with his favorite response to what she would demand: "Whatever you say, Keri."

He admitted that he was excited about having twins, but at first, he didn't see any additional burdens that other parents of more than one child had. Even as very small children, we could see that he was nowhere as uptight about it, which only infuriated Mother more. During our early years, if he forgot and bought something for me and not for Haylee, or vice versa, our mother would become so upset that, in a violent rage during which I would swear I felt a whirlwind around us, she would tear up or throw out whatever he had bought. Haylee felt the whirlwind, too, and, watching Mother, we would cling to each other as tightly as we supposedly had the day we were born.

There was simply no excuse Daddy could use for what he had done that would satisfy her. For example, he couldn't say one of us liked a certain color more or was more interested in something and he had just happened to come upon it during his travels, like someone else's father. Oh, no. Mother would look as if she had accidentally put her finger in an electric socket and would tell him he was wrong and had done a terrible thing.

In his defense, he pleaded, "For God's sake, Keri, this isn't a capital offense."

"Not a capital offense?" she fired back, her voice shrill. "How can you not see them for what they are?"

"They're little girls," he declared.

"No, no, no, these are not just two little girls. These are perfect twins. They see the world through the same eyes, hear it through the same ears, and smell it through the same nose."

He shook his head, smiling but concerned. I looked at Haylee. Was Mother right? To anyone watching us, it did look as if we liked the same foods, the same flavor of ice cream, the same candy. It was true that when we were very young, anything one of us liked, the other did, too, and anything one of us hated, the other hated. Maybe we felt we were supposed to or we would lose our mystical powers. Nevertheless, Mother was shocked Daddy didn't realize that.

"I think you're exaggerating," Daddy told her.

"Exaggerating? Are you in the same house, Mason? Do you see your own children?" she asked him in what, even as a young girl, I thought was a terribly condescending tone. She sounded more like she did when she chastised us.

Mother also had a habit of smacking her right fist against her right thigh when she started her responses to things that upset her this much. Sometimes, she did it so hard that both Haylee and I would flinch as if we felt the blows. After one of her more dramatic outbursts, I saw her thigh when she was getting ready to take a shower. It had a bright red circle where she had pounded it. Later it turned black-and-blue, and when Daddy mentioned it, she said, "It's your fault, Mason. You might as well have struck me there yourself."

Finally, Daddy always managed to stammer an excuse, but he still couldn't ever get away with "I'll buy the other one something tomorrow." Whatever it was that he had bought one of us and not the other, it was gone that day, no matter what he had promised. Sometimes he would take it back and have his secretary return it to the store, but most times, after Mother had destroyed it or thrown it out, he would go back when he could and buy two this time, so he could give both of us whatever it was he thought one of us had wanted. He never looked happy about it. That satisfied Mother, though, and brought what Daddy called "a fragile armistice where we tiptoed on a floor of eggshells." We were all smiles again. Our pounding hearts relaxed and the electric sizzle in the air disappeared, for a while anyway.

In our house, stings, burns, and aches ran around just behind the walls and just under the floors like termites. Haylee and I were in the center of continuous little tornadoes. Sometimes I thought Haylee did things deliberately so she could see these storms brew between Daddy and Mother. It was one of the differences I sensed early between us. Haylee had an impish delight in causing little explosions between our parents.

But she was far from the main cause of it all in the beginning. It wasn't difficult to understand why this turmoil was happening around Haylee and me. In our mother's mind, a minute after we were born, all thoughts about one of us had to be about the two of us simultaneously. She claimed it was practically blasphemous to do otherwise, because the biggest danger for any parent of identical twins was that somehow, some way, he or she would favor one over the other and destroy the confidence of the one not favored.

It was one thing to praise one of your children because he or she had done something spectacular. Everyone knew stories about fathers who favored one son over another because he was a hero on the football field or got good grades. The same was true for a daughter who might please her mother more by being more responsible, being talented in music or art, or maybe just being prettier.

But none of this could apply to identical twins, not in our mother's way of thinking.

According to Mother, Haylee had no talents that I didn't have, and I had none that she didn't have. Certainly, neither of us could be prettier than the other. Our voices were so similar that people never knew which one had answered the phone. Even Daddy was confused sometimes when he called. There was always a question mark in the air first. "Haylee? Kaylee?"

When we were a little older, Haylee often pretended to be me on the phone. I think she worried that Daddy liked me more and wanted to see how he would speak if he thought I was the one answering the phone. I suspected he did like me more than he liked her, and she knew it. Once she said, "If he doesn't know which one of us it is, he'll say your name because he hopes it's you." I didn't know if she was right. I didn't keep as close a count as she did.

Maybe it was simply because he wasn't around us as much as he should have been, but if I suddenly came upon him while he was reading or if Haylee did, Daddy would look at whoever it was, and his eyes would blink for a moment as his mind settled on which one of us was there. Anyone could see that he was struggling with it because Mother had him terrified about calling me Haylee or calling her Kaylee. Mother insisted that he must know which of us was which.

After all, how could our own father not know us? He agreed, and when he did get it wrong, he blamed himself for not concentrating or paying attention enough. However, he admitted that there were times when he was actually mistaken even though he was concentrating.

"They're so alike!" he cried, hoping to be excused when Mother blew up at him for it, but all that did was prove her point and make her even more obsessive about how we were supposed to be treated.

"Of course they're so alike. That's always been my point. You have to try even harder, Mason, and be more careful about it," she told him. "You never liked it when your father called you by your brother's name, and you weren't even twins. He is two years older than you are, but how did you feel, Mason? Go on, confess. You felt he was thinking more of him than he was of you, right?"

Daddy had admitted that to her once, so what could he do but retreat with the look of a punished puppy? I always felt sorrier for him than I did for us. Sometimes I pretended I *was* Haylee if he called me that, just so he would get away with it, but if

Mother was there, that was impossible. She never made a mistake. I never knew why not, except to think that it was true that mothers knew their children better.

There were so many rules of behavior toward us that Mother laid down, with the power and importance of the U.S. Constitution, our own Ten Commandments:

Thou shalt not call Haylee "Kaylee," or vice versa.

Thou shalt not buy one a gift you do not buy the other.

Thou shalt not take one somewhere and not the other.

Thou shalt not kiss one without kissing the other.

Thou shalt not hug or hold the hand of one without hugging or holding the hand of the other.

Thou shalt not say good morning or good night to one without saying it to the other.

Thou shalt not ask one a question you do not ask the other.

Thou shalt not introduce one to someone without introducing the other.

Thou shalt not tell one a story without telling it to the other.

Thou shalt not smile at one without smiling at the other.

Because of all the rules, I often thought our house was more of a laboratory than a home. I think Daddy did, too. Even Haylee admitted to feeling as if we were under observation in a glass bubble while strange new experiments on bringing up identical twins were being conducted. Many of Mother and Daddy's friends often also seemed to believe that. I once heard someone whisper that maybe Mother was giving reports to a special government agency. I know that, like me, Haylee felt this all made us seem strange to anyone who witnessed our upbringing. There were other twins in our community, even on our street, but they were not identical, and they seemed no different from kids who had no twins. They were permitted to wear different clothes and do different things, and their mothers weren't so uptight about potentially devastating personality complexes.

But our mother would point or nod at them and say, "Look how competitive their parents have made them. They enjoy making each other feel bad. You'll never do that," she would add with a confident smile. "You will always consider each other's feelings first." She had no idea about what was coming, crawling along on the tails of shadows toward our home and our family as we grew older.

It was difficult, if not impossible, not to feel that we really were unique, and not just because we happened to be identical twins. Haylee liked to think we did have special powers, and for a long time, I believed it, too. We looked so alike that we could pretend we were looking in a mirror when we looked at each other. In fact, we rehearsed facing each other and moving our hands to points of our faces as if we were looking into a mirror. Mother's friends would roar with laughter, and Mother would look very proud when she had them over for a lunch during our younger years.

"They're so perfect," she'd whisper, her eyes fixed on us. "So perfect, down to every strand of hair."

She would seize our right hands and turn them up so others could see our palms and then say, "Look at the lines in their hands, how exact they are in depth and length. Not all identical twins are this exact," she'd explain.

Both of us did have some sense of difference simmering inside, though, and it grew stronger, of course, as we got older, despite Mother's efforts to smother it. It was destined to boil over, but in Haylee before me. Mother seemed unable to imagine that. She was so confident that she was right about how we would grow up and treat each other.

I was convinced that she truly believed that Haylee and I had the same thoughts simultaneously. If one of us asked her a question, she would immediately look at the other's face to see if the same question was on her mind. Whether it was or not, she assumed it was. Daddy never did, but she was quick to point out how we both laughed at the same things on television and looked sad at the same sad things and wondered about the same things.

"Remarkable," she would say in a loud whisper.

She often surprised us like that, commenting on some ordinary thing we had done together and giving us the feeling that it wasn't ordinary after all. Daddy would look at us again to see what she saw. Sometimes he would nod, but most of the time, he'd shrug and say, "It's not unusual, Keri. Kids are kids," and he'd go on reading or doing whatever he had been doing. More than once, I caught Mother smirking at him with great displeasure when he did that.

I often wondered why Daddy didn't think we were as special as Mother thought we were. Did that mean he loved us less? Why wasn't he as afraid of any differences we might show? In fact, whenever he could, especially when Mother wasn't watching or listening, he encouraged them, and because of that, Haylee loved him more. But I never believed he loved her more than he loved me, which was what she often claimed.

It wasn't easy for him to applaud our differences. Keeping us similar was so important to Mother that we were hardly ever alone when we were very young. It seemed she was always there hovering over us, watching carefully, eager to pounce as soon as one of us began to do something different from the other. If I reached for a cracker and she saw me do it, she would hold the box out to Haylee, too.

"I don't want one," Haylee would say.

"You will in a moment," Mother would tell her, as if only she could know what either of us really wanted. It didn't matter if Haylee wanted one just then or not. She was getting one because Mother insisted.

If Daddy was present, he would say something like "Why don't you just let them eat when they're hungry, Keri?"

"She's hungry," Mother would reply. "I know when she's hungry, Mason. Do you cook for them? Do you know what they like and don't like?"

He'd put up his hands like a soldier surrendering.

The same rule applied to me if Haylee reached for something or wanted something, but I saved trouble by reaching for it, too. As soon as I did, Mother would smile at me, her worried face opening like clouds parting for the sunshine.

"See?" she would say if Daddy was there.

Haylee often noticed how pleased Mother was with me and looked upset. It was as though she was keeping track of how many times our mother smiled at each of us, adding up the points we earned to prove whom Mother would eventually love more. I tried to impress her with how important it was to Mother so she wouldn't think I was doing it to make her look bad or to make myself look better, but Haylee never believed me.

"You want her to love you more, Kaylee. Don't say you don't," she told me.

Maybe I did, but I knew Mother wouldn't let herself do that. She was too strict about how she interacted with us.

I claimed I remembered Mother changing my diaper whenever she had to change Haylee's and her doing the same for Haylee whenever she had to change mine. Maybe it was something Daddy had told us, but the images were very vivid. It still seemed to be true as we grew out of diapers. Neither of us could wear anything fresh and clean if the other didn't. If Haylee ripped something of hers and Mother was going to throw it out, she'd throw out mine along with it. Haylee often got her clothes and shoes dirtier than I got mine, but mine were always washed along with hers anyway.

How many times did Haylee have to eat when I was hungry, and how many times did I have to eat when she was hungry? It got so we would check with each other in little ways before crying out, reaching out, or even walking in one direction or another. If Haylee wasn't ready to go or to do something, I didn't, and the same was true for her. We both knew instinctively that it was the only way we could protect ourselves from doing things we didn't want to do.

Mother didn't realize that we were doing this deliberately or why. Instead, she would always point out our mutual requests and actions to Daddy to prove her theory that we were unusually alike.

"Don't you see? Can't you see how remarkable they are?" she would ask, frustrated at how calmly he took it all in. He'd shrug or just say, "Yes, remarkable," but I could see he wasn't as convinced about it as she was. Maybe he saw how she was often causing us to do things simultaneously, but he hesitated to question her about it, even though I could see him scrunch his face in disapproval. Sometimes he tried to be humorous about it and say something like "Hey, Keri, guess what? They only need one shadow." He'd laugh after he had said something like that, but she never laughed at his jokes about us and soon he stopped trying.

He never really stopped complaining, though. I remember Daddy claiming that I was able to stand and walk long before Haylee could but that Mother wouldn't let me. He said he suspected she would push me down to crawl until Haylee took her first steps. Then, and only then, would she announce our progress to him.

Once, when they were arguing about us, I overheard him tell her that he had seen her breastfeeding many times, one of us at each breast and stopping if one was satisfied, no matter how the other cried.

"It has nothing to do with hunger. You don't

know anything when it comes to that sort of thing, Mason. You're just like any other man."

But from the way he kept questioning her about things she had done with us, I could tell he was growing more skeptical. None of that mattered to Mother, though. She would act as if she didn't hear what he was saying. Once he dramatically turned to the wall and complained, but she ignored him and didn't laugh at all. For Daddy, it was like being on a boat that was sailing toward a storm in the distance but being unable to change direction.

There were just too many things Mother would do with us that annoyed him. Eventually, he complained more vigorously about things that he thought were more serious. If Haylee or I had a cold, she always gave cough medicine to both of us. Daddy objected loudly to that, but Mother assured him that whichever of us seemed fine would soon catch the same cold. "An ounce of prevention is worth a pound of cure," Mother declared.

Often, Haylee would begin to cough when I did, but I couldn't help suspecting that she was just imitating me to make Mother happy and earn those love-me-more points.

"Don't you see what a wonder they are?" Mother would say to Daddy when he didn't react enough to please her after she had told him about something we had done together. Nothing seemed to frustrate her more.

"They're a wonder to me no matter what," he would say, but she would shake her head as if he was too thick to understand.

Sometimes he would try to seem more excited just to please her. Then he would reach to hug us. I saw how he always looked to Mother first so she would see that he was going to lift us both, hold us for the same amount of time, and not favor one of us over the other with his kisses and hugs. That pleased her. She would smile and nod as if he had passed some sort of test. Keeping the peace was obviously the most important thing to him, even more important than standing up for Haylee or me if either of us did something different, something original.

When I was old enough to understand him more, I realized that he wanted his home to be a true sanctuary, a place he could come to in order to escape the pressures and conflicts he had to endure in his work. Sometimes when he came home and I was there to see him first without him knowing, I would see him close his eyes and take a deep breath, as if he had finally reached fresh air. No wonder he let Mother get away with as much as she did when we were younger.

Of course, we had been too young to know what they said about us when they were alone, but later, when we were older, I understood that right from the beginning, Mother often instructed

Daddy about how we were to be treated, especially how he was to talk to us, hold us, walk with us—in short, love us. Loving your children was supposed to be something that came naturally to a father or a mother. It wasn't something that had to be taught. I knew he thought this, but he never came out and said it, at least not in our presence.

Daddy never stopped trying to get Mother to loosen up when it came to us. For our first birthday and every one thereafter, Mother made us each a cake so we would have the same number of candles and one of us wouldn't blow out more candles than the other.

"Don't you think you're carrying this too far?" Daddy would ask from time to time, especially about the birthday cakes. That could set her off like a firecracker and threaten to ruin our birthday celebrations. Those hands of surrender would go up, and he would step back like someone asked to step off the stage and become simply an observer, maybe a student in a class on how to treat special twins.

In fact, when we were old enough to understand some of what she was telling him, we would also listen at the dinner table or in the living room when she was reading to Daddy from books about bringing up identical twins. She did sound like a teacher speaking to a student. It wasn't as clear to us when we were very young that she was talking about us, of course. Sometimes, even after we realized it, it still felt as if she was talking about other children. We would sit there listening and when she paused, Daddy would look at us closely as if to confirm that we were the girls she was describing.

I shouldn't have been surprised at how accommodating Daddy was when it came to her instructions regarding us. It wasn't easy for anyone to challenge her. Mother was an A-plus student in high school and college. Like Daddy, she had graduated with honors. When they first met, he was majoring in business, and she was heading to law school. Daddy admitted that no one could research anything better than our mother. That's why she would be a very good lawyer. In those early days of our upbringing, she simply overwhelmed him with facts, statistics, and psychological studies of children. She'd hand him the books or the articles she had culled and tell him to read them for himself.

"That's all right, Keri," he would say. "I'll take your word for it. I've got plenty to read as it is."

Even so, I caught him gazing at articles from time to time, reading the sentences Mother had underlined. She left them around the house deliberately, I thought, especially near where he sat. When I was older, I tried to read them, too, but Haylee thought they were boring. After all, they didn't have her name in them. Mother knew Daddy was glancing at them at least and would make references to them when he started to question something she was doing. It was enough to stop him, even in mid-sentence.

However, they weren't always arguing about us. No matter what Daddy really thought about how she was raising us, both Haylee and I were always impressed with how much Daddy respected Mother and how much she admired him, at least when we were younger. When she wasn't angry at him for something, she treated him as if he were a movie star who just happened to be living in our house. He was a handsome, light-brown-haired, athletic six-foot-one-inch man with what Mother called "jewel-quality crystal-blue eyes, eyes that help his smile stop clocks."

I didn't understand what that meant, and when I didn't understand something, Haylee certainly didn't, either, although most of the time she would pretend she did just to make Mother happy and pile up those love-me-more points.

"How could a smile stop a clock?" I asked.

"Yes, how could his smile stop a clock?" Haylee quickly repeated. She didn't like me being first with anything, especially questions.

"It means he is so stunning that even time itself has to pause to appreciate him," she explained, but we both still had puzzled expressions on our faces.

Haylee looked at me, worried that this had helped me understand but not her. It hadn't. We were too young yet, but Mother didn't elaborate any further, except to say, "That's why I fell in love with him. I was always very particular about boyfriends." She laughed and kissed us and said, "Don't worry. Someday you'll know exactly what I'm saying. Both of you will have lightbulbs go off in your heads simultaneously."

That was her big word for us, *simultaneous*.

Everything we did had to be done at the same time, and she literally meant the exact same moment. She was so positive about this and made it so important to us that we both worried that we were doing something terribly wrong if one of us did something without the other, even when she wasn't watching us.

"I'm warm," I might say, and indicate that I was going to take off my sweater. I could see Haylee thinking about it. Even if she wasn't warm, too, she would nod and start to take off hers. And the same was true for me whenever she began to do something I hadn't thought of doing. If Mother happened to see this, she would smile and kiss us as if we had done something wonderful.

"My girls," she would say. "My perfect twins. Haylee-Kaylee, Kaylee-Haylee."

Were we really perfect? In the beginning, Haylee liked to believe it, but gradually, as we grew older, Mother let go of "my perfect twins" and replaced it with "my perfect daughter," which made it sound as if we were halves of the same girl.

It was reasonable to accept that every young girl would want her mother to believe that she was perfect. What Haylee never understood was that it was true for every mother except ours. Ours didn't see one of us as perfect without the other.

How sad and troubling was the realization that substituting one word, *daughter* for *twins*, would bring about so much pain and unhappiness for Haylee and me.

And eventually, even for Mother herself.

But by then, it was far too late.

2

Whether it was for our love-me-more points or not, it was always very important to both of us that we please Mother and win her approval of everything we did. She never stopped telling us that she loved us both equally and that everyone who knew us did as well. However, both of us knew in our hearts that someday someone, maybe many people, would love one of us more than the other. I believed Mother when she told Daddy that was going to be the most painful thing of all for us. In fact, because of the way she described it, it frightened me a little.

Would Haylee hate me if I was eventually more popular than she was? Would I hate her? Was envy more deadly in identical twins than it was in anyone else, as Mother believed? From the way Mother brought us up and the things she told us about ourselves, it was easy for us to believe our emotions were different from those of other girls our age. We supposedly felt everything more deeply because we shared so much in our hearts. Therefore, our emotions were doubly strong.

"No one could ever be as sad or as happy for a sister or a brother as you are, and this will be so forever and ever. The things you do to and for each other will always be unusual compared with others your age. But don't ever let the others make you feel weird. Most of the time, they'll wish they had inside them what you have.

"When you are older and someone favors one of you more, perhaps falls in love with you, it will be a deep cut that will mend only when the other one finds the same affection," she predicted.

I wondered if I would be afraid to fall in love first. I didn't think Haylee would fear it. Actually, I didn't think Haylee believed half the things Mother told us.

Although Daddy was obviously unhappy with how Mother was raising us and what she was teaching us about ourselves and how others viewed us, I couldn't help thinking she was only trying to make us stronger so we could deal with the things that were going to happen to us simply because of who and what we were. If we didn't listen to her and obey her, our lives would be full of pain and disappointment, just as she predicted.

Maybe that was why Mother was so careful about where she took us and whom we would meet. We didn't have any real friends until we were in our private grade school. If other mothers suggested having us to their homes to play with their children or bringing their children over to play with us, Mother would simply say, "Thank you, but they're not ready yet."

Daddy overheard Mother say that on the phone one night to Laura Demarco, who lived about a half mile away on our street. Her daughter, Candace, was our age. We had met her and her mother a few times at the mall. Both Haylee and I would have loved to go to her house. We were very curious about other children. There was so much about the "outside world," as Mother called it, that we longed to know.

"What do you mean, 'they're not ready'?" Daddy asked Mother as soon as she had hung up. "It would be good for them to mix with other kids before they enter school, don't you think, Keri?"

"There'll be time for them to pick up other kids' bad habits," she replied dryly.

"What bad habits? They're too little to have bad habits."

"Oh, you're so ignorant when it comes to children, Mason. I know what I'm doing. These are the formative years for any child, especially ours. It's best not to confuse them."

"Confuse them? With what?" he asked more emphatically. He glanced at us. By now, I could see he didn't like to be reprimanded or disrespected in front of us. We were old enough to understand, and I thought it embarrassed him.

We both sat entranced, waiting for Mother's response. How could playing with another girl our age ruin us?

"With their identity, for one," she said. "And all the good habits I'm inculcating."

Daddy grimaced. "Their identity?"

"Their special identity," she corrected. "Other children won't understand how important it is to keep them balanced."

"Balanced," he repeated, shaking his head. "So when will they be ready?"

"I'll let you know," she said. There was that judge's gavel coming down again, case closed.

Daddy left the topic for another day, which was pushed further and further into the future. Haylee and I were disappointed that Daddy didn't try harder for us. We were hoping he would win this argument. But he never won any.

Yet I never believed that Daddy was not as interested in our upbringing and care as Mother was. She convinced him that she had made the greater personal sacrifice once we were born. She had decided not to pursue her legal career and often reminded him of that. She said that if there had been only one of us, she would have eventually hired a nanny and continued with her education and her part-time work as a paralegal.

"I would have agreed to that anyway," Daddy said, "twins or no twins."

Mother would have nothing to do with such a thought.

We'd often sit on the floor listening to them discuss us as if we weren't right there. Or at least I did; Haylee was bored with their arguments about us.

"I thought by now you understood, Mason. Identical twins are a true phenomenon," Mother declared. "They require very special care and nurturing, especially ours, because they are extra special. Besides, it was a blessing to have two of the same. It's a double joy, and if God is going to be so good to me, I have to live up to the gift and be doubly attentive and twice as unselfish."

How could Daddy argue with that, even though he was still trying to get her to be less intense about how we were to be raised? "I understand, but we all have to be a little selfish in order to survive, to keep our marriage healthy, don't we, Keri?"

My ears perked up at the word *selfish*. It was a word Mother treated as profanity. Neither Haylee nor I could ever be selfish. We were to always think of each other first. Why was it all right for Daddy to say they should be selfish?

"Of course, we should think of each other, but

the children and their needs come first. Don't you believe that?" Mother tossed back at him.

"Yeah, sure," Daddy said.

"Sometimes I wonder if you do," she said.

He threw up his hands in surrender and retreated to his little corner of peace and quiet, as he did most of the time. I was disappointed because I still didn't understand what he meant by *selfish* and wished they had argued more. How could it ever be good to be selfish? I wondered for the first time if Daddy really was happy we'd been born.

There was no doubt that Mother did more for us and sacrificed more. She was far from selfish. When she had given up college and her intention of becoming a lawyer for a while, if not for good, she had dismissed the housekeeper and taken on the housework herself. She relented while she was nursing us and permitted a maid, Mrs. Jakes, to come in once a week. She was a woman in her early sixties who had lost her husband and whose own children lived far away. At least, that was what we were told. I remember she had curly white hair and bright cerulean eyes that looked too young for her face and made her smile soft and warmer than those of most women her age. She was fascinated with us, but Mother had her doing mostly housework and very little with us.

Once we were able to do most things for ourselves, Mother let Mrs. Jakes go. In my heart, I thought it was really because she wasn't treating us with equal attention enough to satisfy Mother. She favored me more, talking mostly to me. Haylee didn't like her, maybe for that reason. When Haylee complained about Mrs. Jakes, Mother looked at me to see if I would object. I didn't, because in a weird way, even then I understood that Mother would blame me for letting someone favor one of us more. I even felt a little guilty about it. For that reason more than any other, she didn't want to bring anyone else into our home to do housework.

Even though we could take care of our basic needs, Mother still could have used the help. We lived in Ridgeway, a very upscale community outside of Philadelphia, and had a large, two-story house with a double gable. It had complex rooflines, and the siding was a mix of oiled cedar board and clapboards painted gray-green, which Mother thought played well with the natural surroundings. On the first floor, we had what Mother called the great room, along with the kitchen, its dining nook, and our dining room. The walls had rustic-grade butternut paneling and walnut floors with classic painted trim. There were soaring fir ceilings in the great room, and we had a screened porch. The great room had a large stone fireplace. Everyone who came to our house loved it for its warmth and complimented Mother on her decorating skills. Between the house and us, she didn't have time for much else, which I eventually realized was why Daddy complained. He felt neglected.

More and more, he pointed out how little they were doing with their friends and how many events they had missed. She found fault with every babysitter she hired, even Mrs. Ramsey, who was a retired schoolteacher, and sweet old Hattie Carter, a sixty-four-year-old grandmother herself who could whistle "London Bridge Is Falling Down" or "Puff the Magic Dragon." Mother was suspicious of everyone they hired and everyone who came into contact with us. When she came home after going out, the first thing she would do was come to our room and question us about the sitter, seeking a reason to classify her as inappropriate, especially for us.

"We haven't gone to a movie in months," Daddy told her, "much less enjoyed a quiet dinner together."

"We'll do all that when they're older," Mother told him. "It's difficult to get the proper kind of babysitter."

"Other people don't have so much trouble with babysitters, Keri."

"We're not other people. Other people don't have what we have!" she exclaimed, her eyes looking as if they would pop.

The dwindling of their social activities was another battlefield from which Daddy retreated. That was probably why he devoted more time to his work and our property. He had continued to develop it years after he and Mother had bought it, but about two years after we were born, he stopped. The property was nearly five acres, and he once had plans to build a lake.

Daddy had almost become a professional tennis player. He was a star on his high school and college teams, and he had a beautiful clay court built almost as soon as they bought the house. Sometimes Mother played with him. We sat on the bench and watched. We weren't quite five yet when Mother bought us tennis outfits and tennis shoes. Neither of us could hold a racket well, but I could hit the ball better than Haylee. Maybe that was why Mother discouraged Daddy from teaching us any fundamentals.

"They're not ready," she said. "They're too little, and their muscles and bones are just developing. It might even damage them."

"You can't keep saying they're not ready, Keri. I was hitting a ball at their age," he said.

"That was you. The usual rules don't work with identical twins. Everything has to be special, Mason."

"Everything?"

"Everything," she said, as firmly as usual.

Daddy smirked at that, but he didn't spend any more time teaching us about tennis. Mother always had a reason Daddy shouldn't do something with us. I think that was why he stopped trying after a while.

When Daddy and Mother played tennis, it didn't seem to me that either one of them was having fun. Sometimes Daddy let Mother win or kept their scores close. She wasn't that bad herself and was always quite a competitive person, but it was easy to see how good Daddy was, how gracefully he moved. Mother hated losing to anyone, even to Daddy, and I was sure he knew it. There was no limit to how far he would go to keep the peace. When I was older and looked back, I wished he hadn't thought peace was more important than we were.

Mother was a better swimmer than he was. When he was home early enough during the summer and joined us at the pool, she often challenged him to a race, and she always beat him. She looked at us and cried, "See, girls? Men aren't as superior as they'd lead you to believe."

"Yeah, yeah," Daddy said. "I know. We're all egotists. Women don't take selfies and pamper themselves."

Mother just smiled, as if Daddy was too ignorant to realize what she had known years ago. Daddy could roll his eyes and throw up his hands, but he never got the better of her, and sometimes his face turned crimson and his jaw tightened in frustration.

Both Haylee and I were very impressed with Mother—and not just because she was our mother. As far as we were concerned, besides knowing so many things, she was one of the prettiest women in the whole world. We knew she had done some modeling. She had beautiful cloth-covered albums with snapshots and newspaper clippings that she often let us look at. She was nearly five foot eleven, with thick blondish-brown hair that matched the beautiful amber necklaces Dad had bought her on their first anniversary. Haylee and I had slightly darker brown hair, but we both had the same patches of tiny freckles on the crests of our cheekbones. Mother actually counted them and concluded that we each had the same number of freckles. That plus the matching small birthmarks we had just under our left earlobes were pieces of evidence she always used to demonstrate how special we were when she paraded us before her friends.

"Identical twins don't always have what they have. As babies, when one cried, the other did; when one was hungry, the other always was. Why, they almost pooped at the exact same moment!" she would exclaim, and her friends would look at us, astonished.

"You're so devoted to them," her friend Melissa Clark told her once.

Mother pulled us to her, embracing us and smiling at her friends. "Look at them. Why wouldn't I be devoted to them?"

She kissed us both before she continued. She always kissed us each twice. If she kissed me first and then Haylee, she would kiss Haylee a second time and then me. The next time she did it, Haylee was first, and the same set of kisses followed. I saw how that amazed her friends.

"I wish my mother loved me half as much as you love them," Louise Kerry said.

"If you were an identical twin, she might have," Mother replied, and smiled at us. "All the joy is compounded. Just holding hands with the two of them when we walk, getting double hugs and kisses, making me feel like a mother-in-the-middle love sandwich—it's so special."

I looked at her friends' faces and saw how fascinated they were with Mother and with us. We were riveted to her descriptions of us as infants. Sometimes she told her friends things she had never told us.

"When the doctor announced that I was having twins, I didn't believe him," she said. "They felt to me like one child, not two. I was really surprised, up to the day I gave birth and actually set eyes on the two of them side by side. I remember my doctor saying, 'You've had clones.' Even he was amazed at how identical they were."

"It's true. I've never seen any twins so alike,"

Mrs. Letterman said. She was the oldest of Mother's friends, having retired from being a school business manager. "And I've seen at least five or six sets during my years at Cherry Hill."

"It's easily explained. They have the same DNA," Mother told these friends, nodding at us sitting side by side, dressed in the exact same outfits and shoes. Our hair was brushed the same way and kept the exact same length. "Monozygotic twins develop from a single egg-and-sperm combination that splits a few days after conception. Their DNA originates from the same source. They were a total surprise because no one in either my husband's family or mine had twins, much less identical twins. I began to learn about twins as soon as I could. I mean, to raise identical twins properly, you have to go deeper than Dr. Spock."

"I love the way you know so much about it," Mrs. Letterman said.

"They're my children. Why wouldn't I?"

Whenever Mother explained us to someone, the other person was always very impressed. Once Daddy told us, "As soon as you were born, your mother went after the research on identical twins as if she were about to argue a case before the Supreme Court. I really do believe your mother has become a nationally important expert on the subject." He often said something like that when he was tired of arguing about anything she did with us, but he really didn't sound proud of her. He sounded more annoyed. I even thought he believed she knew too much, if that was possible.

But who else could question anything she did? We didn't have our grandparents nearby to help Mother care for us when we were young. Daddy's parents were living in a Florida development for retired people. Mother's father died when she was in college, and her mother, our grandmother, Nana Clara Beth, had remarried and lived in Arizona. Her new husband had grandchildren of his own, and we sensed early on that Mother resented how our grandmother doted on her new husband's grand-children more than she did on her own. Mother was an only child. She told us that only children were normally spoiled. "But not me. Your nana Clara Beth spoiled no one but herself and criticized my father for doting on me too much. She drove him to an early death," she said, her eyes like hot coals.

I actually imagined my grandfather sitting in the rear of a car and my grandmother driving him to a dark place where death waited, smiling with teeth as sharp as razors.

Daddy had two brothers. The older one, Uncle Jack, went into the military and was stationed in Ger-many. He had a wife and two children, a boy, Philip, who was now eight, and a girl, Arlene, who was ten. Daddy's younger brother, Uncle Bret, was a salesman for a drug company, married with three children, all boys, ages five, six, and seven—Tim, Donald, and Jack. They lived in Hawaii, so we saw little of them.

We didn't see our paternal grandparents much at all, either. Daddy's parents refused to do much traveling anymore, and Mother hated going to Florida, especially where they lived. She called it "God's waiting room, full of bingo games and grandparents with ungrateful children."

"Don't even think about us ever retiring there," she warned Daddy, but I thought the real reason she disliked going to Florida was that our grandmother Mary was always trying to get Haylee and me to be different from each other. She bought us different things, things Mother confiscated as soon as we returned home and then hid somewhere in the basement or threw out. Haylee claimed she saw Mother literally bury two different watches our grandmother Mary had given us. Mine was blue with a silver band, and Haylee's was silver with a blue band. I didn't think Daddy ever knew what she had done with them. When he asked about them, she told him she didn't know.

"They're probably somewhere. The girls weren't that fond of them," she said. "They must have misplaced them."

He didn't pursue it. He asked us, but neither of us would ever tell him something bad about Mother. It was better to just say we didn't know. He looked suspicious, but he didn't keep asking.

Daddy was very much into his own work by this time anyway. He had helped start what was becoming an international software company, Capture Software, and shortly after our birth, he was appointed president of the company. Because we were such a full-time job for her, Mother didn't complain about his long hours, the weekends he had to give up, even the holidays he had to cut short, leaving her alone with us. I always thought she would rather have him busy with his own things than involved with our upbringing. He often apologized for not doing more at home or with us, but he was in the middle of a big expansion with his company by the time we were twelve. He said they were going public and would be on the stock exchange. He wasn't even home enough on weekends to play tennis very much.

When I was twelve, I once heard Mother tell him, "Ordinarily, I would accuse you of committing adultery with your devotion to your work, Mason, but I'll let it go for now because I have so much to do."

Yet, in the early days at least, there were times when they were together and we weren't the subject of their conversation or the focus of all their attention. They seemed to be back to being college sweethearts, at least from the way Mother had described herself and Daddy back then. When Daddy graduated from high school, he was a chamber of commerce award recipient. Mother said the big joke about him was that he was destined from birth to be the hero in a movie. Listening to her talk about Daddy or hearing them reminisce about their childhoods and their romance was like listening to one of the fairy tales Mother read to us. Who could foresee that it would all shatter like Humpty Dumpty?

Speaking about Daddy, she once said, "He made me feel safe wherever I was and whatever I was doing. Neither of you can get married until you both find a man like your father. Promise?"

Of course, we promised. We were only nine at the time, and neither of us realized that Mother was being literal. She actually expected that we would fall in love at the same time and have a double wedding, and even get pregnant at the same time. On afternoons when the three of us were together in the great room, she drew up all these fantasy scenarios for us, detailing how she would plan our marriage ceremonies and receptions and how she would help set up our nurseries.

I felt like reciting, "Once upon a time, there were identical twins who found identically perfect husbands and had identical marriages and identical families. They died on the same day at the same time and were buried side by side in the same cemetery."

Mother was so good at performing what she saw as perfect stories for us, taking our hands and pretending to walk down the aisle at our wedding. She said she would always throw big birthday parties for us, even when we were mothers ourselves. We'd sit at her feet as she waved her hands like magic wands and drew up the scenes before us. It was as if we were in a movie called *The Perfect Twins*.

Normally, Mother exhausted us daily with her attention to every detail of every aspect of our lives. Neither of us could have an inch of space more than the other, whether it was in the car or in the house or even in the yard and the pool. I thought she imagined a yardstick when she told one of us not to crowd "your sister."

For years, even though there were other bedrooms we could use, Mother kept Haylee and me in the same room. We slept in the same king-size bed. We had identical dressers for our clothing, and we shared the closet space equally. Just mentioning that some of our classmates had their own rooms was enough to fire up her eyes.

Then would come that familiar answer. "You're not ready."

It was Daddy who nagged her about it more than either of us, because if we complained, it would seem that we didn't want to be with each other, and Mother wouldn't tolerate that.

"How can they not be ready, Keri? They're becoming young women, aren't they? They need their privacy."

"They are not young women yet, Mason. It doesn't surprise me that you don't know that."

He especially didn't argue when she referred to anything feminine. It wasn't until we were nearly thirteen that Mother finally gave in to our having separate bedrooms.

However, in order to make things as perfect as she wanted, she had our original bedroom redone with the exact same flooring materials, fixtures, and paint for the walls to perfectly match the second bedroom. All our old furniture was given away, and doubles of everything were ordered and installed. We even had the same number of closet hangers. Why wouldn't we? We had the same exact clothes, the same amount of underwear and socks, the same number of shoes, hats, and belts.

Daddy complained about the waste of good furniture. "This is too much," he said, looking at the work being completed. She had ordered everything new while he was on a business trip. "Why does it all have to be exactly alike? Don't they have to feel like something's their own?"

"Not yet," she declared. "I know what I'm doing. One might think the other has better furniture."

"They could pick out their own, Keri."

"It would still happen, Mason. I've explained it to you many times. No child is more susceptible to inferiority and other complexes than an identical

twin," she recited. "It's a vulnerability clearly rec-
ognized in the psychological community."

She made sure we also had the same television
sets and the same computers. Mother didn't permit
us to have our own phones when other kids our age
were getting theirs. She didn't actually come out
and say it, but I don't think she wanted either of us
to have separate friends for as long as possible. If
someone wanted to be friends with me, he or she
had to be friends with Haylee, and vice versa. And
in that case, we didn't need two separate phones.
One of us could talk for the other. We were rarely
anywhere alone anyway.

When she finally permitted us to have separate
phones, we could speak to different classmates. We
were both in high school by then, freshmen, and
some things had begun to change. It was clear that
each of us was trying harder to be her own person.
Haylee wanted to wear different clothes and do different things with her hair, but that was still something Mother resisted.

"Why do you want to do that?" she'd ask with
a pained look on her face. "You should be very
proud of who you both are. You're both remarkable. What parent wouldn't want to double up on
so much beauty and intelligence? Both your father
and I feel very lucky to have you. Don't be so eager
to change anything about yourselves. You'll always
be happier if you don't."

Whenever she told us that, I would look at Haylee to see if she was comforted by it or if it would change her behavior. She nodded just like I did, but I didn't think she was convinced or at all happy about the idea. She was good at hiding her true feelings, much better at it than I was, actually. I was sure in my heart that if Haylee could find something very different from me about herself, she would pounce on it and treasure it.

Sometimes when Haylee looked at me, I could almost see her imagining us being separated in an operation like the one to detach conjoined twins, something we had watched a show about on the science channel. When the documentary was over, I saw the way she was staring at me. We weren't physically conjoined, of course, but I could see that if we were, she would want that operation, even if the operation meant I would die.

This wasn't something I knew for a long time, but when I finally did believe it, it was too late, for I was practically naked and alone in the darkness, waiting in vain for her to rescue me.

3

Until we were eight years old and Mother had decided we were ready to enter the third grade, she homeschooled us. When Daddy first heard her plan, he disagreed, and they had another argument, something that was happening more and more frequently by then.

"They're not having much contact with other children as it is, Keri," he said. "You won't even let them play with the neighbor girls."

Of course, both Haylee and I were hoping he would win the argument, but Mother was determined to give us the "special preparation" we needed, and that required isolation.

"I've told you time and time again how important their development is during these formative years, Mason. They have to be groomed carefully."

"Groomed carefully? Sometimes you make it

sound like they're not special, like they're handicapped," Daddy replied, almost casually, which
resulted in the worst outburst Mother had ever had
until then. It was even worse than the times she
would pound her own leg in frustration.

Haylee and I were having our lunch at the kitch-
enette. It was a Saturday, and Daddy had invited
some of the men who worked with him to play tennis
doubles. Fortunately, none of them had arrived yet.

She began by slamming a dish so hard on the
kitchen counter that it shattered into dozens of
pieces. Daddy stepped back, his eyes wide. Mother
didn't seem to realize what she had done at first.
She started to talk slowly and very low. I felt very
frightened, and when I looked at Haylee, I saw that
her eyes were as full of fear as mine.

"Handicapped? You accuse me of thinking they
are handicapped? The most perfect twins in all
of Pennsylvania, perhaps the country? And why,
because I have the foresight to envision how other
children will treat them, not only other children
but their teachers, and what damage that could do
to them?"

She stepped toward him, a piece of the broken
dish still in her hand.

"Do you have any idea what a curiosity they
will be, and do you even know how vicious and
mean children can be to one another? Do you?" she
repeated, raising her voice.

Daddy stood there, frozen. He was shocked at what he saw in her face. He started to shake his head.

"And what I've been trying to prepare them for and build them up to be strong against all these years?" Her face was so red, the veins in her neck so visible under her skin, that she looked like she might pop out of her body.

"Okay, okay," Daddy said, putting his hands up. "I shouldn't have said that. I'm sorry."

She stared at him so hard I thought she might burn a hole in his cheek, but after a moment of silence that seemed to make our ears ring, she relaxed her body and began to clean up the broken dish.

Daddy moved forward to help.

"Leave it!" she snapped. "Get ready for your playmates."

Daddy looked at us, and he seemed more frightened by the expressions on our faces than by any look of Mother's. He backed up to the doorway. "Sorry, Keri," he repeated. "I'm sure you're right. Sorry." He left, looking like someone happy to get away with his skin still on his body.

It wasn't until he had left that I realized Haylee had seized my hand, and we were squeezing each other tightly. She released mine first. Mother said nothing. She cleaned off the counter and then vacuumed the kitchen floor while we finished eating. When we were done, as we always did, we brought our dishes and silverware to the sink. Both of us were afraid we had done something wrong, too, but she surprised us by smiling and changing her voice into her loving, soft, almost melodic tone.

"What your father doesn't realize," she said, "is that I've been homeschooling you since the day you were born. That's how unaware he is about what is happening here. We're simply going to get more formal about it now. I've studied up on homeschooling, and I know exactly what has to be done. Don't be surprised. Daddies are oblivious to their own families more often than not. It's the way men are built. They never stop thinking about toys and games. It's why most of them are surprised one day to learn their daughters have become little women. When you finally do attend a school outside of this house, you will see very quickly who is handicapped and who isn't." She widened her smile and then hugged us. "I'll let you know soon when we'll start the official first day of homeschool."

She turned back to the sink, and I took Haylee's hand and led her out of the kitchen. Our hearts were still doing flip-flops. I could feel Haylee's body trembling, and I was sure she could feel mine. Neither of us said anything until we heard Daddy's friends arriving. Then we decided to go out and watch them play. One of Daddy's coworkers, Bryce Krammer, was always amused by the sight of us.

He called us the Mirror Sisters and asked us to tell him which one was which.

"Does your daddy ever make a mistake when he talks to you?" he asked.

"Sometimes," Haylee said, and all the men laughed.

"But Mother never does," I added.

Daddy quickly got them all into the tennis, and the argument about homeschooling was forgotten.

Mother decided to add one other thing to our education: piano lessons. What shocked Daddy was that she insisted on each of us having her own piano.

"Why can't they just take turns with the instructor?" he asked.

"That won't work," she insisted. "Eventually, they'll be teaching each other this way. It's natural to identical twins. One always mimics the other. I call it the shadow syndrome, which is a good thing."

He was still against it, but she went ahead and bought two pianos anyway. Our first piano teacher, Joe LaRuffa, a former high school music teacher, was quite impressed with us having our own pianos, but he was also impressed with how quickly we learned and how much Mother made us practice.

So music instruction became part of our homeschooling, something Mother told us was being sacrificed in public schools. "Which is another reason I want you homeschooled first. Your father knows nothing about any of this."

We had as much of a structured day as any school-age child. Every day, even on weekends sometimes, we sat in the den that she had converted into a classroom, blackboard and all. We even had actual school desks that Mother had found at an antiques shop. One had the initials *BB* carved deeply into it, so rather than grind them out, she carved the same initials into the second desk exactly where they were on the first.

We watched her work in the garage. Daddy wasn't home at the time. He was on another business trip. I was fascinated with how she bore down on the desk without the initials and carved them into the wood. Her expression was so intent that I thought she was angry about it. She worked carefully and paused every few moments to be sure they would be exactly the same when she had finished. She wouldn't let either of us touch the desks until she had completed the carving. Then she shellacked both the desks and the chairs and placed the exact same number of pencils and pens in the holders.

When Daddy got home, he was amazed and asked about the initials. "How did you find two with the same initials carved in them and in the exact same place?"

"Maybe it was the name of the school," she said,

"or maybe it was the initials of a boy two girls had crushes on."

He shook his head and stood there smiling like someone waiting to hear the end of a story or the punch line of a joke. I thought she would say she was kidding and tell him what she had done, but she never did, and neither Haylee nor I ever told him what we saw her do. Instinctively, we knew it would upset her. It was always a question of us being more loyal to her than to him, even though we weren't sure why she would have to lie to him about it.

Later, when Daddy wasn't there, she complimented us for not saying anything. "Your father would not understand," she said. "You sensed that, I know. You are so amazing."

I looked at Haylee. I was sure she didn't have that idea. I certainly didn't. I was simply afraid that Mother would be angry, but I had no real thought about why. Maybe we *were* amazing.

When we began what she called our formal homeschooling, Mother spent most of her time continuing to teach us to read. Once she felt we had achieved a certain level, she had our school day divided into subjects: English, math, science, and social studies, with thirty minutes for each. Our music instruction was on Tuesdays and Thursdays. In order for us to get used to the idea of separate classes, she had a clock timed to ring after thirty minutes. We had our lunch period, but even that was like a class, because she taught us proper dining etiquette, including how to softly dab at our lips with our napkins. If I did it one more time than Haylee did or if she did it one more time than I did, Mother pointed it out so we would do it exactly the same. After all the subjects were done, we had to spend another half hour in what she called a study session, during which we would mostly read. I read faster than Haylee, but I knew that if I finished too soon, Mother would make me start again until Haylee caught up.

"You might have missed something," she would say.

Every Monday, Wednesday, and Friday, we also had what she called physical education class, even if it was raining or snowing. We would go out back and do exercises, and then we were allowed to kick a ball or just run in circles. I could beat Haylee in a race, but the first time I did it, she started to cry, and Mother looked very upset. She made us race again, and this time, I deliberately lost, something I often saw Daddy do when he played tennis with Mother.

Exercise was usually the end of school on those days. Of course, we had homework to do before we could watch television or play a game. Mother compared our handwriting and pointed out that Haylee wasn't finishing her Qs as well as I was. She made her practice just writing Qs until she did it the same way I did. After we were seven, she decided to add French, because she spoke French well. Once, when Haylee couldn't remember how to ask in French to go to the bathroom, Mother made her stand in the middle of the room and hold it in until she got it right.

"You'll thank me later," she assured both of us. "They won't teach you a language in grade school, even at the private school we've been considering for you when I think you're ready to attend. Forget the public school. A good education is a luxury here in this country and not a necessity. Even after you begin at the private school, we'll continue our work here at home, especially with French. I want you to always be miles ahead of your classmates."

She smiled. "They'll think you're special simply because you're perfect twins, and they'll expect you to be superior, perfect in everything. That's fine. You know why? Because you *will* be," she said. "You'll be so far ahead when you do enter school that your teachers will not know what to do with you. Why, I expect that on graduation day, you'll be so close in your averages that you'll make the speech together. Wouldn't that be something? You'll alternate lines. There'll be enough applause to make everyone deaf for a few moments."

I was the first to realize that Mother tried her best to avoid referring to us as two. She wouldn't say "the two of you." It was always just "you."

When I realized this, I told Haylee. Mother was right. We were already way ahead of children our age when it came to the study of English grammar, so I pointed out the use of the pronoun. "She's using the plural *you* whenever she refers to either of us. It's almost like she sees double." That was something many people joked about when they first saw us.

Haylee shrugged, but then she thought about it again, and despite what Mother believed about our simultaneous habitual gestures, Haylee narrowed her eyelids into slits of suspicion and showed a touch of anger. I never did that with my eyes. I didn't think I ever looked as mean as Haylee could look.

"I don't care about the plural *you*. You're just trying to show off. She looks mainly at me anyway," Haylee said, "and she means me anyway when she says 'you.' She can't help it, no matter what she says. I'm the better student, so I understand everything faster. She knows."

How could she say that? I wondered. Mother never gave her a higher grade on a test than she had given me. In fact, neither of us ever had a different grade, higher or lower, on anything. Contrary to what Haylee claimed, I was usually the one who came up with the answers to Mother's questions first.

I was about to disagree with her when Mother

entered our bedroom, and I practically glued my lips together so none of my protest would escape, because that would have caused a furious argument right in front of Mother.

If Haylee and I got into an argument about something, no matter what it was, she always blamed us both and punished us equally. Neither of us could ever be right or wrong. In fact, both of us had to be a little wrong if we disagreed. If Daddy made a comment that favored one or the other of us in an argument, Mother practically clawed him to death. There was one thing she stressed above all else. I was surprised she had never had it on a plaque above our bedroom door: *Never blame your sister for anything; never make her look foolish or stupid, or you will look foolish and stupid, too.*

Once, when we were only six, she brought us down to the living room after Haylee had shouted at me for spoiling her drawing of our house that she was going to show Mother and Daddy. I had added the porch light by the front door. She had forgotten it, and I was just trying to help. Mother could hear Haylee scream and came rushing in.

"What is it? Why is only one of you screaming?"

"She ruined my picture! She ruined my picture!" Haylee cried, pointing her finger at me and pumping the air as if she could poke out my eyes.

"Stop!" Mother shouted, so loudly her voice

seemed to bounce off the walls. Her eyes looked like they were about to burst like egg yolks.

She rushed forward, took hold of us by our earlobes, and marched us out to the stairs, ordering us down to the great room.

"Sit," she commanded, and we did. Despite her exclamations of double love for us, she could get as angry at us as she got at Daddy. A cloud of red rage hovered over her, threatening to drown us in cold, hard rain. Haylee kept her head down, and I lowered mine. Although Mother never hit us, we couldn't help anticipating that she might—and as hard as she hit herself.

"How many times have I told you?" she began, in a much calmer tone than I'd expected. "Don't you know how important it is that you defend each other and protect each other? You will never, ever have a friend more loyal or caring than your sister. If someone attacks one of you with a nasty word or does something physical to one of you when you attend school, you must defend and attack together. You must always think of yourselves as one.

"Let me tell you why," she continued, her voice becoming more like her teacher voice, patient and reasonable. Haylee looked up, and so did I. "Because you are so close and so dedicated to each other, jealous girls and boys will try to get you to hurt each other. They will try to . . . to wedge themselves between you." She pressed her hands together and sliced the air. "They will whisper terrible things in your ears, claiming one of you has said something nasty about the other.

"Some," she said, now strutting up and down like she did when she gave us a lecture in our home classroom, "will be very, very clever about it. They will act as if they really don't want to tell you these things about your sister. Oh, how much pain they'll pretend to be in. They'll make it seem as if you demanded that they tell you something so they can't be blamed for starting trouble."

She smiled. "Think about the way I explained how Adam and Eve lost the Garden of Eden. The snake whispered into Eve's ear and made it seem as if God was afraid that she would realize how beautiful she was, how much like a goddess she was. The snake, which was the devil, made God seem bad. Remember?"

We nodded simultaneously.

"Good. Well, other students, and, I'm sorry to say, other girls mostly, will want to ruin your beautiful relationship with each other. They'll be whispering in your ears. They won't have anything like what you have as sisters. Every friend they've trusted has betrayed them, but you will never betray each other, because that would be the same as betraying yourself. See?"

Again, we nodded. She reached down to stroke our hair and pat us on the heads.

"You are my precious," she said. She didn't say precious *what*, just "precious," because we were her precious everything. "Now," she continued, "this is why whenever there is an urge to disagree or argue, you must battle it, smother it, stamp on it, beat it to death. Those bad urges will be fanned by the snakes around you. So I don't want to hear you raising your voices to each other, and I especially never, ever want you telling stories about yourselves. If you break something, you don't tell who broke it. You both broke it, understand? Don't tell on each other, even to your father or me.

"Yes. I saw the look on your faces when I said 'even me.' I know too well how a child can get her parents to favor her by constantly running to them to reveal something bad that the other child did. In my time in school, among my girlfriends, I saw many sisters—who weren't identical twins, of course—try to get their parents to favor one of them over the other. Of course, they were nowhere near as close to each other as you are. Jealousy and green envy. That's what caused it. You're too young to fully understand this, but it's scientifically called sibling rivalry. In time, you will fully understand what it is and why it is the worst sin of all for you. Then you'll remember what I told you today and be grateful.

"However, the truth is that you don't need to worry about sibling rivalry, because there is no way

I would favor one of you over the other. That would be like my favoring my right leg over my left. I want both my legs to be equally strong, don't I? Otherwise, I would limp. That's how you must think," she said, obviously excited about the analogy she had just made. "Yes, yes, that's it. You must think of yourselves as parts of the same body, the invisible you, the Haylee-Kaylee you or the Kaylee-Haylee you. If you don't, you will always limp through life. Do you understand?"

We nodded. I understood a little, but I didn't think Haylee even wanted to understand any of it.

"Good. I knew you would," she said, and then, as she always did when we were side by side, she knelt down, embraced us both, and hugged us both against her breasts and her face, actually kissing us with one kiss, her lips touching Haylee and me simultaneously. "Now, go back to your room and think about all this. Cherish it."

We rose, and I took Haylee's hand so we would walk out together. Mother loved to see us do that. The more we touched each other, the happier she was, and we both wanted Mother to be happy, almost more than we wanted happiness for ourselves. Or at least, I did.

Now, though, when Mother stepped into our bedroom this time, she looked very upset, even though I hadn't had the chance to argue with Haylee about whom Mother looked at more for the right answers when she asked questions. Something else was obviously bothering her, something far worse.

"Somebody went into my jewelry box and played with my bracelets and necklaces," she said. "They are not where they are supposed to be, and for a little while, I thought something very valuable was missing. Who did this?"

I looked at Haylee. I knew I hadn't done it, but I didn't know for sure that she had, and even if I did, I would never say it.

"She did," Haylee said, and pointed at me. "I told her not to. I saw her go into your bedroom and go to your jewelry box."

I held my breath. I had never done that, and Haylee knew it. It was shocking to hear her accuse me, and for a few moments, I had trouble breathing. It was as if some very heavy thing had been put on my chest.

Mother stepped forward, her eyes looking like sparkling ashes in the fireplace. I wanted to shake my head and say that Haylee was lying, but I didn't, because then I would be accusing her of something. Mother looked at me as if she expected me to say it. When I didn't, I was surprised to see a small smile on her lips, but then she reached out and pinched Haylee's earlobe, practically lifting her off the floor. Haylee screamed.

"You're in detention," Mother declared. "March out."

"Why?" Haylee protested. "I didn't do it. She did it."

Mother stopped. "This was a test," she said. "No one touched my jewelry. Didn't I tell you never, ever to hurt each other, blame each other, or get each other in trouble? Didn't I?"

"Yes," Haylee said through her tears.

"Well, you just did it. You disobeyed a very special and important rule."

"I'm sorry."

"Sorry isn't good enough. You're in detention for the rest of the day," she said. "Go."

Haylee didn't look back. She lowered her head and left the bedroom to go downstairs to the pantry, where Mother put us if we disobeyed her about anything. She would not let the light be put on, either, and there were no windows. There was nothing to do but sit in the dark. Just having to stay in there for ten minutes was horrible. The rest of the day meant that Haylee would be in there for hours!

I did feel sorry for her, even though she had tried to get me in trouble. I felt sorry for her for two reasons. She just didn't listen when Mother forbade us time and time again to say or do anything to hurt each other. Either she couldn't obey that rule or she was just too stubborn to do it. This meant that she would get Mother angry at her again and again and would be punished again and again. No matter what, when one of us did something that displeased Mother, she was too angry to be nice to the other one, so I would have to keep myself from looking at her. It was best to stay away until Haylee was forgiven.

And of course, I felt sorry for Haylee sitting alone in the darkness. I couldn't help it. Ever since we were infants, if one of us suffered some pain and began to wail, the other would, too. Once, when Haylee cut herself on a piece of glass she had picked up outside, Mother looked at the wound and then, using the same piece of glass, cut me on the same finger. She said she did that so we would always feel sorry for each other and understand what each other suffered.

Daddy saw the Band-Aids on our fingers and was curious.

"They both picked up broken glass outside," Mother told him.

"Amazing," he said. "And cut themselves in the exact same place?"

She looked at me to see if I would tell, but I didn't, just as I wouldn't tell him what she had done to the second classroom desk.

"I'm not surprised," she said. "And you shouldn't be. What one does, the other does. They have since the day they were born. Your children are very, very special, Mason. When are you going to realize it?" She sighed deeply, as if she felt sorrier for him than for us.

He shook his head and didn't continue to ask questions, which was what he did more and more.

Mother was right, though. After that, I did feel the same pain that Haylee felt, and she seemed to feel the same pain that I felt, although sometimes I thought she was pretending just to please Mother. For me, at least, it was almost supernatural the way I imagined myself suffering whatever Haylee suffered. But I could also enjoy whatever she enjoyed. If she took a piece of chocolate, I tasted it when she put it in her mouth. I would get myself a piece even if Mother wasn't watching, but sometimes I didn't and still felt as if I had eaten it. Would this always be? Would the enchantment last forever?

Right now, I could easily imagine how uncomfortable and even afraid Haylee was in the dark pantry. It was as if I was in the darkness, too. When Mother wasn't looking, I sneaked into the kitchen, went to the door of the pantry, and whispered through the crack.

"I'm here, Haylee. You can whisper to me. Mother's busy. She won't know."

She didn't respond. I wondered if she was crying, sobbing to herself the way she sometimes could without making a sound. Sometimes her body would shake so hard she looked more like someone freezing. That would frighten me, and before long, I would be shaking, too.

"Are you all right, Haylee? You know what

you can do to pass the time? Play that word game Mother taught us yesterday. You remember. Think of a number of letters, and then think of something like a tree. What on a tree has four letters? Remember? That would be either leaf or bark. Tell you what, I'll give you some to think about." I rattled off ten more examples of Mother's game. She still didn't whisper back. "Mother's up again," I said, hearing the sound of footsteps. "I'll come back later."

I slipped away and went back up to our room. I tried not to think of poor Haylee below in the darkness, but no matter what I did, the image of her sitting in the dark pantry alone kept coming back. Did she hear mice scurrying under the floorboards? We had heard that from time to time, and occasionally, especially in the pantry, we would come upon an ugly, scary spider. Whenever either of us was in there doing detention, just the thought of that made us itch and jump at the sensation of something crawling on us.

If we were placed in there together, we were forbidden to talk. Mother would listen at the door, and if she heard whispers, she would add another hour of detention. The first time we were in there together, we held hands, but the next time, we didn't. Usually, it was because of something Haylee had done, but we both had to be blamed, even if I couldn't have done it, too. Mother would get angrier if I tried to claim innocence while Haylee was guilty. The worst thing to do was be angry at Haylee for getting us in trouble and then have Haylee yell at me once we were in the pantry. There was no telling how much longer our punishment might be.

I heard Daddy come home early that afternoon and hurried out and down the stairs, hoping his arrival would mean Haylee would be let out of the pantry early, but Mother didn't make any move to do so. I found them both in the great room. It looked as if she hadn't even told him Haylee was in the pantry. He was telling her about something good that had happened at work. He paused when I stepped into the doorway.

"Kaylee? Where's your sister?" he asked instantly. He was so accustomed to us greeting him together.

I looked at Mother.

"She's being punished," she said.

It was rare for one of us to be punished and not the other, so Daddy's eyebrows rose like two question marks. "What did she do?"

"Mainly, she didn't defend her sister but instead lied about her and blamed her for something," Mother said. "My perfect twins don't do that."

"What did she lie about?" he asked.

"Playing with my jewelry."

Daddy sat back, his face tightening. "Why lie about something like that? Was something broken, missing?"

"No, and in fact, no one played with my jewelry."

"I don't understand," Daddy said, shaking his head. "No one played with it?"

"It was a test to see if one of them would lie about the other. Haylee did. She blamed it on Kaylee. She won't do that anymore," she added.

There was a look on Daddy's face that I hadn't seen before, a dramatic look of disgust, as if he had put something very bitter or spoiled in his mouth. He looked at me, and then he turned to Mother.

"Test? What do you mean, test?"

"It's part of their education," she said.

I was still just standing there, listening, waiting, and hoping that Daddy would disagree and put a stop to it.

"Sounds like entrapment," he said, softening a bit the way he would when he was trying to make a joke. I wouldn't say it was a complete smile, just an expression on its way to becoming one. To me, that was disappointing.

"Hardly the same thing," Mother said firmly. "Entrapment is a practice whereby a law-enforcement agent induces a person to commit a criminal offense that he would not likely otherwise do. The key word is *induces*."

"My wife the would-be lawyer," Daddy said, but she wouldn't even tolerate the shadow of a smile. There was no doubt that she didn't see anything amusing about it. He grew serious quickly. "She was probably just frightened," he offered.

"She would never be if she defended her sister and her sister always defended her. It's a very important point, Mason. I won't let them enroll in an outside school until I'm confident that they will behave correctly in relation to each other and other students. I never believed in that sink-or-swim philosophy that my parents, especially my mother, imposed on me. A mother's duty is to provide her child with as much preparation for the nasty outside world as possible before turning that child loose in it. Those problems and issues are doubly important here because of what and who they are. Besides, I showed you that study done on orphans compared with children from a solid family. Everything is twice as intense for identical twins."

He nodded, but he didn't look as convinced or accepting of Mother's technique as he did about most other things. In fact, he still looked quite upset. "Setting her up to lie. I don't know," he said. "That still seems to fit your definition for entrapment, counselor."

"It most certainly does not," she countered firmly. "If you want an analogy, think of it as a fire drill."

"It's not the same thing," he insisted, despite the look she was giving him. I thought something was changing a little. The wall Mother had built around her methods for bringing us up had suffered a small crack. "You have her in that pantry doing detention?"

"That's right." She looked at her watch "One more hour."

"One more hour? How long has she been in there, Keri?"

"Almost four hours," she replied.

"Four hours!"

"Don't act so shocked. They've both been there that long before, Mason."

"Have they?" He looked a little stunned, not as much because of what was happening to Haylee as because he never realized what punishment Mother had imposed on us previously. "That seems a little too much," he said. "What if she has to go to the bathroom?"

"This is exactly what psychologists warn about!" Mother cried, practically leaping off the settee and waving her upturned palms at him. "Parents abdicating their responsibilities because those responsibilities are too difficult for them to carry out, especially enforcement of rules. If we're not strong, they won't be. It's as simple as that."

"Nothing is as simple as that," he said. "What if she's claustrophobic?"

"Kaylee isn't, so Haylee isn't. I think I would know, Mason. I'm not surprised, however, that you don't. Besides, you don't give in to weaknesses, you attack them, confront them. It's called building backbone. I know what I'm doing, Mason. I don't appreciate being criticized."

"Okay, okay," he said. "I'm going up to shower and change. I thought we were going to take them out to dinner tonight."

"We were, but that's been postponed."

"So we're all being punished for what Haylee did?" he asked calmly.

"We must think of ourselves as one, Mason. Like any chain, a weak link can bring it all down." She sat back. "You, a company president, should know all this without me explaining."

"I know how important morale is, too," he said.

She stared at him. Whenever Mother focused her eyes with a steely glare on anyone, including Daddy, it was as if an earthquake were about to happen. In fact, she looked like she could start a fire with her eyes and burn him up, like Joan of Arc being burned at the stake. Mother had been practically in tears when we read that story with her. "Strong women always suffer somehow," she had told us, "ever since Eve."

"Okay, okay," Daddy said quickly, like someone putting out a fire. "I'm still going up to shower and change. Whatever." I saw him shake his head and heard him mumble to himself as he left the room and headed for the stairway.

Mother watched him leave and then looked at

me, her eyes suddenly as suspicious and angry as Haylee's could be.

"Did you go into the kitchen and whisper through the pantry door, Kaylee?"

How could she know? Why hadn't she stopped me when I was doing it?

"Yes," I said. There was, as I just had seen, nothing as terrible as lying to Mother.

"Because you felt sorry for Haylee even though she tried to get you into trouble?"

"Yes."

"That's good, Kaylee. You cared about her despite what she had done. We have to make sure she behaves the same way toward you, has compassion for you, too, understand?"

"Yes, Mother," I said, happy I wasn't being put into detention, too.

"You go and let her out now, and tell her that I was so pleased with how much you felt sorry for her that I decided to reduce her punishment. She'll see that it is important to care more for you and that by caring for you, she's really caring for herself. Go," she said.

When I opened the pantry door, Haylee, who was curled on the floor, slowly raised herself like a cobra. She had dried streaks of tears along her cheeks, and her hair was quite messy because she had been running her fingers through it nervously, something I would do, too.

"What do you want?" she said, spitting her words at me.

"Mother said that because I felt sorry for you and tried to comfort you even though you blamed me for something I didn't do, you can come out now," I said. "She said you should think about it, especially about caring more for me like I cared more for you." I tried to recite it accurately as Mother had dictated it.

Haylee stood there in the pantry, strangely defiant even though she was being released. She folded her arms across her chest.

"Didn't you hear what I said? You can come out."

"She tricked me," she said. "That wasn't fair. I shouldn't have been put in detention alone."

"It wasn't a trick. Like she told you, it was a test. She's only trying to help us help each other all the time, Haylee. Don't you want her to let us go to school? She won't if she doesn't think we're ready to protect each other. I just heard her tell Daddy that. You've told me so many times that you want to go to school, and I've told you the same thing. Don't you see? We'll never get there if we don't listen."

She nodded, lowered her head, and walked out. I closed the pantry door.

"You should go thank her," I said.

"Thank her?"

"Thank her for helping you understand. She likes that."

She narrowed her eyes in that angry and suspicious way again but then smiled. "Okay," she said. "I will. I know just what to say. I'll say what you would say."

I followed her to the living room. Mother was sitting back on the settee, her arms spread over the top, waiting.

"Thank you, Mother," Haylee said. "I'm sorry for what I did and what I said. I made a terrible mistake." She looked at me. "Sorry, Kaylee." She leaned over and kissed me on the cheek.

Mother's face brightened, making her look younger and even more beautiful. "That's very good. Perfect, Haylee. You understand now? You understand why you must always protect each other?"

"Yes, Mother," Haylee said. "I appreciate what you did for us."

Mother's smile deepened because Haylee said "us" rather than "me." Haylee glanced at me, looking pleased with herself.

"Go wash up. We're going to a restaurant for dinner," Mother said. "You two can order your favorite pasta with meatballs."

"Okay," Haylee said.

I smiled. Haylee didn't know it, but Mother was going to make Daddy happy, too, and no matter what happened, I always liked it most when everyone in our family was happy.

"And maybe we'll all go for frozen yogurt for

dessert afterward, and you two can get your favorite, blueberry," Mother added.

Wow, she is pleased with us, I thought.

"I think I want chocolate tonight," Haylee said, swinging her eyes toward me.

"Me, too," I added quickly.

Mother nodded. "That's fine. Go on, Kaylee. You get cleaned up, too. I'll be up in a while to pick out your outfit and brush your hair."

We started to turn.

"Wait!" she cried, and we looked at her. "What's that on your right ring finger, Haylee?"

Haylee looked at it as if she had never known it was there. It was a piece of green ribbon. "Nothing. I was just pretending I had a ring," she said.

"Get it off this instant. Never put anything on that Kaylee isn't wearing. That includes make-believe jewelry. You know how I hate it when someone gives one of you something and not the other."

Haylee ripped it off quickly.

"Okay, go on," Mother said.

We walked out quickly. At the bottom of the stairway, Haylee turned to me and smiled. "You don't really want chocolate more than you want blueberry, do you?" she asked.

"It's all right."

She widened her smile. "See? I can make you do anything I want," she said, and laughed.

"I can do the same to you," I countered, even though it was something I wouldn't even think of doing.

She rushed ahead of me up the stairs. Daddy poked his head out of their bedroom when he heard our footsteps.

"Hey, what's up?" he asked. He was in his robe and was rubbing a towel over his hair.

"We're going to a restaurant after all," I said. "And maybe for frozen yogurt for dessert."

His face brightened. "Way to go, girls, whatever you did," he said.

"We helped each other," Haylee told him. "We will always do what's better for both of us. We'll never be selfish."

She said it with such assurance that I actually believed her, until I saw her turn away and smile, and something about that smile sent a chill through me. It was so different from any smile I might make, even the impish smile she had flashed at the bottom of the stairway. Maybe she knew that, too, because she kept it off her face the rest of the night.

As usual, at the restaurant, people who knew Daddy would stop by and comment on how perfectly identical we were. Even strangers did it. One man paused to say, "I'm going to my optometrist. I'm seeing double again." He laughed, but neither Haylee nor I did. We had heard that so many times that the humor had long since been washed away.

However, Mother soaked up all the compliments like a flower absorbing sunlight. I saw the way she looked at Daddy each time, as if to say, *See how well I'm doing with them? Never challenge me again.*

He seemed to be in full retreat now anyway, and that moment of defiance I had seen in the great room earlier was a fading memory. He talked more about his business, his plans for the future, and some vacation ideas. Mother listened, but her eyes were always on us, especially noticing the way Haylee was fidgeting. This was something I didn't do nearly as much as she did. Despite how good a student Haylee believed she was, she had a more limited attention span than mine. Instinctively, because I knew Mother was looking for it, whenever Haylee grew bored, I tried to look just as bored. I knew that if I didn't, she would be angrier at Haylee than normal, and that could end with another punishment we'd both endure. We were supposed to protect each other even from boredom.

"Stop playing with your food," she muttered. "Don't swing your legs under the table. Wipe the food from your mouth. Don't lean over your plate so much."

These orders were always meant for us both, even though I didn't do those things as much. She gave the commands while she listened to Daddy describe some new project he was working on. It was easy to see that her snapping at us in the restaurant bothered him, but criticizing her for criticizing one of us would only make things worse.

That night, however, I woke from what I thought was a bad dream. It was really the sound of our parents arguing. It was rare to hear Daddy raise his voice, especially this late in the evening, but that was what was happening. I looked at Haylee. She was in a deep sleep, so I rose and tiptoed to the slightly opened bedroom door to listen better. They were in their bedroom.

"Don't you see?" Daddy said. "Haylee lied because she wants you to like her more. It's only natural. You don't have to be a psychologist to figure it out, Keri."

"No, it's exactly the opposite. It's unnatural. If she wants me to like her more, then she wants me to like Kaylee less. That's harmful. She shouldn't want to harm her sister, ever."

"But isn't it natural for them to be somewhat competitive? They have no other children to compete with as long as you keep them homeschooled. So they have to compete with each other. It's human nature. I appreciate how you're teaching them, how much they've learned, and how much further along they are, but they'll have to compete with other students in many ways eventually. There are social hurdles, especially for kids today."

"Exactly. I'm training them to be a team for

just that reason. Don't you see how careful I am to protect them, to be sure they have self-confidence? Since when do you question the way I'm bringing them up? You're doing it more and more lately. Who's been talking to you? I sensed it this afternoon when you heard what Haylee had done and learned about her punishment. Well? It's that secretary of yours, that woman who looks like a chipmunk, isn't it? I've seen the way she looks at me every time the girls and I visit you at your office. 'They're so exact,' she says, as if that was a mistake. 'You keep them so exact. I would never know who was who.' Like that was something terrible. Well? Was it that woman?"

"Stop it," he said. "Of course not. There's no reason to call her 'that woman.' She's been with me for five years. Her name is Nancy Brand."

"Why isn't she married with a family of her own so she doesn't have to sniff like a chipmunk around ours?"

"I don't get into the personal lives of our employees. And she doesn't look like a chipmunk. Let's just forget it. I'm tired," Daddy said, his voice strained with defeat and frustration.

They were quiet. I waited, listening. I was just about to turn away when Mother said, "I'll look into enrolling them in Betsy Ross. But not this semester. The next. It's coming up very soon."

"That's good, Keri. It will give you a chance to spend more time with your friends, too. You should get out more."

"Oh, that's so shortsighted, Mason. It's when your children begin school and start to socialize that you need to spend more time with them."

"Whatever. Whatever you think's best," he said, sounding like he was waving a white flag.

I waited, but I heard nothing more and returned to bed. Haylee woke when I crawled back under the blanket.

"I just heard something important," I said.

"What?"

"Mother is going to look into enrolling us in Betsy Ross next semester, and she said that was very soon."

"Good. I'm tired of only looking at your ugly face."

"It's your face, too," I said.

"You don't see it because you don't want to," she said, raising herself on her elbows, "but our faces are not really exactly alike. I'm prettier. When we go to school, you'll see I'm right. I'll have more friends, especially more boyfriends."

"Don't let Mother hear you say that. You'll be in the pantry for days, and I won't come to keep you company through the door."

She lay back again. I was so angry that I didn't think I could fall asleep.

"Don't worry about Mother," she said. "Someday she'll think I'm prettier and nicer, too."

I didn't think there was anything she could say that would hurt me more.

But we were still young.

She would have lots of opportunities to come up with worse ideas.

And she did.

4

During the days that followed, Haylee thought I had lied to her, because Mother didn't come right out the next day and tell us she finally was going to enroll us in the Betsy Ross school. Although I had caught Haylee lying to me many times, I had never lied to her, and she knew it. Nevertheless, she turned on me one afternoon and with a hateful look said, "You lied to me about our going to school, Kaylee Blossom Fitzgerald. That was mean."

"That's silly, Haylee. Why would I lie to you about it?"

"You want to be more important than me," she said. "Mother would never tell you something and not tell me."

"I didn't say she told me, Haylee. I said I overheard her talking to Daddy. You were asleep."

She pursed her lips as she always did when she

didn't like something I had said. It was something else I rarely did, but somehow Mother never noticed. Maybe she didn't think it was important. If she did see something one of us did differently, something that bothered her enough, like scowling or chewing the insides of our mouths when we were nervous, she would tell us to stop, or else "your sister will be doing it, too." It was impossible to believe that one of us would do something that eventually the other wouldn't. Mother had drummed that into our heads from the moment we could understand what she meant. However, I believed it more than Haylee did, I thought, which was why I was always frightened by some of the things Haylee did.

Haylee didn't really care what was true and what wasn't about what I had told her anyway.

"You just want to be more important," she repeated. She was good at hearing what she wanted to hear and being deaf when something displeased her. Sometimes she could make me so angry and frustrated that I did feel like getting her into trouble, even if it meant I would be in trouble, too.

"You'll see that I'm right and not lying," I said, but now I wasn't sure myself.

Mother had promised that she was going to do things for us in the past, especially things Daddy wanted her to do, and then she had never done them or had put them off so long that Daddy simply forgot about them. But us going to a real school was something Daddy often mentioned. I hoped he wouldn't forget or give up. Being with others our age was something Haylee and I really wanted, although Haylee always told me she wanted it more, because I was more afraid of it than she was. She repeated that now.

"Why am I afraid of it?"

"You're too shy," she said. "I overheard Mother say that to Daddy. And that's the real reason we're not going yet, so it's your fault."

"Now who's lying? Mother would never say that."

She gave me that Haylee Blossom Fitzgerald shrug, widening her eyes. She would do that only when Mother wasn't looking. It was something she did instead of laughing at me when she was teasing me, especially when she was caught in a "lie without clothes," as Mother put it.

"Yes, she did, Kaylee."

"No, she didn't. I'm the one who talks about going all the time. You're the shy one, the one who's afraid to ask Mother questions," I fired back at her.

It was true, and she knew it. As always, when she knew she'd been caught lying to me, she would just smile and go on to something else, leaving my frustration dangling in the air like a spider. My insides certainly felt as if spiders were crawling all over me. I hated letting her do this to me, but I was also frustrated about school.

The Betsy Ross private school was not far from where we lived. Every time we drove past it, Haylee and I would gaze at the redbrick building and the children outside with great curiosity and longing. They seemed so much happier than we were, so much more excited about everything as they called to one another and walked and ran over the beautiful grounds with the tall maple and oak trees. Sometimes we saw children on the ball field. If we had to stop at the traffic light in front of the school, their laughter rolled toward us in waves and drew us to lean a little out of the car windows, as if we were begging for a little of their social activity.

I often asked when we were going to attend Betsy Ross, and Mother would always say, "You'll go when you're ready."

"But why are they ready and we're not?" I had asked recently. "So many of them are younger than we are."

"Are you wondering that, too?" Mother asked Haylee.

"No," she said, shaking her head, even though she was wondering even more than I was.

"I don't know why I have to repeat this. I've told you so many times," Mother said, looking more at me, "that you are special and very different from those children. When you are there eventually, you will see exactly what I mean, and you will thank me for making you stronger before you entered the school of . . . plain fish."

I looked at Haylee. She was smiling. She loved it when Mother spoke to me as if I were dumber than she was. Nevertheless, my mind was full of challenging questions, like *Why are they plain fish? And if they're so plain, why are they in school and we're not? We're smart enough to attend classes and do well, right? You've said so many times.*

Of course, I dared not ask those questions. I was quiet instead, and I would close my eyes and roll up the car window whenever we were driving past the Betsy Ross school now. I didn't want to see or hear how happy the "plain fish" were. I felt like a poor, starving little girl who could only stare through restaurant windows at the wonderful and delicious things other children were eating. It was torture to look. However, because of what I had overheard Mother tell Daddy, I was far more interested in going to school now, and despite how she pretended otherwise, so was Haylee.

One day two weeks later, Mother finally told us. Daddy was home, and we had just sat down to have dinner. She said she had visited the grade school and had spoken with the principal, Mrs. Green.

"Since they are beginning a new marking period at Betsy Ross and you've both been doing so well in our home classroom, I've decided it is time to enroll you."

I looked at Haylee to see if she would feel sorry for doubting me, but she didn't show it if she did. Instead, she looked as surprised as she could and avoided looking at me.

"Betsy Ross is the best of all the private schools in our area," Mother continued. "However, I've insisted on a number of things. You will be in the same classroom, of course, and sitting side by side. If your teacher finds one of you falling behind the other for any reason, I will be informed immediately so that I can help bring you up to your full capabilities.

"I've decided," she added, before either Daddy or we could say anything, "to volunteer as a teacher's assistant. I will not assist your teacher, however. The principal has a rule against that, a rule I couldn't bend. I almost threatened not to enroll you, but then I realized that I wouldn't be that far from the situation anyway. I'll assist the second-grade teacher. This way, I will personally bring you to school and take you home every day, and if there is any sort of problem, which I don't anticipate, I will be there to jump right on it."

"What's that? Teacher's assistant?" Daddy said. "Why would you devote your new free time to that, Keri? You could return to your law studies or—"

"It's too late for that, Mason. Besides, I've lost

interest in it. There are many other women with children at the school volunteering for things and even fathers who help with the high school sports program."

"I know, but—"

"This is how it will be for at least the first year or so while they are in grade school, Mason," she said firmly. Mother could declare something and end her sentence with the sound of a judge's gavel. It was as good as saying "Case closed," which was something she did say from time to time.

"Well, if that's what you want . . ." Daddy conceded, happy that at least she had finally given in and arranged for us to attend the school.

"Of course it's what I want. I'm not going to start needlework or join some ladies' book club," she said. For a moment, her eyes blazed, and then she softened her whole body and smiled at us. "We'll go shopping this weekend for some new clothes for you and some things you'll need for school. I have the books that you'll be using in the third grade, and we'll work from them now, although they look a little simplistic for you. Well? What do you have to say?"

"Thank you, Mother," we both replied, with that amazing synchronicity she always pointed out to Daddy and anyone else who heard us.

She smiled. "My girls," she said. "My girls will be outstanding. Haylee-Kaylee."

"Kaylee-Haylee," we both said, and she laughed. Daddy widened his eyes and shook his head.

Mother held out her arms, and we got up and went to her for a hug. I looked at Daddy. I expected that he would be very happy for us, too. We were finally going to attend a regular school, as he wanted, but when Mother hugged us, he looked very troubled for a moment. It sent a chill through me. Why did he look so afraid for us? He lost the expression quickly when we returned to our seats and finished our dinner as Mother lectured us about how we were to conduct ourselves at school.

"Most of the time, when your teacher asks a question, I'm sure you will have the answer before any other students. Don't hog the answers. No one else will get a chance to shine, and everyone will resent you. Even your teacher will begin to ignore you and pretend not to see your hands waving. So, first, share the answers with each other."

"Isn't that cheating?" I asked.

"No, I mean take turns so one of you doesn't answer many more than the other."

"Isn't that a lot to ask of them?" Daddy asked softly. "Keeping track of who answered what and how many times, I mean?"

"They can do it. They do it here in our classroom, don't you?"

We both nodded. We'd agree to anything if it meant we could go to school. Daddy gave his usual shrug, and Mother went on, listing what she liked and didn't like about how things were being run at the school. She threatened to run for the school's board, at least while we were attending.

Afterward, we went up to our room, almost unable to contain our excitement. Haylee started to think of the clothes we could wear and sifted through her closet, declaring this was for a Monday and this was for a Tuesday, planning outfits for every day of the week, including shoes. She knew Mother wouldn't let her wear something different from me, so she tried to get me to like what she liked for each day at school.

"Don't bother, Haylee. She's taking us to get some new clothes, and she will decide what we wear every day, just like she does now."

"Not if you want to wear what I want," she insisted. "That always pleases her. You just have to agree right away. That way, we can do things *we* want to do. It's important, Kaylee."

Why was choosing for ourselves what to wear suddenly so important? I wondered. Although I didn't fully understand what Haylee was saying and hoping at the time, it did give me some warning. Once we were out from under Mother's complete control, Haylee was going to push against the restrictions Mother had set down around us, and I would always have to go along with it, or else. The seeds of Haylee's rebellion were just being planted. I would be confronted with many kinds of choices in the months and years to come. Haylee always would blame me for her not getting what she wanted. It would always be "If you would do it, too, she would let us do it." What was going to happen actually was the opposite of what Haylee believed and feared. She wasn't going to be forced to be like me. On the contrary, I was going to be forced to be more like her so she would not be in trouble so much.

I was certain that Mother would find a way to blame me for the things Haylee did anyway, just as she often did now. It went back to her belief that we were two parts of the same person with the same thoughts and feelings. Whatever Haylee had done, whether breaking some school rule or speaking back to a teacher belligerently, I was surely about to do the same thing. If Haylee couldn't have dessert or couldn't watch television, I couldn't, either. There was what Mother called punishment and precautionary punishment. Daddy questioned it, of course, just as he had done in the past, but she was adamant. She was convinced that the potential for doing something wrong couldn't be in one of us without being in the other. She cited psychological studies, which usually drove him into retreat. "Besides," she said, "if Kaylee shows more self-control, then Haylee will."

"But she has," Daddy protested when this

eventually happened. "She didn't talk back to their teacher. Haylee did."

"She will, Mason. Why wait for something we know is going to happen? If two of anything are made the same way with the same parts and one develops a problem, it's a certainty the other will. It's simply logical."

He shook his head as always, but he looked more disgusted than ever.

"We brought them up to respect their elders," she said. "Haylee weakened and became more like one of the other students than her sister. They were warned about exactly this sort of thing. They've got to constantly think about how they can help each other."

She was referring to what she had told us when she took us to Betsy Ross that first day. "You are each a role model for the other," she explained. "This is more important than ever now. When good children enter school, they are more influenced by their peers than by their parents."

"What are peers?" Haylee asked, before I could.

"Peers are people who belong to the same age group or social group. The children in your class will be your age, of course, but as far as similarities go, that will be it. So even if a child is brought up well, is polite and kind and respectful toward his or her elders, peers might change him or her. The worst children are often seen as heroes by their peers. But you are your own heroes. You look to each other for guidance and not to any other classmate, understand?"

"Maybe they'll look to us," Haylee suggested.

Mother smiled. "Very good, Haylee. Yes, they might just do that. You bring them up to your level, and never stoop to theirs. That's exactly what I mean."

Haylee practically glowed like a pumpkin with a candle inside its cutout face. Mother didn't see the way she smiled gleefully at me, or she would have bawled her out for it. It was, as actions by either of us were soon to be called, "unsisterly" of her.

There was so much to remember, so many more rules for us to obey, now that we were going to be with other children. Any child would be nervous about entering school for the first time, but here we were, identical twins who had never been in school, and we were entering quite a bit later than the others. It made us a greater curiosity, not only to the others in our class but also to the teachers. I could almost hear their whispers. The way their eyes followed us made me so nervous and afraid that I started to walk with my head down on the second day of school, whereas Haylee looked back at everyone with glee, her eyes full of defiance. She seemed anxious to have someone say something nasty or stupid, eager for it, like someone with a chip on her shoulder. I was nervous, because I knew that if she got into an argument or a fight, I had to come to her aid immediately, or our mother would be doubly upset.

By the time we entered the third grade at Betsy Ross, we hadn't accumulated many of those memories that people live with most of their lives, but that first day of school was one of them.

Daddy looked as excited about it as we were the night before. He told us how he had cried when his mother left him on his first day at kindergarten, a life memory he would never forget. "I wasn't the only one," he added. "There were wailing, frightened children all around me, but I got over it quickly and began to enjoy it. In fact, I hated missing school and tried to hide being sick whenever I was."

"We'd hate it, too," I said.

Haylee nodded. "If you get sick," she whispered to me later, when we were told to go to bed, "you'd better keep it a secret, or else Mother won't let me go to school that day, either."

"So should you," I said.

Mother had spent a great deal of time deciding what to buy us to wear for our first day. In fact, she took us to three different department stores until she settled on a cable-knit sweater dress dip-dyed in candy colors with 3-D bows near the neckline. The dress was long-sleeved, with a ribbed neckline, cuffs, and hem. She bought us candy-colored socks to go with it and a pair of red sparkly shoes for each of us.

"I'm glad I have two the same size in stock," the saleslady said.

Mother smiled at her. "If you didn't, you wouldn't sell one to me."

"I know it's cute to dress them alike, but don't they each want something different?" she pursued.

"I think you should concentrate on serving your customers and not on giving advice about things you wouldn't know about," Mother told her, with those sharply pronounced consonants and vowels that could feel like tiny razors in your ears.

It looked as if the poor woman was going to lose her face. It seemed to ripple and drop as she turned and quickly packed up the two matching dresses.

If there was any doubt about whether we'd attract attention with our identical faces and bodies, our identical colorful outfits put that to rest. No other student at Betsy Ross looked as dolled up as we were. In fact, even though it was expensive to attend the private school, some of the older students we saw entering the building were wearing ordinary, everyday, inexpensive clothes. Mother thought they looked a bit sloppy and muttered that she would say something about it.

"Maybe if I get on the school's board, I'll make a point of it," she said. "It wouldn't hurt them to have a decent dress code."

Haylee looked at me, obviously realizing that it was going to be more difficult than she had thought for her to choose our clothes after today.

Actually, I wondered why Mother couldn't clearly see the difference between Haylee and me when she brought us to school that day. I wasn't going to cry like Daddy had done in kindergarten, but I was certainly very nervous and, at the least, timid about everything I did, whereas Haylee was eager to attract attention, parading a little in front of me, acting like she was some child star.

When our teacher, Mrs. Elliot, greeted us and told us what desks to take, Haylee practically leaped into hers. I lowered myself into my chair the way I would into a hot bath. I was trembling, secretly longing for the security of our own desks back home, the ones with the initials *BB* carved into them. Right now, it felt more like putting on someone else's clothes, someone else's shoes. I looked at Haylee. She was obviously not suffering a moment of anxiety. She looked as pleased as what Mother called "a bee drowning in pollen." Mother stood in the doorway of our classroom for a few moments, watching us.

Other students took their seats with the assurance that comes from doing something often. I envied how far ahead of me they were in most ways, despite what Mother thought about us. I told myself that I would willingly give up being smarter if I could be more self-confident. There were fifteen students in our third-grade class. Five were boys. These other students knew one another from attending first and second grades together. Just about everyone was watching us. Haylee looked back at as many of them as she could, challenging them with her smile. She was acting as if she really was the prettiest girl in the class.

"I've seen twins," a boy with short sweet-potato-colored hair leaned over to tell Haylee, "but you're really, *really* twins." He was on her other side. He had a mischievous smile and eyes the color of fresh grass.

"Yes. We're perfect twins. Monozygotic twins develop from a single egg-and-sperm combination," Haylee recited, with an air of superiority.

"Mono what?"

"Monozygotic. It's DNA. Don't you know what DNA is?"

"No, but I know what D-U-M-B is," he replied. He kept his smile, looked over at me, and then turned to whisper something to the girl on his other side. They laughed until Mrs. Elliot clapped her hands, and everyone settled down.

I looked back. Mother was still standing in the doorway. Her eyes were small, like Haylee's could get. Was she angry already? Would she come charging in and tell us to get up to leave, that the class wasn't good enough for us, just because she saw what had happened between Haylee and the boy sitting next to her? I held my breath.

"Okay," Mrs. Elliot said.

She looked at least twenty years older than Mother, maybe old enough to be her mother. She had gray strands like ribbons in her hair and wore no makeup, not even lipstick. Our mother looked like a movie star compared with her, I thought. Mrs. Elliot was a little stout, too, and had eyes the color of black spiders. I thought of that because of the thin wrinkles that seemed to explode through her temples like webs when she squinted.

"I'd like to introduce you all to our new students, Kaylee and Haylee Fitzgerald," she said, nodding at us. "How about a nice welcome?" she added, and the other students clapped, the boy with the mischievous smile clapping the loudest.

Haylee seemed to burst like a flower blossoming in slow motion on one of those television science shows. Mother made us watch those shows in our science class at home. I just smiled slightly. When I looked back, Mother nodded and left to go help the second-grade teacher. I breathed easier.

"Which one is Kaylee, Mrs. Elliot?" the boy asked. "I can't tell them apart."

"That's enough," Mrs. Elliot said when the class laughed. "Okay, yes. Kaylee, please stand."

I did.

"Thank you. Haylee?"

Haylee rose more slowly and turned so everyone in the class could have a full view of her. I hadn't done that.

"Thank you," Mrs. Elliot said.

"I still can't tell," the boy said.

"Why don't you write that out five hundred times after school today, Stanley Bender?" she said, and he wilted a little.

While Mrs. Elliot passed out a booklet of school rules, however, Stanley Bender, still wearing his mischievous smile, leaned toward Haylee again. "Do you two always wear the same things?"

"Yes," Haylee said, without skipping a beat. "We do everything together, like a team. But I usually choose what we'll wear." She glanced at me and saw how astonished I was at her bold lie.

Stanley's smile widened as the girl in front of Haylee and the one on the other side of him leaned over to listen. "Oh, yeah? Do you pee together, too?" he asked. Everyone who heard him laughed.

"Why do you want to know? Do you like to watch girls pee?" Haylee fired back. Even I was surprised at how quickly she could be brazen with strangers.

The girls looked at the boy, whose face almost matched his sweet-potato-colored hair, and laughed again, only this time at him.

"Quiet," Mrs. Elliot demanded, and Stanley Bender sat back.

Haylee turned to me and smiled as if to say, *Don't worry. I'll protect us . . . always.* I saw that the other girls who had heard her were also smiling at her. She glowed in their appreciation.

However, Stanley Bender turned out to have asked a question that was less silly than everyone first thought. It was odd to the other students, I'm sure, but whenever I raised my hand to go to the bathroom, Haylee did so instantly, too, and vice versa. Years later, when we were in seventh grade, we were still doing that. Some teachers became annoyed with it, and one, Mrs. Plunket, our math teacher, refused to let Haylee go one day. Haylee peed in her seat, and that created a very big scene. Mother almost had Mrs. Plunket fired.

But many things like that were waiting for us in the future. For now, we were in school, and we could finally meet and find friends one way or another. Usually, it would be Haylee's way. She made instant decisions about the other girls in our class and especially the boys. If she didn't like someone, I couldn't like him or her. If I talked to someone she didn't like, she would tell Mother that I didn't listen to her when she told me why not to be friends with that person. She didn't make it sound like she was telling on me; she was clever enough to make it sound like she was worried about me.

Two weeks after we entered school, a girl named Mary Braddock invited us to her birthday party.

Haylee didn't like her and told Mother she had made fun of us, even though she hadn't, but that was enough for Mother to hear. I couldn't challenge what Haylee had said. We weren't permitted to go to the party. I was surprised that it was more important to Haylee to decide things for us than to go to our first party hosted by a classmate.

The table was set. I would for the longest time have to eat the dinner Haylee wanted. She was simply more aggressive at finding friends and disliking others. Her decisions were instantaneous, and it did no good to ask her to reconsider. Haylee Blossom Fitzgerald never gave any other girl a second chance. If anything, that kept us from making many friends.

Mother was right about our schoolwork, however. In the beginning, neither of us achieved much less than a ninety-eight on any test in any subject. I often heard Mrs. Elliot compliment Mother on how well she had done with us in our homeschooling. Mother gloated about it to Daddy. If he wanted to express opposition to anything she had decided for us, that diminished even more now. Look at how successful her planning had been.

Before our first year of private-school attendance ended, we went to three birthday parties for girls Haylee did like because they were in awe of her. Two of them, Melanie Rosen and Toby Sue Daniels, became what she declared were "our best friends," even though they weren't really that close to me. The truth was, I didn't like either of them very much. They were always complaining about other students, making fun of other girls, and eager and willing to do anything Haylee told them to do. Because we were doing so well in all our subjects, she offered to help them, which actually meant that I would be doing most of the tutoring. In exchange, they gave Haylee things our mother would never want us to have, from candy to magazines and, eventually, when we were in sixth grade, cigarettes. Haylee smoked only at their houses and tried to get me to do it, too. Melanie and Toby Sue showed her how to get rid of the smell, but Mother finally did detect it on our clothes.

I'll never forget that day, because it was the first time I saw Mother fall for one of Haylee's serious lies. She sat us in the great room as usual and began her cross-examination just like the lawyer she had once set out to be.

"Let me see your hands," she began, and inspected our fingers. Melanie and Toby Sue had shown Haylee how to scrub off any traces of nicotine, and I hadn't given in and smoked a cigarette that afternoon. Mother squinted suspiciously when she saw nothing. She leaned in closer so she could smell our breath, but Haylee had gargled with mouthwash before we left Melanie's house.

Mother still looked skeptical and suspicious. "Which one of your friends gave you cigarettes?"

she asked me. Although she wouldn't ever tell us so, she must have believed that I would be more truthful.

But before I could answer, Haylee spoke up. "It wasn't a friend, Mother. It was Melanie's father."

"What? He gave you cigarettes?"

"No. He was the one smoking. He likes to do magic tricks," she continued. Mr. Rosen did like to perform for us. He worked in a bank and, according to Melanie, hated his boring job. He had always wanted to be an entertainer. He was very funny sometimes. I liked him much more than I liked Melanie.

"So?" Mother asked.

"Well, he was smoking when he performed in Melanie's room for us," Haylee continued. "The windows were open, so we didn't notice it that much. He always has a cigarette dangling from his lips, right, Kaylee?"

That part was true, so I nodded, expecting Mother to start shouting at us for lying. She didn't, and Haylee continued her fabrication with more confidence than I had ever seen her have.

"The teachers have a room for those who want to smoke," she said, "and when you walk by, you can smell it in the hallway. Our clothes could smell from that, too, I bet."

"Really? That should be stopped," Mother said.

A really clever liar gets someone distracted from

the main questions as soon as she can, I thought. At this moment, Haylee looked like she had taken lessons in how to deceive. She was doing so much of it at school as it was.

"It's just like you say, Mother, very dirty," she said, nodding and grimacing. "I can see how yellow it makes their teeth. It's ugh."

"Good," Mother said. "Next time Mr. Rosen comes near you with a cigarette in his mouth, I want you to tell him how upset I was about the stench on your clothes. If he wants to get lung cancer, fine, but I won't let you go to Melanie's house if it happens again."

"Oh, we'll tell him, won't we, Kaylee?" she said.

There was a part of me that wanted to end the lying, to tell Mother that Haylee—and I, because the three of them were demanding that I do it—smoked cigarettes from time to time, but I was now more afraid of Haylee's anger than Mother's at my snitching on my sister.

"Yes," I said.

"Good. My girls are still perfect," Mother said, smiling. I couldn't believe we were getting away with it. Mother was still cautious, however. "I want you to have friends, but remember, real friends don't force their friends to do bad things."

"They don't, Mother," Haylee said, with more of a confident grin than a smile of relief. "If anything, Melanie Rosen and Toby Sue Daniels do what we tell them, not vice versa. We never forgot what you told us about keeping our standards higher and making them become more like us."

She's talking too much, I thought. *Mother's not stupid*. I waited, expecting her to really cross-examine us now, but she surprised me. She rose, smiled at us, and went off to prepare dinner. I didn't move, half-expecting Mother to return now that she had thought about it a little more.

Haylee was watching me. "That was close," she said. "You did well, Kaylee."

"I don't like lying to Mother," I said.

"Sometimes she makes us lie."

"What? Why?"

"She's too strict with us, so it's her fault if we lie," she replied. It was another example of how Haylee was going to lay blame for everything at Mother's feet.

"That doesn't give us the right to lie," I insisted.

She rolled her eyes. "You know, I have a hard time getting the girls in our class to like you because you act like such a goody-goody, Kaylee," she said. "All right. From now on, if Melanie and Toby Sue want us to smoke in their rooms or anywhere else, they'll have to loan us clothes to wear."

"It will get into our hair, too, Haylee. Mother will smell it on us."

"Then we'll just shampoo and blow-dry before we come home."

"Just to smoke? That's stupid."

"If I do it, you'll do it," she ordered. "Or we won't have any friends at all, ever."

"I don't like your friends."

"They're *our* friends, Kaylee, don't you re-member?" She lost her smile. "Don't ruin it for me. Just . . . grow up." She rose to go to our room and paused in the doorway. "Don't think I'll be a baby like you just to please Mother," she warned.

"I'm not a baby, Haylee."

She smiled again. It was almost as if she knew what was coming next and was preparing me to do things I would not even have thought of doing.

She couldn't beat me in a race, and she couldn't get a better grade in any subject, but she would be in charge of us, or else.

It was the *or else* I never saw coming that really put her in charge.

5

Haylee would never let me forget that she had her first period almost a month before I did. In her mind, it was like finally beating me in a race. We were just finishing our sixth-grade year at Betsy Ross. Although most of the sixth-graders were eleven and some very close to twelve, we knew that a period could come as early as eight and as late as eighteen and still be considered normal. Our school nurse had told us that. Two other girls in our class, one of them Haylee's friend Melanie Rosen, had also had their first periods, or what Mother called "the stork's first visit." She was still treating us like little girls, and although we were learning a lot about sex from our girlfriends, or I should say Haylee's friends, Mother had yet to have a real mother-daughter talk with us, a talk that wasn't scientific and delivered with anatomical illustrations.

Mother was prepared for our first periods, however. Despite what we were taught to expect, more girls were getting it at earlier ages these days. The nurse told us that there were some theories involving hormones in our foods. It was all scientific gobbledygook and quite boring. It seemed to take the *X* out of *sex*. Who wanted to be able to identify fallopian tubes on a chart? What did that have to do with boyfriends and parties and romance? A first period was more than some historical biological event.

All of us girls both feared and looked forward to it. It was impossible not to anticipate the pain and discomfort but at the same time look forward to feeling mature, almost escaping from childhood, where you were seen as a little girl, innocent and protected, then stepping into adolescence with all the excitement that awaited us.

Sometime during the night before Haylee's happened, she was having cramps. She complained and moaned, refused to eat, and wanted only to curl up in the fetal position. Mother kept asking me how I was, but I had nothing to say, no complaints. She seemed concerned, but more like disappointed, and kept asking me if I was sure.

"No cramps at all?"

"Maybe a little," I said, more to make her happy than anything.

"Then it's probably just an upset stomach,"

Mother concluded, going by her belief that if some-thing like a period wasn't happening to us both simultaneously, it wasn't happening. She gave us each a tablespoon of castor oil.

However, Haylee had trouble sleeping that night, and almost as soon as she got out of bed in the morning, she shouted for Mother, who came running to our room. Haylee was crying now. Mother looked at me. I shook my head. She gri-maced, took Haylee's hand, and led her into the bathroom. Daddy, who was getting ready for work, stepped into our room. I was staring in awe at the red spots on Haylee's bedsheet.

"What's happening?" he asked me. Mother was still with Haylee in the bathroom.

I shook my head. I didn't know how to tell Daddy. He had little to do with anything intimate about us, and according to Mother, he'd never even changed a diaper when we were babies. I suspected she never would have permitted him to do it any-way.

"Keri? What is it?" he called.

Mother poked her head out and said, "The rea-son some men give thanks they've had sons instead of daughters."

"What?"

"Just go to work, Mason. As usual, I have ev-erything under control when it comes to the girls," she said, and disappeared back into the bathroom.

Daddy looked at me, still concerned, and I decided to mouth, "She's having her first period."

He widened his eyes and nodded. Then he flashed a smile and fled, as if having a period was catching and he might be the first man to experience it.

When Mother came out of the bathroom with Haylee, who looked calmer, she held out a pad for me, even though I hadn't had a period and wasn't even having stomach discomfort.

"She doesn't need it!" Haylee cried out in protest. She was happy I hadn't had mine.

Mother glared at her. "She will, now that you have," she snapped back.

Haylee looked away quickly but muttered, "I'm just saying what's true."

"I don't need you to tell me that, Haylee. Wouldn't it be stupid, embarrassing, for me to ignore that it will surely happen to her very soon, too, and send her along with you to school unprotected? Well?"

"Yes, Mother. I'm sorry," Haylee said quickly. She sneaked in an angry look at me even so. Mother then gave me the same instructions I imagined she had given Haylee in the bathroom. All the while, Haylee stood off to the side, her arms folded tightly across her chest, pouting.

The moment Mother left us, Haylee grabbed my right wrist, almost twisting my arm, and said,

"You'd better not lie about it and tell the girls you had your period, Kaylee. You're still a little girl."

"I'm not a little girl."

"Of course you are," she said with glee.

Haylee finally had something that made her different from me, and she didn't want to lose it too quickly. Until I had my period, she was going to use hers to prove to her friends that she was more mature than I was, even though nothing else physically about her was any different from me. Both of us had begun to grow pubic hair and develop breasts. Haylee claimed I had less hair and smaller buds. She wanted to count hairs and measure the way Mother had counted our freckles, but I wouldn't do it. That satisfied her, because she could claim I was afraid to see that she was right.

She wasn't, of course, but I did look at her when I could to be sure. Sometimes when I gazed at myself naked and saw Haylee undressed, I felt as if we were being sculpted more intensely and frequently, as if God came to us during the night and made subtle changes with his miraculous fingers that were becoming more and more pronounced. It caused me to become more curious about myself and even a little thrilled with the changes I was seeing. I could almost feel the child in me dwindling, sinking in a pool of toys and picture books.

Despite Haylee's claims up to the day of her first period, neither of us seemed to be moving into adolescence faster than the other. What I was seeing in her I was also seeing in myself. Mother measured us regularly to confirm it. Haylee and I were exactly the same height, four feet eleven inches, and we each weighed ninety-two pounds. Haylee was just a few ounces heavier, but Mother didn't count them. We still had the same shoe size, too, and remarkably, neither of us yet had any of the skin blemishes we saw on other girls occasionally. Unlike our classmates, neither of us had a single cavity. Our dentist, Dr. Baxter, always remarked about how perfectly identical our teeth were and how healthy, too. Mother told him that it shouldn't surprise him. She was compulsive about our brushing and flossing together and forbade us to chew gum or eat candy.

"My girls always will be perfect," she insisted. "Unlike other siblings, they look after each other."

She was right about that. During our early school years, Haylee was always watching me and I would watch her to be sure neither of us accepted gum or candy from anyone. When other students, especially boys like Stanley Bender, teased us about it, Haylee was more upset than I was, but while Mother was hovering in the hallways or in our classroom doorway, she didn't dare disobey. When I was teased, I bragged about our dental health, and eventually, Haylee, seeing how that took the steam out of any ridicule, did the same.

"It's like they have one mouth, isn't it?" Mother had commented when we had our most recent checkup. She was always looking for her view of us to be reinforced.

Dr. Baxter nodded. "I could never tell you whose teeth I'm working on," he said. "Not a single tooth is different from the other's."

His dental assistant, Shirley Camp, said similar things, all of which pleased Mother but annoyed Haylee, even though only I could see her displeasure when Mother wasn't with us or wasn't looking at us. Haylee so wanted her own eyes, her own mouth, and her own nose and ears.

"I hate mirrors!" she once exclaimed, reluctantly admitting that when she gazed at herself, it was like looking at me through a window. We never played that game anymore where we pretended to be looking into a mirror when we looked at each other and touched our noses and ears with opposite hands perfectly. Once when I bumped my head and had a tiny bruise, she was as happy as a bee drowning in pollen, even though hardly anyone but her could see it. She dared not mention it in front of Mother. I think she was afraid Mother would have her bump hers in the exact same place. I wondered myself, recalling how she had cut my finger with that same piece of glass years ago.

I understood why Haylee avoided looking at herself. I supposed it was as if we had a mirror walking beside each of us, but finally, Haylee had something very different about herself to cling to. Getting her first period was like being admitted to a private club that I couldn't join. It was populated not only by her friend Melanie and the two other girls in our class who had their periods but also by three other girls in the seventh and eighth grades who were friends with Melanie. Now the seven of them had something special in common. They sat together in the cafeteria as if something magical had occurred and so changed them that they were almost a different species from the other girls their age.

Haylee saw the look on my face when she first sat with them and made no room for me to sit beside her. I stood there dumbly for a moment, holding my tray.

"Go sit somewhere else, Kaylee. We have more mature things to talk about, things you wouldn't understand," she said, dismissing me.

I couldn't help the tears that came to my eyes.

Haylee went on, "I don't know if you even realize it because you're still a little girl, but boys look at us differently. We have sex things to discuss now, things you can't appreciate or might be embarrassed by."

"That's not so," I said. "Boys can't tell unless you or someone else tells them or you suffer bad cramps in front of them."

Haylee looked at Melanie and shook her head, as if to say, *Don't pay attention to her. She's a child.*

It felt as if a pot of boiling water was steaming in my chest. "We're not supposed to say bad things about each other," I reminded her.

She shrugged. "It's not something bad, Kaylee. It's just a simple truth. You're still a child." She turned to Melanie. "She's very jealous, of course. She's been wearing the same pad for a week and studies it for a drop every night."

They both laughed.

"I do not!"

"You're not wearing a pad without having a period?" Haylee asked.

I was so shocked that she would talk about what Mother wanted me to do that I couldn't speak.

"See?" she told Melanie.

They laughed again.

"Mother would be very mad at you for saying that, Haylee."

"I don't think you'll tell her just to get me in trouble, will you? You know how she hates the idea of one of us trying to get her to love her more. You'll end up in the pantry with the jars of pickles and jelly."

Melanie laughed again, and they walked away before I could think of something nasty to say. The frustration felt like a belt being tightened around my chest until I couldn't breathe. She was right. I would never tell Mother anything bad about her, even though I felt such a strong urge to do so and have that smug look wiped off her face.

There wasn't any other way Mother would learn about this quickly, either. She had stopped assisting the second-grade teacher after our first two years and did not know that Haylee was making a point of not sitting with me at lunchtime. Without Mother in the school, Haylee tried to avoid me all day. She was always whispering and laughing with the other girls, none of whom I particularly wanted to be with anyway. She started flirting with some older boys, too, and couldn't wait to tell me who liked her.

"That should tell you something about us, Kaylee," she said. "They don't even look at you, do they?"

I didn't answer, because she was right, but I did think the reason they were looking at her was that she was practically throwing herself in front of them.

Despite not wanting to, I did feel left out, even immature. The more Haylee gloated, the more miserable I felt. I was afraid I might never catch up to her socially. I did become best friends with Sarah Morgan, whose grades were as good as mine and Haylee's, even a little better. Although she looked like she wouldn't get her first period for another ten years, Sarah was pretty. She had what I thought of as an angelic face because of her soft, gentle, and caring eyes, her porcelain complexion, and her perfect nose and lips. She had diminutive, doll-like features and was a good two inches shorter than we were. I thought she might still look like a girl only ten years old even when she was a senior in high school.

In the fifth grade, Sarah suddenly had to wear glasses. Haylee was ready to pounce on that and make fun of her, but her mother bought her very stylish frames, and contrary to what Haylee thought, most of the girls admired them. Sarah seemed incapable of getting into an argument, and whenever Haylee said something unpleasant to her, which was often, she simply smiled, as if Haylee was someone to be pitied. Of course, that only made Haylee angrier. I liked Sarah's wit and the way she couldn't be intimidated, something I longed to master ever since we had entered Betsy Ross.

Haylee and I hadn't been given our own rooms at home yet, so it was still especially important to Mother that neither of us brought home someone the other didn't like. Whoever it was had to be shared and equally liked. I had to make a deal with Haylee in order to invite Sarah over on a Friday to have dinner with us and spend the night.

"You can have her this Friday, but I have Melanie on Saturday," she proposed. I was actually a little afraid of Melanie Rosen by now, and not just because she and Toby Sue had gotten us to smoke and look at dirty magazines. She had developed faster than we had, and I heard stories about her seeing boys in the junior high, meeting secretly and "doing things."

"You shouldn't be friends with her after the trouble we almost got into because of the smoking, Haylee. Melanie is one of those peers Mother warned us about. She'll get you into more and more trouble, and you won't be able to lie your way out of it like you did with the smoking. We'll both be grounded for weeks, even months!"

"Don't you say anything like that ever, especially in front of Mother," she warned me, with those big eyes and clenched fingers. "You'll be sorry if you do."

I didn't, but Haylee wasn't shy about saying negative things about Sarah in front of Mother. She was so clever and careful about it, though, that it looked as if she was telling Mother things just to protect us.

"We're her only friends," she told Mother. "She's so shy that she's actually someone to be pitied."

"Well, then, maybe it's nice that you're being her friend," Mother said, which disappointed Haylee.

"Other girls and even boys ask all the time why we're friends with her," she whined. "We're afraid we'll lose friends because they don't like to be around her and don't invite her to anything."

Mother looked at me.

Although I wasn't going to speak up and say that Haylee was lying or even exaggerating, I was sure Mother could see my unhappiness with what Haylee was saying.

"What did I tell you about not letting your peers pressure you into making bad decisions?" Mother asked Haylee. "You don't look to them for advice or guidance. You look to each other. I've brought you up to have each other's best interests first and foremost, not the interests of your friends."

"I know," Haylee said. "We do."

"Then there is no problem. Kaylee likes Sarah, too, don't you, Kaylee?"

"Yes, Mother."

"Haylee?"

"She likes my friend Melanie Rosen, too," Haylee quickly inserted, so that I would not get what I wanted while she didn't get what she wanted. "We both do."

"Then you mean *our* friend Melanie, don't you?" Mother corrected.

"Yes, Mother."

"You don't want any friends who don't like your sister as much as they like you, and your sister doesn't want any friends who don't like you as much as they like her. Is that clear?"

Haylee nodded. Mother looked at me, so I nodded, too. It was like swallowing some bad-tasting medicine to have to pretend to like Melanie. For one thing, she made fun of Sarah whenever she could. She cheated on tests, stealing answers willingly given by Haylee, answers I had given her. So she was really cheating from me, too. Some of the things she told us when we were at her house disgusted me, especially about what her older brother was doing in the bathroom. I could see that Haylee enjoyed all that and even enjoyed my discomfort at hearing the details, which she now blamed on my being less mature.

"He doesn't know it," Melanie said proudly, "but I can see him reading magazines with pictures of naked women and then playing with himself. You know what I mean by that, don't you, Kaylee? It's not like he plays ring toss or something," she said, grinning at Haylee, who grinned back.

"I know," I said, even though I wasn't as sure as Haylee was.

Sometimes I thought Haylee was conspiring with Melanie to make me feel uncomfortable and help her differentiate herself from me. I was sure she said things about me to her new friends. I did hear that she was telling them how much she had to look out for me because I was so trusting and innocent. She made it seem like I was a big burden.

Mother, who was unaware of all this, was pleased at how we were supposedly making friends together. I didn't like the way we were deceiving her, but if I didn't go along with it, I wouldn't have any of the friends I wanted to have. They would all be Haylee's friends.

Now Mother looked at us both for a moment and then smiled and nodded. "You'll both be just fine if you depend on each other the way your left hand depends on your right," she said. "You can depend on your sister, Haylee." We waited for her to say the same to me, but she didn't. It was so unusual, but I didn't want to do anything to remind her.

Haylee looked down rather than at me. She was afraid I would gloat the way she would at the way Mother had singled one of us out for a warning or what seemed clearly to be a compliment. Then she surprised me by looking up with a little more defiance than usual and said, "Sometimes we need our peers to teach us things, right, Mother? Things neither of us knows because we don't have the same experiences or haven't been to the same places. That's okay, isn't it, Mother?"

Mother's eyes narrowed with suspicion. "What places, Haylee?"

She shrugged. "Places. I don't know."

Mother nodded to herself as a suspicion emerged. She looked from me to Haylee, who could clearly see that she had said too much. "Do any of your girlfriends have boyfriends already?" She looked quickly at me first for our response.

"Not steady boyfriends," I offered.

"I think," Mother said, nodding to herself again, "that the time has come for us to have a serious talk about the stork and his first visit."

She indicated that we should go into the great room. Haylee looked up at me quickly, suspecting that I might have said something more to Mother secretly. I hadn't, but I tried to look more surprised than she was so she wouldn't think that.

"We can't depend on what you learn in science and health classes," Mother began, after we had sat beside each other on the settee. She took her usual teacher position.

Haylee almost groaned. She was afraid that Mother was about to turn something exciting into another biology lesson.

"You know more about the human body than most of the other students in your class, I'm sure. Even before Haylee got hers, you already knew why you have a period every month and what that leads to. You knew that before anything about it was explained to you in school. You were always way ahead of the other girls your age because of the homeschooling," she said proudly.

"She still doesn't have one," Haylee pointed out.

Mother closed and opened her eyes. Then she turned to her slowly. "Don't you believe she will have it soon?"

"Yes."

"Then why mention that at all, Haylee?"

"I don't know."

Mother took a deep breath, the way she did when she was annoyed by something Daddy had said.

"I'm sorry," Haylee said quickly, and lowered her head.

"You need to think more before you speak. Your tongue can get too far ahead of you and get you into trouble. Understand?"

"Yes, Mother," Haylee said.

I didn't think I had to say anything.

"All right. Where was I? Boys, although they mature slower than girls in every way, are usually more aggressive when it comes to having sex," Mother continued. "It's been that way since the caveman days. In fact, some men behave as if they are still back there when it comes to having sex for pleasure."

Haylee looked up quickly. This was the first time Mother had mentioned "having sex" and "pleasure" in the same sentence, revealing that it was something you could do for other reasons than having babies.

"That doesn't mean they enjoy it more," Mother quickly added. She smiled at our looks of astonishment.

Both of us were thinking, *What other mother but ours would come right out and say such a thing?*

"Sex is something a man and a woman can both

enjoy. Look at it this way, my precious, if it wasn't enjoyable, human beings might not do it enough to have children and keep the human race going."

"So every animal enjoys it?" Haylee asked. "I mean, we learned in science that they have sex. I mean, Mr. Boyton didn't call it sex. He called it reproduction," she added, with twisted lips as if the word itself was distasteful.

"I think that's safe to say, yes, they enjoy it. Now, here comes the most important part, dear Haylee and Kaylee. You can enjoy it too much, or you can forget that the most important reason for it is to make children."

"You don't make children every time," Haylee blurted. Her conversations with her "special group" were showing.

"Okay, Haylee," Mother said, sitting back and crossing her arms over her breasts. "Why don't you tell us why not?"

Suddenly, Haylee looked frightened. I couldn't help the way my lips were starting to smile. I could help her, but I wanted her to struggle with her lies.

"We learned that a woman has to be ready to make babies inside," she said, practically stuttering.

"Yes, but she could be unaware of how ready she is. Then what could happen?"

Haylee pressed her lips together.

Mother looked at me, so I had to answer. "She could get pregnant," I said.

"How?" Mother asked.

"The man's sperm gets into her and meets an egg."

Mother nodded. "And who do you think would suffer the most after that?" Mother asked us, looking more at Haylee now.

"The girl," I said when Haylee hesitated. I had to wonder if she had any doubt.

Haylee nodded.

This conversation was already going places Haylee had never anticipated we would go with our mother. It was fun to talk about these things with her girlfriends. I had to admit that even I enjoyed listening to them talk sometimes, but showing too much excitement about it when your mother discussed it was a definite no-no.

"All of this doesn't just happen out of the blue. There are places on your body that a boy could touch, even touch with his lips, that would make you so excited that you might forget what you know could happen, so you have to be very, very careful," Mother said.

"Lips?" Haylee said, now smiling. I knew she already was quite acquainted with that activity. Melanie had recently described the experience when she made out with Bobby Lester in his basement den. I had seen Haylee's eyes brighten when Melanie described how it had taken her breath away. She was bragging about how far she had gone. She told us that if Bobby hadn't gotten excited so quickly, she might have gone further. She even knew the term for it, *premature ejaculation*. "So if we say PE, Kaylee," Melanie had said, turning to me with a wide smile smeared like whipped cream on her face, "we don't mean physical education class."

Of course, everyone had laughed, mostly at me. Even Haylee had laughed at me. I felt like bringing that up right now but kept my mouth shut.

"Yes, Haylee. It's part of foreplay," Mother said.

"Why four?" Haylee asked, grimacing.

Mother smiled.

I knew Haylee was pretending. She had heard the term. We both had. She was just trying to appear innocent. I was surprised at how good she was at it, but instead of appreciating her ability to deceive, I was worried for us both.

"Not *four* as in the number four, Haylee. *Fore* as in before."

"Oh."

"I don't expect you hear the term from any of your friends. They would probably just say 'making out,'" she said, "or 'hooking up.' Something like that." She looked at me, too. "Anyway, foreplay involves touching, kissing, and even licking."

"Licking!" Haylee exclaimed. She knew about that, too, but she continued putting on a good act, an act Mother accepted because she believed she was that innocent or maybe wanted to believe it.

She did look happy that the idea wasn't immediately attractive to Haylee, but I knew from Haylee's conversations with Melanie that it was—all of it, what Melanie called L and S, licking and sucking. She glanced at me to see if I might give away the truth, but I didn't change expression. The way Melanie had described it disturbed me. It was all I could think about at the time, and I imagined doing things like that with different boys.

"It's all a way to arouse you or for you to arouse a boy someday. I hope not soon," Mother added. She paused and looked at us more carefully. I think we were both holding our breath. "Other mothers would never discuss this with daughters at your age, but you are older, wiser, and more mature than their daughters, I'm sure, and will benefit from what I'm telling you."

"Arouse a boy," Haylee repeated, as the images began to settle into both our minds, thanks to Melanie.

"Well, when I was a teenager, we called it being turned on, and I imagine that still is something you will hear. When you're turned on, you're more apt to make a mistake. Understand?" she asked, looking first at me.

I nodded, so Haylee nodded quickly, too. She wanted to appear older now, even in front of Mother.

"And if you're turned on and make a mistake,

you can get pregnant," Haylee said, anticipating that I might say it first.

"Exactly. Any boy who doesn't want you to be careful and doesn't want to be careful himself is not a good boy to be with. If one of you knows of such a boy and sees that he's interested in you, what should you do?"

"Warn each other," I said immediately.

"Very good. I'm depending on you both to do just that as you grow older. Now," Mother said, relaxing her arms, "I want you to have friends who are boys, and someday, as you know, you'll have a real boyfriend and you'll go to dances and parties, but you'll always remember that mistakes can spoil your whole life, right?"

We nodded.

"I have told you never to come to me to tattle on your sister, but I'm going to make a big exception to the rule starting today," she said. "I want either of you to tell me if one of you is close to making a mistake. Until you're on your own out of this house, I want you to remember that new rule. Understand?"

We nodded.

"Good," she said. "From this day on, whenever you have a question about sex or boys, you ask me, not your peers," she added, looking mostly at Haylee. "There are girls who might enjoy seeing one of you in trouble. That's the bottom of the barrel when it comes to jealousy between girls. Beware of it."

"We will," Haylee said quickly. She looked at me to see if I would as much as suggest that some of her girlfriends fell right into Mother's definition of jealous girls. I was so tempted, but I didn't do it.

"All right. That's enough for now. See how fathers get away with everything when there are daughters? Not that your father would have the time to have a good, healthy discussion with you even if you were boys. Especially these days," she added unhappily.

Daddy had been gone for nearly two weeks on a major business trip to London. He had told us that his company had a chance to get a very big international contract. Haylee wasn't as aware of it as I was, but Daddy was away more often, and even when he was home, he missed many dinners because of working late at his office.

"Do you have any questions?" Mother asked.

Haylee looked at me.

"I don't," I said.

"Me, neither," Haylee said.

"My girls," Mother said, smiling. "My perfect girls. Haylee-Kaylee, Kaylee-Haylee." She hugged us as usual and then left.

The first thing Haylee did when we returned to our room was to seize my arm again. Her teeth were clenched, and her eyes were full of threat.

"Don't you ever tell Mother I'm with a boy who might not be careful, Kaylee." She gave me her superior look. "You don't know enough about boys to decide who I should be with and who I shouldn't. Is that clear?"

I pulled my arm out of her grasp and surprised her by smiling back. "Of course. But there's no reason for you to worry. You're just as smart as I am, Haylee. You won't ever be with such a bad boy, either, will you?" I said. "Right now, you have to worry about it more than I do because you could get pregnant, so you won't make a mistake, right? You certainly don't need me watching over you." It was something my friend Sarah would say, and with the same sort of smile on her face.

Haylee looked a little stunned and then quickly regained her composure and said, "Of course not."

But she looked at me a little differently for the rest of the evening. She was like someone who wasn't quite sure she knew the person she was with, and there were no two people on earth who supposedly knew each other better.

A week later, what she had hoped wouldn't happen for a long time did happen. I had my first period.

Although Mother didn't notice her behavior, Haylee went into a sulk. What really annoyed her was that I didn't have cramps as bad as hers. What pleased Mother, however, was that I had my period the same day of the week exactly three weeks later and almost at the same time. I knew that whenever we did something simultaneously or something happened to us simultaneously, Mother felt she was right about us.

"That's not just a coincidence," she told us at dinner that night. "Now you're both the same again and you can support and help each other as usual with the new problems and questions that come up."

Daddy had come home late and looked uncomfortable with all the talk about periods and cramps.

Mother rattled off a list of things she had found worked for herself to relieve the pains, like drinking lots of water to avoid bloating. She said her grandmother used to give herself and her mother cinnamon and ginger. When she got into more detail about blood flow, Daddy cringed.

"Do we have to discuss this at dinner, Keri?"

"See, girls, men are just built weaker," she declared, smiling.

Haylee smiled, too, but I didn't.

Daddy looked even more annoyed. "It's not a matter of being strong or weak. It's what's appropriate," he said, with a sharper tone than usual. "You'd think with how you stress dinner etiquette, you'd be teaching them that."

Mother despised being criticized in front of

us. Her face would blanch and her neck tighten. More than Haylee, I knew how many times she and Daddy had argued about how we were being raised and how Mother's devotion to us had affected their relationship and their social life. On two occasions I knew of recently, she had decided not to accompany him to a business dinner, citing the need to help us with some aspect of our schoolwork, mainly, it seemed, to bring Haylee up to my level.

"Why does she have to be getting the same grades as Kaylee?" Daddy demanded. "She's doing as well as, if not better than, I was in school."

"If either of them falls behind the other in anything for any reason, it will be damaging," Mother insisted.

As usual, their argument had ended with Daddy just walking out of the room. Silence seemed the best way to stay married, but whether either of them wanted it or not, the static we used to see frequently, static that seemed to have disappeared from our home, had returned. It began to occur more often. Sometimes I expected to hear thunder roll through the house. Mother was even saying "your father," as if she had nothing to do with him, as if he was no longer also her husband.

Arguments between them had come and gone over the years. I expected them to happen at least once a week, usually because of something she was doing with us. Now their arguments were more about their relationship, the little they were doing together, and the friends Daddy said they were losing. The static those fights created resulted in more silence between them, and soon it felt as if we were all walking on eggshells again.

And this time, it wasn't going away, even after Daddy left for good.

6

Years later, I would wonder if Mother realized how bad things finally had become between her and Daddy or if she always knew but didn't care as much as Haylee and I would have expected her to care. It did seem like she either missed clues or deliberately ignored them, all in the name of bringing us up perfectly. Any mother would tell her husband that their children came first, but the sacrifices our mother was willing, even eager, to make were not ones Daddy was willing to make. Gradually, what social life they had thinned out, until their attending parties, meeting people for dinners, and going to shows with friends dwindled to almost never.

The periods during which Daddy would be gone for business trips grew longer. It was clear to me, at least, that he welcomed any opportunity to stay away from the home he had once so loved. In fact, there were weeds showing on the tennis court, and it was easy to see how our property was being neglected, not to the point of being outright shabby but without the loving pride that Daddy had once had in it. Mother didn't seem to notice or care, either, and if I asked her about something like the unkempt flower beds, she would say, "That's your father's responsibility, not mine. I have enough to do with you and what needs to be done inside the house."

By the time we entered the tenth grade in high school, Daddy had drifted so far from us that he almost forgot our birthday, something Mother pounced on like a panther. He was supposed to return from a business trip the day before but called to say he was being delayed. It was then that we heard Mother reminding him that he would miss our fifteenth birthday. The plan had been for us all to go to the London House, an upscale restaurant outside of Philadelphia that, though built to resemble a pub, was very expensive and far too formal to make anyone who had lived or traveled in England think they were in that kind of neighborhood place. The rich cherry paneling, brass bar, hardwood floors, and chandeliers in the dining room, along with the maitre d' in a tuxedo, gave it the elegance to justify the high prices. There were some traditional English dishes on the menu, such as shepherd's pie and, for lunch only, fish and chips, but everything else was gourmet. The chef, in fact, was not English but French.

Mother liked it, but the restaurant wasn't Haylee's or my favorite. We thought it was too stuffy. None of our friends had ever gone there with their families, but we knew Mother liked parading us past the upscale crowd, the men dressed in jackets and ties and the women in designer clothes bedecked with expensive-looking jewelry. We'd walk through the dining area to a center table, which for us was like a stage. Still identically dressed and with identical hairstyles, we turned heads and created a pause in conversations. Although Haylee hated sharing it with me, she enjoyed the attention. Normally, Mother soaked in the compliments we received from strangers. But this time, from the moment we left the house without Daddy, I knew she was very agitated.

Nevertheless, as usual, she went on and on about the importance of our birthday, making it sound like a national event. I was embarrassed by how special she made our birthdays appear in front of people, especially strangers. I knew Haylee always enjoyed the attention and sat listening, entranced about her own significance. Despite Mother's mood concerning Daddy, all was going well until Mother spotted Bryce Krammer and his wife entering the restaurant.

Mr. Krammer was an executive in Daddy's company. He was part of the group who came over to play tennis sometimes and had been the one to call us the Mirror Sisters. Neither he nor the other men had come to play tennis for some time, which partly explained why the court looked neglected. He and his wife had been to our house for dinner at least a half dozen times through the years, and when Mother was socializing more, she and Daddy had been to theirs. It was the Krammers, in fact, who had turned Mother and Daddy on to the London House restaurant. They saw us immediately and came directly to our table.

"Well, what do we have here?" Mr. Krammer said. He was a tall, thin, dark-haired man with graying hair. Despite being in his fifties, he had what I thought was the sort of impish smile more comfortable on the face of a teenage boy, a modern-day Tom Sawyer. I knew that his amused look at Mother whenever she talked about us annoyed her. She believed there was nothing remotely amusing about the things she was pointing out about us. "Surely these aren't the little girls I remember. These are two beautiful young ladies."

His wife stood there smiling at us and then turned to Mother and exchanged greetings. "I just told Bryce the other day that he should speak to Mason about us getting together soon. It's been so long since we've seen the twins, too. I had no idea they were so grown-up and so beautiful!"

"Today is the girls' birthday," Mother declared, ignoring her and directing herself to Mr. Krammer. Mother thought very few women these days deserved her attention and time. The truth was, Daddy had tried to get them together with the Krammers, but Mother always found a reason not to be able to make the date.

"Oh, wow!" Mr. Krammer declared. "How old are we?"

"*They're* fifteen," Mother replied.

Mr. Krammer ignored the subtle criticism. "So it's not just another dinner. It's a celebration. Happy birthday, girls."

"Thank you," we said, so perfectly in unison that it was comical.

Mr. Krammer looked around. "Mason in the bathroom?" he asked.

Mother hesitated, her forehead folding so deeply that the wrinkles looked more like deep slices. "Don't you have a possible merger with a company in Texas going on?" she asked.

"That fell through last week," he said. "Why?"

"Mason isn't here tonight," she said, without giving any more details.

I saw the way the Krammers looked at each other. To me, it suggested that they already knew a lot more about Daddy and Mother's strained relationship than they pretended. Daddy's absence only confirmed what they believed, but, like most people, they chose to ignore something unpleasant.

"Oh, well, he's so hard at it most of the time that he makes the rest of us look like pikers," Mr. Krammer said. He forced a smile, but it was clear he didn't want to linger another moment. "Once again, happy birthday, girls."

"Yes, happy birthday. We'll call," his wife promised, her words as empty as a deflated balloon. She touched Mother's hand, and they walked off to their table in the rear, both with hoisted shoulders, looking as if they had just stepped out of a walk-in freezer.

Mother stared ahead, the anger rippling through her face from her forehead down and settling in the tightness of her lips.

Where was Daddy? I wondered. Why did he lie about where he was going, especially when he was reminded about our birthday? Haylee was more interested in what she would eat and wasn't even looking at Mother, nor did she care one iota about the Krammers and their reaction to Daddy's absence.

Mother's face seemed to lose the brightness she could generate when talking about us. Her eyes would surge with an energy that normally captured the interest of most people. In fact, Mother would treat our birthdays the way most people treated New Year's Eve. She would talk about our future, predicting all the good things that were to come and the achievements we would surely enjoy. Inevitably, she would reminisce about our births and early days, bringing up one anecdote after another to emphasize how alike we were.

When Daddy was with us, he would look at her as if he was just learning about us himself. Because she would so dominate the conversation at our birthday celebrations, it was almost as if he wasn't there anyway. He always appeared worried about what he would say and what gifts he had gotten for us. Because Mother was so in control of it all, he surely felt unnecessary.

He wasn't unnecessary to me. I could see how hard he was trying to please Mother. Sometimes it seemed she didn't want to share us with him. We were all hers. I knew she loved it when someone would comment on how much we looked like her, calling us clones. If Daddy was standing by, I would quickly glance at him and see his eyes lower. He stood beside us, wanting to hold our hands, but Mother was always in between us when the four of us went anywhere. He was more like someone going along for the ride. And when we were older and no one had to hold our hands crossing the street or walking on the sidewalk and going into the mall or a store, he looked even more lost.

If he asked either of us a question about school, he had to ask the other. We had set answers for the obvious questions, like how we were doing in some school subject, how we liked attending Betsy Ross, whether we'd made any friends. I could see his displeasure in the recited reactions, but I could also see Mother's satisfaction. She said "They're so alike" so many times that Daddy looked as if he wanted to put his hands over his ears and scream.

I read stories about daughters who were "Daddy's little girls," but the chances of either Haylee or me ever becoming that were nonexistent. Too often, in fact, he looked at us as if we were strangers. It seemed Mother had made him feel that we were beyond his understanding. Rather than deal with all the psychology she had imposed, he drifted further back and became an observer and not a member of the family.

Now I glanced again at Haylee. I was confident that I missed him at our birthday celebration more than she did. Over the years, it was rare for us to be alone with him, and if we did go somewhere with just him, all of us were subjected to Mother's vigorous cross-examination about what we had done, where we had gone, and even what we had eaten. No matter how strongly Daddy adhered to her rules for us, there was always something for her to criticize. It was no wonder that he began to do less and less with us alone.

"I'm starving," Haylee said. She looked at both of us, and I realized she really had no clue about what was happening with Mother and Daddy. And she was the one who thought she was more sophisticated about male-female relationships.

Mother signaled to the waiter. I was sure she had already ordered a special cake for us. For the last two birthdays, she had stopped making two identical cakes and simply had a chocolate line drawn down the middle with Haylee's name spelled out on one side and mine on the other. She had ordered that for us tonight. It was a big cake, because she had insisted we have fifteen candles on each side. It looked like it was on fire. In fact, someone yelled, "Get the fire department!" And there was lots of laughter.

When it came time for us to blow out the candles, the whole restaurant joined in to sing "Happy Birthday." Afterward, many of the other customers called out to us as we left. Haylee made sure to give any young man, even if he was with a girlfriend or a wife, a special flirtatious smile. Someone had taught her to lower and raise her eyes when she flirted. Normally, Mother might have noticed, but she was occupied with her own thoughts, dark and red with rage.

It wouldn't be long before we realized that what Mother had learned from Bryce Krammer was the catalyst for the impending break in our parents' marriage. So much began to happen between them behind closed doors right after our birthday. Daddy didn't raise his voice, but I could hear the mumbling, and the tone of it was clearly colored with anger. They hardly looked at each other whenever he was home. Finally, she was on the phone and then visiting with her lawyer. She kept the truth from us as long as she could, and then one night, when Daddy wasn't home again for dinner, she asked us to go into the great room after dinner and wait for her.

"I have something very important to tell you," she said.

Haylee's first worry was naturally that she had done something to upset Mother. I hadn't really talked with Haylee about the cold war between Mother and Daddy. Every time I suggested that something was happening, she immediately changed the topic, like someone who didn't want to waste time on something that didn't have her at the center. She was far too into herself at this point, and other conflicts were developing between us almost daily now, mostly around boys or her girlfriends.

Like anything else that Haylee believed involved competition between us, capturing the interest of many boys in high school was very important to her. Consequently, she wasn't getting involved with any one boy more than the others. She flitted about as if she was collecting smiles, expressions of romantic interest, and invitations for dates, something Mother was still reluctant to let either of us have and most certainly not one of us without the other. We could attend school parties and parties other girls had, but even then, we had yet to be permitted to stay out until the Cinderella hour. Of all our friends, Haylee's especially, we had to be home the earliest, which was always before midnight.

Daddy had tried to loosen the strict rules Mother imposed on us, but because she was more often than not the one who drove us places and picked us up, his opinion carried little weight. Telling her that other girls weren't as restricted did no good. Even reminding her that she was going on dates at our age didn't change her mind. According to her, other girls, even her, weren't as "special" as we were. Of course, other girls didn't live under the same rules. She always stung Daddy with a final comment, like "I'm not surprised you don't realize it."

Haylee was smart enough not to complain much more about it than I did. In fact, I had to complain about things that really didn't matter that much to me, especially how long we could hang out at a friend's house or where we could go afterward if we went to a movie with friends.

"You've got to complain more about not being allowed to go on a date, Kaylee," she told me. "It's not that she doesn't think we're old enough. She doesn't think you want to do it as much as I do. You know that's it, Kaylee. I wish you were more interested in having fun."

I was, but her ideas for having fun and mine were growing further apart.

"If you don't start wanting to do the things I want to do, I won't want to do what you want," she threatened.

Whenever we were alone, she began to sulk about it. Now that there was real trouble brewing between our parents, I thought she would stop thinking about herself so much. Actually, she was happy that Mother was distracted with her marital problems. She could get away with more. One thing she began doing was hiding an article of clothing in her book bag so that after we were brought to school, she could go into the girls' room and change. She even brushed her hair differently and began to wear a different shade of lipstick. She restored everything before Mother came to pick us up. Ordinarily, I was sure Mother would learn about it, but she was too distracted or angry about Daddy at this point.

For my part, I wasn't unhappy about the changes Haylee was making for herself daily. There was so much about her now that I didn't want associated with me. I was hoping that our classmates, and especially our teachers, would see the differences and start thinking of us not as twins but instead as just two ordinary sisters. It got so that I wouldn't smile when someone commented on how alike we were. "We're really not," I began to risk saying. Although Haylee didn't believe it, especially now, I wanted to develop my own identity as much as, if not more than, she did. I was confident that anyone who spent any time with us would eventually see the differences in our changing personalities.

For one thing, Haylee was becoming more sarcastic and egotistical. The way she spoke to our teachers often got her reprimanded. When Mother was told about something Haylee had done or said, she would lecture us both, and when a punishment was levied, even now that we were older, we both still endured it. If she couldn't go to a movie, I couldn't. It was no good complaining about how it wasn't fair. We were to look after each other, weren't we? Reluctantly, I tried to do just that, but Haylee was no longer listening to me or was simply ridiculing my warnings in front of other girls.

Haylee didn't work as hard on our schoolwork as I did, but I had to do what I could to help her keep up. If we had a reading assignment, I had to explain it to her before we stepped into class, and because we were still seated close to each other, we had developed ways to share answers on tests. I wanted to stop, but I was afraid of Mother's reaction to Haylee falling so far behind me. Because I was doing well, she would blame it on me and see it as evidence that I wasn't being a "special" sister.

Ironically, the luckiest thing to happen from Haylee's point of view was my growing interest in Matt Tesler and his interest in me. Haylee was usually jealous of any attention boys gave me, even ones neither of us would ever want to date when we were finally permitted to date. Some of them called me to talk about schoolwork and, I knew, to see if that would lead to anything else. I didn't encourage any of them until Matt began to call.

There was nothing glamorous about Matt Tesler. He was about an inch taller than we were, and although he dressed neatly and never looked sloppy, he wore plain, solid-colored shirts and dark blue jeans, clothes that Haylee called monotonous. She didn't like his short, almost military haircut, either. At the time, he was one of the top five students in our class. He preferred exercising on his own, especially biking, and was well built but never went out for any school teams, even though the coaches tried to get him to do so.

It was easy to see why they wanted him. In gym class, he was as skilled as anyone else when it came to basketball fundamentals or soccer and baseball, but he was smart, too, and could easily be a team's playmaker or captain. His lack of interest was annoying to other boys at school, but I liked his indifference, not only to the pursuit of personal glory on the sports stage but also to the social rejection. He seemed more mature, and that caused me to want to know more about him. Why wasn't he like every other boy? What had happened in his life to make him the way he was?

Haylee wouldn't give him the time of day, and every time she saw me talking to him, she complained as if it was hurting her reputation.

"He's a few floors below nerd," she said. "Who wants to talk about computers or the environment? He thinks Taylor Swift is some kind of cheese," she added in front of other girls, who all laughed.

At first, I liked the fact that she wasn't interested in Matt. If I had shown the slightest interest in any other boy at school, she was at him so aggressively that she usually turned him off both of us. After a while, I avoided saying anything nice about any of the boys, but Matt was different. I sensed that what some others, especially Haylee, viewed as snobbery was really his greater stability and self-confidence.

He had a sister in the fourth grade, and his parents were both professionals. His father was the head of radiology at Pennsylvania General, and his mother was vice president in charge of commercial loans at Stuyvesant National. The gate in the wall he put up between himself and most of the students at our school gradually opened wider when it came to me, especially this year. At first, we talked mostly about our schoolwork, but we were soon exchanging opinions about almost everything. I discovered he had eclectic interests in music, authors, and movies. He loved jazz and had recordings of the greats, and yet he could also talk about some new song that had attracted his interest. I knew some of the older teachers liked talking with him about music and classic movies.

Despite her opinion of him, I suspected that Haylee never really looked at Matt. She never realized how blue his eyes were. She never saw his smile the way I did. When she made up her mind about someone, she wouldn't change it. I tried not to talk him up too much. If she saw how much I really liked him, she would do something to ruin our relationship for sure. But suddenly, as my interest in him became clearer, she realized how she could take advantage of it.

I knew she was plotting something when she came into my room to thank me for helping her with the math quiz. Usually, she treated whatever help I gave her with schoolwork as something expected, what Mother had early on described as "sisterly." That Mother didn't see how much Haylee took advantage of that surprised me. She was so keen and perceptive when it came to almost everything else about us.

"I know you really like Matt Tesler," Haylee began, after she had flopped onto my bed. She liked walking around in just her bra and panties now, especially when Mother wasn't around. "You'd love to have sex for the first time with him, wouldn't you?"

"I'm not thinking of it like that, Haylee."

"Sure you are. I don't blame you, and I wouldn't tell Mother if you did," she said. "Just like you wouldn't tell if I did." She looked sharply at me to see my reaction.

"We're supposed to tell her if either of us is with a boy who might get us to do it," I reminded her.

She sat up and pounded her thighs the way Mother would when she was displeased with something. "You've got to stop being such a goody-goody. Everyone is making fun of us because of how you are. No one wants to invite us to anything good because of you. They think you'll tell on them, Kaylee. You probably would. You tell Mother every little thing as it is."

"I only tell her what she wants to know. It makes things easier for us both."

"She wants to know too much! Jesus," she said, pouting. "Having you as a sister is like walking around with a bowling ball chained to my ankle. Maybe Mother doesn't notice how ignorant you are when it comes to sex."

"I am not."

"You didn't tell me you masturbated when I told you I did," she charged. I was a little shocked that she assumed it to be true. "Well? Did you?"

"Yes, but not in so many words. You didn't listen."

"Well, if you did, you were too embarrassed about it to just say it. How was I to know you had turned it into a . . . a metaphor?"

I nodded, smiling. "At least you're remembering our English literature lessons."

"Very funny. So? Were you dreaming of Matt Tesler when you did it? Confess at least to me. I'm not telling Mother, Kaylee."

"Maybe," I admitted.

"Okay." Suddenly, she calmed down and smiled, which to me sounded warning bells. "This is the deal. We'll get Mother to finally let us go on a double date. You'll go with Matt, and I'll go with Jimmy Jackson. We'll say we're going to the movies, but we'll go to Jimmy's house. It's all planned," she added, as if that was that. She got up to leave.

"Matt hasn't asked me to go on a date."

"Well, get him to. When we discuss it with Mother, I'll talk up how great he is, and you'll talk up Jimmy." She paused in the doorway. "If you don't, I'll tell Mother that Matt Tesler wanted me to do it with him and now he's trying to get you to," she threatened. "She won't even let you talk to him on the phone."

She smiled and left, her threat hanging in the air like a rotten odor. I sat back on my bed and folded my arms under my breasts. Ironically, Haylee was driving me to do something I had wanted to do anyway. Actually, I was wondering why Matt hadn't been more aggressive about it. It was disappointing. Sometimes I had the sense that he was about to ask me to meet him somewhere, maybe at the mall or a movie, but he didn't. Was he just shy, or didn't he like me the way I hoped? He wasn't pursuing any other girl. Could it be that he didn't like girls?

Before she went to sleep and again as soon as we rose and were off to school, Haylee reminded me that she wanted our double date to happen this coming weekend. It had to, because Jimmy's parents were going to be away overnight, and he would have the house to himself.

"Mother wouldn't let us go there if she knew that," I told her.

"So? I'm not telling her, and you're not, either."

"She might check or find out later."

"We'll tell her we didn't know."

"I don't lie as well as you do, Haylee, especially to Mother."

"Well, improve," she said with a laugh.

I was still undecided about how to get Matt to ask me on a date. I was afraid that if I was the one to suggest it, he might think less of me. As it turned out, neither of us had to be courageous about it. Haylee and Jimmy approached us while we were talking in the hallway before going to lunch.

"Hey, you two," Jimmy began. I could see from

the expression on Haylee's face that she had put him up to whatever he was going to say. I held my breath. "My parents are visiting my aunt Friday night. I was thinking of having a little party with just the four of us, maybe. Can you come?" he asked, mainly addressing Matt.

Matt quickly looked at me. I didn't say anything. He had to be the one to speak, I thought.

"I can," he said. "Kaylee?"

"She can," Haylee answered for me, "if I can, and I can."

"We haven't asked Mother yet," I reminded her.

"So we will . . . together," she emphasized.

"Great. We'll order in some pizzas," Jimmy said. "Nothing formal," he told Matt, and walked off laughing with Haylee.

"He's not my favorite guy," Matt said. "Are you sure about this?"

"If you are," I replied, and he smiled.

"Okay. We'll do it for the cause."

"What cause?" I asked.

"Us," he said, smiling.

I didn't know whether what I was feeling was what Mother had described as arousal, but it did feel good.

Now I was more nervous than ever about asking Mother to let us go to Jimmy's house. I decided Haylee could take the lead. She was, after all, better than I was at deception.

"It's a party with all our friends," Haylee began. "We're going to help make the cheese dips and stuff," she added, which was a nice touch. Mother had taught us how to make different things in the kitchen almost as soon as we could reach the counter. When we were ten, we would help her prepare dinner. She made sure that we alternated responsibilities like making salads, peeling potatoes, or stirring soups and cake batters.

"Jimmy Jackson," Mother said, thinking. "His father is an accountant?"

"Yes, Mother," I said, because she was looking to me for that answer.

"Doesn't his mother work in the public library?"

"And she makes Jimmy read all the time," Haylee offered. "Can we go?"

"*May* we go," Mother corrected. She had such a suspicious look on her face that I felt certain she would be calling the Jacksons, but suddenly, she relaxed. "I don't want to hear about any drinking," she said.

"Oh, Jimmy's parents are very strict about that, right, Kaylee?"

"Yes," I said. I wasn't sure if they were or not, so it didn't seem like a big lie to tell.

"How late can we stay, Mother?" Haylee asked.

"I'll be there at eleven . . . thirty," she said, adding thirty minutes to our usual curfew.

"Thank you, Mother," Haylee said quickly, and looked at me.

"Thank you, Mother," I said.

That was on a Tuesday. On Wednesday, she walked into the great room where we waited and announced that she and Daddy would be getting a divorce. The reality of what had been building in our house finally settled on Haylee's face. She looked at me and matched my sad and frightened expression.

Mother hugged us both and then sat across from us. We were on the settee as usual, sitting side by side.

"It's for sure?" I asked.

"Oh, yes. It's for sure," Mother said. She gave us a weak smile before she continued. "I know the two of you have noticed how long and how often your father has avoided you and me, especially these past few months. I have done my best to protect you from the ugly truth."

"What ugly truth?" Haylee asked, because Mother paused so long, and her face went from anger to sadness and then back to anger.

"Your father has been with another woman, a woman who has her own child from another marriage, too. Apparently, he's been a better father to her daughter than he has been to you."

"Why?" Haylee asked.

Now Mother smiled, but it wasn't a happy

smile. It was a smile full of anger. "Why? Men more than women are always looking to see if the grass is greener somewhere else."

"Grass?" Haylee looked at me.

Did I dare explain?

"Attention deficit disorder," Mother said, which did nothing to help Haylee understand. "He has wandering eyes. He always did, even before you were born, but I tolerated it. His pleasure is so important to him that he'd even sacrifice being with you. You'll understand more when you are older."

"But you always told us we should look for a man like Daddy," Haylee said.

"And I regret that now. I was trying to make this a happy home, despite his . . . indifference."

Haylee looked at me, but I just stared ahead, pushing my thoughts back like someone trying to keep a spring from popping out of a mattress.

"Anyway, it's beyond understanding at this point. I had to get a lawyer, who has met with your father's lawyer, and we've agreed on a settlement. I will have full custody of you. He can visit on certain days, but until you're eighteen, you will not stay with him."

"He agreed to that?" I asked.

"Oh, he didn't have much choice," Mother said with a cold smile.

"Where is he?" I asked.

"He's moved in with his concubine."

"What's that?" Haylee asked first.

"A whore," Mother said bitterly. She stared ahead, looking through us, and then her eyes seemed to snap, and she sat forward. "Nothing will change for us. In fact, you might not even notice a difference. We'll talk more about it, but for now, that's enough."

She rose. Then she lunged forward to hug us, before turning to go make dinner.

Haylee looked even more upset than I did, but it wasn't until later that I learned that was because she thought Mother might now change her mind about letting us go to Jimmy Jackson's house.

7

I suppose people would say there could never be anything "normal" about identical twins, and now, being the children of divorced parents seemed to confirm it. If anything, once our classmates learned that our parents were divorcing, it was bound to lead to more teasing and hurtful remarks, like "Which one will live with your father, or doesn't it make a difference? Maybe he wouldn't know which one of you was living with him."

None of this seemed to upset Haylee nearly as much as it did me. I could almost say it didn't bother her at all. She was so busy planning our social life that she deliberately ignored what was happening at home. The reality did eventually settle in with her, but she was determined not to let it depress her before or during the date at Jimmy

Jackson's house. She constantly worked to build up expectations for me and for herself.

"We've never been alone with boys, Kaylee. There are no jealous friends to interfere and no chaperones with their disapproving eyes. It's like maturing overnight!"

I couldn't really blame her for being more excited than any other girl our age might be. Mother had hovered over us for so long and so firmly, ready to pounce if either of us violated one of the strict rules she had imposed not only on our behavior but also on our very thoughts.

Nevertheless, it was difficult for me to get enthusiastic about a party, even a small, private one, because I was so down about what was happening between our parents. Haylee kept at me about my lack of excitement. After school on Thursday, she finally came into my room, her eyes full of that blazing anger I had long ago nicknamed Haylee's Comet.

I was lying there thinking and wondering how bad Daddy really felt about it all. He had yet to ask to see us to discuss it and defend himself, and he couldn't telephone one of us without telephoning the other. Mother's point about us not noticing much difference in our lives wasn't so far-fetched. Daddy had been diminishing his involvement with us for some time, but more so lately. It really bothered me that the reason might be that he'd adopted a new family and, like our grandmother Clara Beth, he now cared more about his new family than he did about us. At least, that was what Mother had told us about her relationship with her mother. Now the same thing was coming true for us and our father.

"What?" I asked when Haylee continued to stand there glaring at me.

"There's no problem telling the difference between us these days, Kaylee. Your face is so long that your chin slides along the hallway floor when you go from class to class like a zombie. You're taking all the fun out of this. Jimmy is worried you'll be a downer and ruin our night."

"Oh, I'm so sorry for him," I said, with exaggerated sympathy. "Maybe you should just go by yourself."

She dropped her hands to her hips and once again looked as if she might start pounding her thigh the way Mother did when she was in a rage.

"You know Mother won't let me go if you're not going. Besides, you should be sorrier for yourself. And you should be more grateful. You finally have a real date, thanks to me. Everyone was wondering why you and Matt weren't seeing each other outside of school. All I hear all the time is 'your sister is so shy, so socially backward.'"

I sat up, my eyes probably as steely as hers now. "Socially backward! And what do you tell them,

Haylee Blossom Fitzgerald?" I knew I sounded just like Mother, who often used our full names whenever she was upset with us.

The fury and the look of superiority in Haylee's face dissipated like smoke. "I defend you, of course."

"How?"

"I tell them you're just . . . just being careful. Don't you go telling Mother something different, Kaylee."

I shrugged and lay back. "Why should I? You were right. I was being careful, just like you are," I said. "You're just better at hiding it than I am."

She studied me to see if I was being serious. I didn't smile, but I enjoyed how confused and insecure I was making her. Did I really envy her? She wanted that to be true so much that she was eager to accept it. If Sarah Morgan could hear this conversation, she'd be laughing, I thought.

"Whatever. We're going to have a good time tomorrow night, Kaylee," she said, as if she had to convince herself as much as me.

"I hope so."

"You don't need to hope so. We will! Don't dare back out of this at the last moment because you're sad or something. That would make Mother mad, too."

"Make Mother mad? Why?"

"She'd think you've taken Daddy's side or something. You'll make it seem like it's all her fault, and she won't like that, not one bit."

That was a clever way to twist things around, I thought. Perhaps I was underestimating my sister.

"Is that why you act like you don't care what's happening, Haylee? You don't want Mother to think you like Daddy enough for it to matter?"

"I don't want to talk about sad things," she said. "You heard what Mother said about that. 'Dwelling on sadness is like watering poison ivy.'" She turned to leave and then paused. "It's that Sarah Morgan."

"What is?"

"Causing you to be the way you are. She's such a loser. She wants you to be one, too. Losers need company," she added, pleased with herself, and left.

I hated to give her credit for a sharp insight, but she wasn't all wrong about Sarah. It was easy to see how upset she was by my spending more time with Matt than with her lately. If the three of us were together, he practically ignored her, and that made it more difficult to keep her in our conversations. She was always asking me if Matt had asked me out or if I was going to meet him somewhere and wouldn't see her on a weekend. When I told her about our Friday night date, she just nodded and said, "Have a good time," but not like someone who was happy for me. She seemed more like someone who felt sorry for herself.

I did try to hide this from Haylee. I knew she would pounce on it the way she had in the beginning and cry to Mother that Sarah was more of a burden than a friend for us. On more than one occasion, she had made a point of telling me that Sarah would never get invited to parties we were invited to. She'd always be on the outside looking in.

"You're wasting your time being friends with her and forcing me to pretend I am, too," she insisted incessantly. Before I could respond with criticism of her friends, she would quickly add, "But I won't say anything about it to Mother. You'll get tired of Sarah on your own. If you're smart enough, that is."

On Friday after school, Haylee got up the nerve to ask Mother if it would be all right for us to dress differently for the party. "It's just a party like others we've gone to, Mother, but we're older now. We'll each wear something you bought us and approve of," she said.

Actually, I was hoping Mother would agree. She still had no idea how differently Haylee dressed after she arrived at school, and I did not want to be mistaken for her.

Mother looked as if she wasn't going to answer. She seemed to be in deep thought about something else, something I was sure had to do with the divorce. Then, as if the words had just arrived in her ears, the way the sound of a jet plane doesn't come down to earth until the plane is way off in the distance, she looked at Haylee and said, "What's that? What would you wear?"

"I don't know, Mother. Maybe you could help us pick out something," Haylee said, with such sweet timidity you could gain weight hearing her.

Mother relaxed her shoulders. I thought again how clever Haylee was at manipulating people, even our mother, who right now looked overwhelmed and vulnerable. She thought for so long that I believed she wasn't even going to respond. Maybe she was simply tired. She did look older. Despite how strong she tried to appear about the divorce and Daddy's adultery, her face was showing more wear and tear. This breakup of their marriage hadn't just happened, either. She had kept so much from us, but that didn't mean she was keeping it outside of herself. It had been swirling inside her for a long time, tearing at her in little ways.

The wrinkles at her eyes were deeper, and the shadows were darker under her eyes. She had let her hair go, not going to her salon for more than two months, and I could see strands of gray sneaking in. She wasn't wearing much makeup when she went out on errands or when she took us someplace, the way she always used to. Because she had once been a model, her appearance was important to her. She was always coordinated with her outfits and shoes, her jewelry and makeup.

"You two look so beautiful when you dress alike," Mother said, sounding mournful. I thought she was close to tears, and Mother never cried in front of us.

"Oh, we won't change anything else about us. We certainly won't change our hair, will we, Kaylee?"

I looked quickly back at Mother to see if she could tell how sneaky Haylee was being, but it was as if her eyes had glazed over and the world she saw was on the other side of smoked glass.

"Very well," Mother said, after a sigh as deep as the Grand Canyon. "I'll go look in your closets and choose something for each of you."

"Thank you, Mother," Haylee said quickly. "You can go to Kaylee's closet first. I'm going to take my shower. What color are we doing our nails?" she asked me, as if she had forgotten what we had decided, when in truth we hadn't discussed any of our preparations for the party.

"Whatever you do with your nails," Mother said, "depends on what you wear. I've told you often about the harmony you must have in your appearance."

"Oh, right," Haylee said.

"You have to pay attention to these things," Mother said.

I knew what she meant, and so did Haylee. She was just being too anxious and too ingratiating. I thought she was way over the top, and I remained surprised that Mother didn't pick up on how phony Haylee was being.

"Oh, we know, Mother," I said quickly. "We were going to do a neutral anyway."

Mother nodded. "Of course you know what to do. I've brought you up the way a mother should bring up her daughters today. Little was your father aware of what work has to be done raising girls to be perfect ladies. He thinks, like everything he does, it's just a simple click of the computer mouse," she said. "Click, and you delete a wife." She pretended to press a button. "Click, and you delete a family. Click, click, click, and the past is gone!"

Haylee looked halfway between amused and confused. She glanced at me. I was wondering if everything we did and everything we said would somehow, some way, wind its way to a nasty comment about Daddy. Was Mother going to become one of those man haters now, comfortably blaming what happened to her on the gender and not the individual? The romances and marriages she had once dreamed up for us like a master storyteller would be lost and forgotten or filed away with other childhood fantasies. No matter whom we liked and eventually loved, Mother would find fault with him. I had seen this in some of my classmates, too, as if it somehow made them feel better when someone was poisoned with the same bitterness. They had to share it and make someone else feel miserable. After an argument with Mother, Daddy often would walk out, leaving the saying "Misery loves company" floating in his wake like ugly car exhaust. I hadn't fully understood it until now.

Mother followed me to my room reluctantly. She was muttering to herself, which was also something I caught her doing much more lately. Sometimes she was so loud I would look in on where she was, expecting to see someone else with her, a visitor. But visitors, especially her friends, had become almost nonexistent. When she was a teacher's assistant, she'd rarely had time for any of her friends, even on weekends.

"I don't know why I agreed to this," she said, shaking her head as she sifted through my clothes. She paused. "What kind of a party did Haylee say it was?"

"Just a party, Mother. No special occasion."

"Hmm," she said. "You both look so beautiful in this." She took out a black jacquard rose fit-and-flare dress with pink and cream panels. "You'll both at least wear the pink fleece jackets. It's spring, but the nights still have a winter chill."

"Thank you, Mother."

"You know what shoes go with this," she said. "You both have those sterling-silver white-sapphire bracelets with the earrings that match. I wouldn't wear anything more."

"Okay, Mother," I said.

No matter how depressed she was now, I would always trust her when it came to fashion. Before she and Daddy had become so estranged, she would buy him his clothes, especially his shirts, sweaters, and jackets. She would often bring home a new shirt or a new sports jacket for him and tell him it was what he must wear. He didn't mind, or at least I didn't think he did. He appeared grateful and behaved as though it was all perfect. He did look handsome in anything she chose. Who would choose his clothes for him now? Was his new girlfriend as good at it? How could she be?

Mother left to pick out Haylee's dress and tell her what else I was wearing and what she would have to wear. There would be no objections. Haylee would wear a crown of thorns if it meant she could get to this party.

The dress Mother picked for her was an all-over sequin skater dress. I suspected Haylee had influenced Mother's choice. I knew Haylee thought she was very sexy in that dress. Afterward, she came into my room so we could be sure we did our hair as close to each other's as possible, and that we used the same lipstick shade and the same perfume.

"She'll look us over like a drill sergeant before we leave," Haylee said, fixing a strand of my hair.

Jimmy and Matt had decided that Matt would pick up both of us, since we were going to Jimmy's house. When Haylee told Mother, I expected she would say no and insist that she bring us to the party and pick us up, but the divorce had begun to make subtle changes already in how she would manage our lives. I suspected that Daddy's complaints about how controlling she was had struck a note with the attorneys. She was going to prove that we were, despite all the preparations and special upbringing, healthy, normal teenage girls. He was just so oblivious to us that he didn't notice.

I hoped Mother was right. That would be one argument in which I would support her. I so wanted Haylee and me to be what anyone would call normal teenage girls, despite what made us so different from everyone else. I knew this was something Haylee wanted even more.

Just before Matt arrived, Mother did exactly what Haylee had predicted, inspecting us with microscope eyes. She fixed Haylee's hair where there was a slight difference from mine with her bangs, something neither of us had caught. Then she stepped back, smiling and nodding.

"You're so alike that even in different dresses, you are like one, my Haylee-Kaylee, Kaylee-Haylee."

Neither of us said anything, but I could see that Haylee wanted to scream.

Fortunately, Matt pressed the door buzzer just at that moment.

Mother immediately began to attend to herself. "I look like a disaster," she said, fluffing her hair and straightening her blouse. "I didn't even put on any lipstick today."

"Don't worry, Mother. Matt's Kaylee's date. He'll only be looking at her."

"Date?"

"Sorta," Haylee added quickly. "Right, Kaylee?"

"We're both fond of him," I said.

"I see," Mother said. Matt pressed the buzzer again. "He's quite anxious. Anxious boys often turn into abusive men. Remember that," she warned.

Haylee squinted as if she was in pain. Was something going to stop our night out after all? I could see that she was holding her breath until Mother turned slowly and went to the front door. We followed, both of us trying not to look too eager.

I could have kissed Matt right then and there. He had brought a bouquet of red and white roses, not for me but for Mother. He was also wearing a dark blue sports jacket, a matching tie, and blue slacks, instead of jeans and a sweatshirt. He looked a century away from how most teenage boys dressed for dates. I could see that he'd had his hair trimmed today, too.

"Good evening, Mrs. Fitzgerald. I'm Matt Tesler," he said.

Mother looked lost for words.

"Oh, these are for you, Mrs. Fitzgerald," he quickly added, holding out the flowers.

"For me? Why?" Mother asked suspiciously, hesitating. If there was one thing she wouldn't tolerate, it was pity. Her fear was that word of her impending divorce was out and might be the subject of gossip. *Poor Keri Fitzgerald, left to care for identical twin teenage girls.*

"I thought anyone who had daughters as nice and as beautiful as yours should be rewarded," Matt said. Then he leaned in, looking past her at me, and added sotto voce, "My father said it was the proper thing to do."

His confession made Mother laugh. She took the roses and stepped aside. Matt entered.

"I've always admired your house, Mrs. Fitzgerald. And the way you keep the grounds."

"Thank you, Matt. These are very pretty. Now," she said, returning to her stern demeanor, "I want you to drive very slowly and carefully. You have quite valuable cargo, double the value."

"Oh, yes, ma'am, I will."

"They have to be home by eleven thirty," she

said firmly. Haylee groaned. Mother glanced at her, and Haylee quickly wiped the disappointment off her face.

"I'll make sure of that," Matt said.

"And there had better not be any drinking or any drugs."

"My parents laid out the same rules, Mrs. Fitzgerald. We have a no-tolerance policy. I'd lose my driving privileges even if there was suspicion."

"Yes, well, let's hope the parents of everyone else attending this party laid down the same rules," Mother said.

I could see that Matt was just about to say, *Everyone else?*

"We should go," I said. "We're helping to organize the party."

Matt raised his eyebrows but opened the door quickly.

Mother looked at us, looked at her flowers, and then stepped back for us to walk out. "Have a good time," she said.

"Thank you, Mother," we replied in our usual synchronized way. I saw Matt smile.

Haylee hurried out ahead of me, moving like someone who was making an escape.

Matt waited for me. "Good evening, Mrs. Fitzgerald," he said. "And don't worry."

"That's impossible," Mother told him.

"I know," Matt said. He smiled at her and closed the door behind us.

"Let's get out of here before she changes her mind," Haylee said, and continued to rush ahead to get into the back of Matt's car, a black late-model SUV.

He went around to open the front passenger door for me and then got in, smiled at me, and started the engine. My heart was pounding. Were we really going on a date? I kept my eyes on our doorway as he backed out, anticipating Mother charging out and putting her hand up to stop us and say she had changed her mind. But she didn't come out, and moments later, we were off to Jimmy Jackson's house.

"Did you tell him to bring Mother the flowers?" Haylee asked me.

"No."

"Good move, Matt," Haylee said. "I think you've done this before."

"Done what before?"

"Stroked some girl's mother," she said.

"I wasn't stroking her. I was telling the truth," Matt said, without taking his eyes off the road. "Get used to it."

"To what?" Haylee said.

"The truth," he replied, and I laughed. He did, too.

"Oh, that's hysterical," Haylee said, not liking

that she was outside the small circle Matt and I had begun to create around us, a circle that looked as if it would get even smaller tonight.

"So what was that about helping to organize the party?" Matt asked.

"My mother thinks there are more kids coming to Jimmy's house," I said.

"Oh, I see."

"Our little lies are just temporary," Haylee declared. "We have special circumstances these days."

"I know. I'm sorry about your parents divorcing."

"We don't want to dwell on it. We want to have a good time. We deserve it," she said.

He looked at me and smiled. "Deserve it?"

"Yes. It's not our fault our home has become the *Titanic*," Haylee said.

"Okay," Matt said. "We'll avoid icebergs."

"It's too late. Just concentrate on being a lifeboat," she said.

I looked back at her. That was very clever, I thought. Maybe Haylee was smarter than I was in important ways.

She smiled and reached for my hand. "Our first double date," she said.

I looked at Matt. He glanced at me just long enough for me to see that he was really happy, too. He also kept checking his rearview mirror.

"Worried our mother might be following?" I asked.

"You bet," he said. "She looked tough enough to give me a ticket if I broke the speed limit."

Haylee laughed harder than I did. I sat back, smiling. We were, somehow, going to have a good time.

Jimmy was expecting that, too. The Jacksons had a custom-built ranch-style house on a lot half the size of ours but with more elaborate landscaping, lighting, and fountains. There was a three-car garage and a driveway lit with beautiful pewter lanterns. When we stepped out of Matt's SUV, we heard a dog barking.

"That's his mother's Pekingese, named Chin," Haylee said. "Jimmy told me that she loves her dog more than she loves him. He also warned me that Chin can nip, so don't try to pet him if he's running loose in the house."

"Thanks for the warning," Matt said. "I've grown fond of my fingers."

"There's a big media room, five bedrooms, and a home office his father uses," she continued as we walked to the front door.

"You sound like you've been here before," Matt said.

"No, she hasn't," I said.

"Maybe I have. Maybe you don't know everything I do, Kaylee."

"Well, when could you have done that?"

"Maybe when you and Mother were sleeping, I sneaked out," she replied. Before I could say anything more, Jimmy opened the door. He was holding the dog in his arms so he would stop barking.

"Keep that monster away from me," Matt joked.

"My mother made me promise I wouldn't lock him in the laundry room or something. He can scratch up a door and bark until his throat gets so hoarse, you could put a saddle on him."

Haylee laughed as if he had made the best joke she'd ever heard. His smile widened, and he stepped back for us to enter. I didn't think Chin was as nasty as Haylee claimed Jimmy had said. If anything, the dog looked happy to have someone else in the house.

"Hi, Chin," I said, and held my hand close enough for the dog to smell it, my fingers turned downward.

We had always wanted a pet, either a cat or a dog, but Mother opposed it, even when Daddy offered to get two of the same breed from the same litter. She was probably afraid that I would spend more time with them and they would take to me more than to Haylee, creating jealousies that would be very damaging to our personalities.

After sniffing my hand, Chin licked it, and Jimmy looked surprised and happy.

"Here," he said, handing the dog to me. "You're in charge of him tonight."

I held the dog gently, and he seemed to settle comfortably in my embrace.

"You want to hold him, too?" Jimmy asked Haylee.

"No!" she said.

"He senses it," Matt said. "He can easily tell the difference between the two of you."

"Oh, I think Jimmy can, too," Haylee countered, and put her arm through his. "Give us a tour of the house, and then lead us to the pizza."

He laughed and brought us into the living room. There were always little things about other people's homes that intrigued me, even when I was only four or five. In our house, there were only a few pictures of Mother's parents and Daddy's with his brothers and their families. Most of the framed photographs in our home were of Haylee and me, but there were no pictures of either of us alone. When the school photographer took individual shots of us, Mother placed ours side by side in a bigger frame. Haylee wanted to have pictures of herself, especially in her own room, but Mother didn't permit it. Any picture we had with Daddy always included both of us, too.

So it was the family photographs that intrigued me in other people's homes, especially those who had pictures of great-uncles and great-aunts and great-grandparents. There was more of a sense of family. The pictures proved their lineage, their history. It made our classmates seem more like somebodies. Perhaps I felt this way because there were no other twins in our family heritage, or at least any Haylee and I were told about. It all made me feel like a planet without a solar system, out there floating through the darkness.

Family photographs gave my classmates' homes a warmth that ours didn't have. There were always so many hand-me-downs, clocks, needlepoints, figurines, paintings, and artifacts of all kinds that had some history attached to them. "This was my great-grandmother's." "This was my father's uncle's." Our house was pretty and well decorated, but it wasn't until I visited homes of my classmates that I realized that ours was a showcase, a model yet to be embellished with the familial warmth and love that made a house a home.

The Jacksons' living room was almost as large as ours but without a fireplace—not that we used ours very much, especially lately. Daddy had always been in charge of it. Mother was thinking of cleaning it out and putting flowerpots in it.

This living room had large wall mirrors beautifully framed in the same cherry wood that the curved settee, the coffee table, and the armchairs were made of. The family photographs and knickknacks were on shelves. A glass-doored armoire contained beautiful figurines that drew my attention.

"My mother's Lladró collection," Jimmy said.

"Beautiful."

"Yeah, if you like that sorta crap," Jimmy said.

"Let's look at the media room," Haylee said.

When we stepped in, I saw why she was interested in it. There were two very comfortable-looking sofas, a large-screen television, and elaborate audio equipment. The room had a malt-colored shag rug.

"We can watch something good and have our pizza in here," Jimmy said. "As long as we don't leave a mess."

"Oh, don't worry. Kaylee is a perfectionist when it comes to cleaning up," Haylee announced.

"And you're not?" Matt asked.

"We are different, Matt. I make the mess; Kaylee cleans it up. Right, Kaylee?"

"You do make the mess," I confirmed, and Matt laughed.

Even Jimmy widened his smile. "Make a mess of me," he told her, and they kissed, right there in front of us.

I hadn't known Haylee could kiss like that. It looked like a movie kiss.

"Let's move on to the kitchen," Jimmy said. "I think we'd better get the food ready. I'm going to need my strength tonight."

He took Haylee's hand and started out.

I looked at Matt, who shrugged. "I didn't think it took all that much strength," he said, and we both laughed.

We followed them, me still holding Chin, who seemed just as curious about what this night would bring but also a little fearful.

Maybe he sensed it in me.

8

When Jimmy had said we could "watch something good," neither Matt nor I suspected that he meant something pornographic. I assumed Haylee knew, because she wasn't that surprised. She had that impish little smile bubbling on her face as Jimmy set it up. The moment the movie began, I could see immediately that the story was going to be stupid. It didn't take more than three minutes for the first woman in the film to take off all her clothes. Jimmy and Haylee were laughing when the man did the same, but neither Matt nor I could utter a sound.

"It's not what I'd call a movie to watch while eating," Matt said.

"Where did you get this?" I asked. "Is it something your parents watch?"

"Hell, no," Jimmy said. "Bobby Lester sold it to me for twenty bucks. My mother would have heart failure if she knew we were watching it, so don't tell anyone."

"Why don't we just listen to some music?" Matt suggested.

"Really?" Jimmy asked. "You don't want to watch this?"

"It feels more like someone's bachelor party. Kaylee's uncomfortable, and to be honest, so am I."

"Oh, you poor dears," Haylee said. "So sensitive."

"Maybe you should be, too," I said. You could have sliced the anger in the air between us. It was that thick.

"It's all right. Haylee and I can watch it ourselves. I have a TV in my bedroom," he said, and turned it off. He flipped another switch, and we heard jazz. "My dad's collection," he said. "More comfortable?"

"Fine with me," Matt said. "That's Dave Brubeck."

"Brew, like in beer?" Jimmy said.

Haylee and he laughed and kissed. Chin was lying at my feet now. The way he watched my sister and Jimmy suspiciously brought a smile to my face.

"You're embarrassing your dog," Matt said.

Jimmy paused and looked. "Yeah, well, did you ever see two dogs at it? *That's* embarrassing."

Haylee laughed. It seemed to me that she would laugh at anything he said. They began whispering to each other. They ate some pizza, whispered and kissed, and then drank what I suspected might be something besides Coke. When they offered it to us, Matt and I shook our heads.

"Help! My grandparents must have snuck in," Jimmy joked, and Haylee laughed with more abandon. They devoured more pizza. After another few minutes, Jimmy stood. "I'm going to show Haylee more of the house, more of my part of it," he said, "before we watch the unappetizing movie." He took the disc out of the DVD player. "Can you amuse Chin for a while?"

"I don't know. You had him so fascinated," Matt said.

"So put on the same kind of show for him," Jimmy said, and he reached for Haylee, who stood. She looked at me with eyes so full of excitement I thought they might start to crackle and pop like firecrackers. Laughing again, she walked out with Jimmy.

"Your sister was right," Matt said.

"About what?"

"It's easy to tell the difference between you."

"She likes to say that these days, and I don't stop her."

"I can see why." He rose and looked at the movie collection neatly stacked in alphabetical order on the shelf beside the TV. "Want to watch something really good?" he asked.

"Sure."

He held up *To Kill a Mockingbird*. "Makes my mother cry," he warned.

"There are good cries and bad," I said.

"Exactly."

He inserted the DVD and then sat beside me, put his arm around my shoulders, and kissed me softly on the forehead. I turned my face up to him, and we kissed on the lips, again softly, almost tentatively, both of us a little unsure. It was nothing like Haylee and Jimmy's kiss. They had both looked like they would ravish each other's faces. Matt smiled and brought his lips back, and we kissed more like we meant it. Then I turned and cuddled up in his arm as the movie began. Chin sprawled out below us and almost immediately fell asleep.

Haylee and Jimmy did not return until the movie was almost over. Chin rose quickly and actually barked at them. I picked him up again.

"You don't spend much time with your dog," I said.

"That's not a dog. It's a stuffed animal with batteries." Jimmy looked at the TV screen. "Bor-ring," he declared from the doorway. Haylee was beside him, looking like she had been tossing and turning in her sleep for hours. She looked flushed, too, her eyes wide, as if she had a great secret and was bursting inside with her eagerness to tell me.

"How about we wake this party up?" Jimmy asked. "I have a couple of joints we can share."

"No, thanks," Matt said rather quickly.

I glared at Haylee. My message was coming through loud and clear.

"Not tonight, I'm afraid," Haylee told him. "But don't smoke them without me."

"I'll smoke one at least, and I can get more," he said. "You guys just sat here and watched this movie?"

"We also finished off the pizza," Matt replied.

"Could you stand the excitement, Grandpa?" Jimmy kidded, followed by Haylee's now very annoying giggle. "You should have watched my film. You'd learn something new to do."

Our movie ended, and we had missed the wonderful conclusion.

"Oh, Matt," I moaned.

"We'll watch it some other time," he promised me. "It's a movie you can see many times."

"Sure, come over anytime," Jimmy said. "I've got it, too."

"Great. You'll have the next party at your house," Jimmy said.

Matt didn't respond. I rose, put Chin down, and began to clean up the dishes, the silverware, and the pizza boxes. Matt started to help. When I looked back at the doorway, I saw that Haylee and Jimmy had disappeared again. Chin had remained with us.

"I think they went outside," Matt said.

"If they went out there to smoke that joint, we'll

both be in trouble. You can be sure my mother will be waiting for us at the door with all sorts of detection devices."

Matt checked the time. "You're okay time-wise. We can check outside to see if that's what they're doing. If they're not around, let's take a walk anyway. I could use the fresh air. I don't think they'll miss us, do you?"

"After we finish this," I said, indicating the cleanup. We took everything to the kitchen, where I rinsed off the dishes and silverware and put them all in the dishwasher. He found the garbage disposal and took care of what was left. "It's a very nice kitchen," I said, admiring how well kept it was and the beautiful paneling and marble counters.

"Is your sister like this at home? Letting you do all the work?"

"No, but only because my mother wants us to do everything together."

"Somehow I think you still do more."

"No comment," I replied.

He smiled and took my hand. We walked out and paused in the hallway for a few moments to listen for Haylee and Jimmy, but we didn't hear anything. Matt shrugged, turned, and went down the hall to check the other rooms.

"They must be outside," he said.

Now concerned that Haylee really was smoking that joint, I went quickly to the front door, and we stepped out. Again, we listened for their voices or laughter but heard nothing.

"I doubt they'd be this quiet," Matt said. "They're hiding somewhere. He probably has his private hideaway to do things his parents can't see."

We walked around outside the house. The Jacksons had a pool and a cabana. The pump was off, so it was very quiet. We made our way toward the chaises that were under an overhang. Matt pulled two out farther and placed them side by side.

"Good night for stars," he said. We lay back on the lounges and looked up at the dazzling sky. "Virgo is usually visible by late April. There," he said, pointing. "It's the largest constellation of the zodiac and second largest overall."

"What's the largest?"

"Hydra. I have this great telescope my father bought me when I was twelve, and I got into stargazing."

"I'm not sure I recognize Virgo," I said, looking up.

"It's difficult to make out the winged maiden holding an ear of wheat in her left hand." He slipped off his chaise and onto mine. I moved over for him, and he pointed again. "That sparkling blue-white star, Spica, helps locate it. You star-hop from the handle of the Big Dipper. See?"

"Yes!" I said, now excited that I could see where the constellation was.

"It's fun."

"We never did much of this," I said.

"Well, maybe we can change that," he said. I turned to him again, and we kissed longer, more passionately. "There's a problem, however."

"What?"

"You're so beautiful, Kaylee. You easily take my attention from the stars."

I started to laugh, but he was being very serious. This time, I brought my lips to his. He slowly moved his hands over my shoulders and then over my breasts and down to my hips. The warmth that moved through my body made his fingers feel like they were under my dress. I was drawn to his touch, eager to have his lips on mine, and then moaned softly, welcoming his kiss on my neck, my cheeks, and back to my lips. I was turned in to him now, pressing my body to his.

I really didn't think we'd go much further anyway, but a loud peal of Haylee's laughter shut our passion down. I turned to look toward the house.

"Where, oh, where are you two? Oh, where has my little sister gone?" We heard her sing, and then Jimmy laughed. "Are you swimming nude?" she shouted. "Did you get ideas from Jimmy's movie after all?"

Before they came around the corner of the house, Matt had moved to his chaise.

"And what are you two doing?" she asked when she spotted us. They kept walking toward us.

"Looking at the constellations," Matt said.

"Right," Jimmy said. "The constellations."

Haylee giggled.

"I can show you Virgo, if you like," Matt offered.

"I'd rather look at Venus," Jimmy said. "Think I have," he added, and Haylee giggled.

"Did you smoke that joint?" I demanded. "Haylee!"

"Just a drag or two," she said. "Big deal. Mother won't smell anything."

"I knew it. You're going to ruin everything for us."

"Oh, chill out. Maybe you should take a drag yourself. We always do whatever the other does," she told Jimmy.

"Oh, really? She always does whatever you do?" he asked.

"But not the same way," she said, giggling.

"I'll have to discover one day if that's true," Jimmy quipped.

"Like hell you will," Haylee told him, and playfully punched him in the shoulder.

"Ow! She's so cruel," he told us.

"What time is it?" I asked Matt.

"Quarter to eleven," he said.

"We'd better go."

"It doesn't take that long to get home," Haylee said.

"If we're there just in time, she won't like it, and we won't get out again so easily," I said.

"What are you, in prison?" Jimmy asked.

"Prison is better," Haylee replied, now sounding sober and bitter. "You still have some rights."

"I can take you home," Jimmy offered. "You can let Matt bring your sister home, and we'll be there ten minutes later. We can do a lot in ten minutes."

"Haylee," I said, my voice full of warning.

"No, sorry, we can't do that. Mother would be angry," she said.

"Why?"

"It's a long story," Haylee said. "It goes back to birth."

She turned away, and he followed her as she returned to the front of the house.

"You all right?" Matt asked.

"Yes, very much all right. Don't worry," I said. He took my hand, and we followed them.

Haylee and Jimmy kissed good night so passionately, his hands moving all over her, especially her rear end, that Matt and I looked away, embarrassed. We got into his SUV and silently stared ahead.

Jimmy came around and knocked on Matt's window when Haylee got into the rear after another passionate kiss. They looked more like two vampires drawing blood out of each other's lips. Matt rolled the window down.

"I hope you saw more than some constellation tonight," Jimmy said.

"I did. I saw something more beautiful."

"Yeah, yeah. Save it for your emails. Later," he said, and stepped away as Matt backed out of the driveway.

Jimmy waved to us. Haylee barely waved back. "It's so embarrassing having to go home so early," she said. "I hope you two had a good time, at least, although I doubt it was as good as we had."

I turned around. "We did."

"Sure. At least we made a party out of it."

"I don't think we should give Mother too much detail about our party, Haylee. You know you can say the wrong things when you brag."

"Don't worry. You tell her about the party. I'll be too tired," she promised, and sat back. She was sobering up quickly now, and I could see that made her even angrier than having to go home early.

I turned back and looked out my window as we passed more homes. It was interesting how houses could look as tired as people at the end of the day, their lights dimming, with fewer signs of activity in and around them. Inside most of them were families asleep or going to bed, families with parents who still loved and cared for each other and lived to protect and enjoy their children. I felt more like a foreigner dropped in a strange land and told to find her way alone, protected and strengthened only with past memories that were dwindling. I feared the truth: tomorrow might not replace yesterday. No matter what I was told, it could be disappointing.

"The Jacksons have a nice house," Matt said. I thought he was uncomfortable with the silence and would say anything that might revive conversation.

"It's all right," Haylee said, making sure that Matt knew she wasn't impressed. "It's half the size of ours, I think."

"I guess you wouldn't be impressed with mine. It's not bigger than the Jacksons'."

"Invite me over, and I'll see," Haylee countered. "I might even watch that movie with you."

I looked back at her. How could she leave one boy and flirt with another within minutes, and my boyfriend to boot? She smiled gleefully, but after that, no one spoke until we were home. Matt drove slowly up the driveway and stopped.

Haylee groaned. "Home sour home," she said. "We've got to get her to let us stay out past midnight, Kaylee. We're the only ones in our class with this stupid curfew."

"I wouldn't push it tonight," I said.

"No, I know you wouldn't," she replied bitterly, and opened her door. She paused. "Well? Give him a real kiss good night so he dreams of you, at least," she said.

"I'll dream of her, no matter what," Matt said.

"Oh, you're so easy," she told him, and got out.

"Sorry," I said. "I hope Mother can't tell what she's done."

"I'll call you tomorrow, and you can give me a full report." He leaned over and did kiss me softly. "I had a great time, Kaylee."

"So did I. Despite my sister," I said. He smiled, and I got out.

Haylee was standing and waiting for me, obviously wanting me to be the first one Mother greeted. Matt waved and backed out. I watched him drive off and then turned to her.

"Just be tired but not so tired that she'll decide we were out too late or something," I warned.

"I can't stand this. No other girls in our class have to go through this third degree, I'm sure. Their parents trust them."

"Or they're too selfish to worry," I said. I started away, but before we could reach the door, Mother opened it the way she would open our bedroom door or our bathroom door when we were younger. It was always as if she expected to catch us doing something she wouldn't like us doing. Whether we were or not, it made us both nervous and made us feel guilty just brushing our teeth or washing our faces.

"Why are you two taking so long to come in?" she demanded.

"We were waving good night to Matt," I said.

In the glow of the front light, her face took on a yellowish tint filled with that usual suspicion. She was wearing a light blue robe and blue slippers, and her hair looked as if she had been running her fingers through it for hours.

"Get inside," she ordered, and stepped away. Heads down, we entered the house, and she closed the door as if she was afraid we'd be followed in by some evil spirit. She approached us quickly and ran her gaze over our faces. "Well? Did you drink anything alcoholic or do any drugs?"

"No, Mother," I said, speaking for myself but making it sound like I was speaking for us both. "It's a nice house. We were practically the only ones who helped clean up, but we left earlier than just about everyone, so we don't know how they'll leave it."

"That's the Jacksons' problem. They approved having a party in their home," she said. I think she quickly realized how cold that sounded. "But it was nice that you showed some responsibility. You didn't get that from your father. What you'll learn, and I hope quickly, is that men and responsibility are almost antonyms."

"Antonyms?" Haylee said.

"Opposites," I muttered.

"Oh, right. That's funny, Mother."

"It's not meant to be funny. It's reality." Mother studied her a little more. "What did you do at this party?"

"Oh, we watched a wonderful movie," I said. "*To Kill a Mockingbird*."

"You watched a movie?"

"The Jacksons have a great media room. We had pizza and sodas, and there was music afterward," I told her. Nothing was a lie.

"Well, your father was always talking about constructing a media room, but that was just another empty promise. You'd better go to bed now," she said. "I want to go shopping tomorrow and spend some of his money. I need some new things, and so do you."

I glanced at Haylee. She still had her eyes down, which I feared was fanning the flames of Mother's suspicions.

"Thanks, Mother," I said. "Good night." I reached for Haylee's hand. "We had a nice time," I added, nudging her.

"Thanks, Mother. Good night," she mimicked, and we walked quickly to the stairway. I felt like a smuggler who had successfully gone through the TSA checkpoint.

Haylee rushed up ahead of me. I thought she was going to collapse into bed, but she surprised me. She turned to me, her face full of fresh excitement, eyes lit again like candle wicks that had been blown out moments ago.

"I can't stand holding it all in."

"What?"

"I'm getting into my pajamas, and when Mother goes to sleep, I'll come into your room."

"Why?" I asked. "What is it?"

"I did it," she said.

"Did it?"

"Twice!" she said, and rushed off to her room, leaving me standing there stunned. I moved quickly to my room when I heard Mother turning lights off and heading for the stairway. I knew she would look in on us before she went to bed. She stopped in my doorway first. I had just slipped into my pajamas and was heading for the bathroom to brush my teeth and wash my face.

"It was so much easier and more wonderful when you two shared a room," she said.

"We can't be little girls forever, Mother."

"I know. It's a pity," she said. "Families should be frozen in time when they are the happiest. Time has a way of eroding things."

She stepped in to kiss me good night and brushed back my hair, smiled at some memory, and went on to Haylee's room. I hoped she had at least washed away any traces of smoke and brushed her teeth before doing anything else. She had to; I didn't. I kept listening for Mother's voice being raised, but I heard nothing out of the ordinary. She dimmed the hallway lights and went to her room.

When I came out of the bathroom, Haylee was waiting, sprawled on my bed. The happy expression of excitement, revealing how she was nearly exploding with the need to tell me something, annoyed me. I had enjoyed my time with Matt. I liked him very much, and thinking about how we were together made me feel warm all over, eager to go to sleep and to dream. Haylee, on the other hand, looked like she would stay up all night talking. There was also that familiar "I'm ahead of you" look that irritated me so much.

"So what did you mean?" I began, folding some clothes I had left out and putting away my shoes.

"Sit down, for God's sake, Kaylee. I have a lot to tell you."

"It's getting late," I said. "Mother is going to wake us up early. You heard her."

"Will you stop being such a child? I lost my virginity tonight," she blurted. "That's what I meant."

I knew it; I just didn't want to hear about it, but I could see that would be impossible. "Why did you do that? You hardly know him," I said.

"That's not important. He's not bad-looking, and he's no virgin. He was a good boy to lose my virginity with. I've heard stories girls like Toby Sue and Melanie tell about how painful it was and how they bled and how they were so sore afterward.

They made it sound more like losing a tooth or something. Melanie hasn't had sex since, for example. How good is that? The boys they were with probably were losing their virginity at the same time, so they didn't know what they were doing. They were like 'slam, bam, thank you, ma'am' lovers, if you could even call them lovers."

"What does that mean?"

"It's an old expression Toby Sue told me. It means the boy has an orgasm before you do and then just says thanks and good-bye. Selfish and inexperienced boys, that is. I knew Jimmy was experienced."

"How?"

"Val Hepworth told me she did it with him a few weeks ago at her house, and it was great. She did it with him because Paige Blackman had done it with him and told her about it and how good it was."

"So that's why you began flirting with him?"

"He was flirting with me," she said, insulted. "I didn't give him the time of day until I wanted to."

I sat on my bed, and she sat up and backed up against my pillow and headboard, spreading her legs.

"I'm a little sore, but I didn't bleed," she bragged.

"I thought that always happens."

"If your hymen has not been broken, it usually does, but I have one of those vibrators."

"What?"

"You remember. I showed you pictures of them in that magazine at Toby Sue's."

"How did you get one?"

"Paige gave it to me. Her mother had three of them, and she swiped one for me."

"Ugh," I said, recoiling. "You took someone else's vibrator?"

"I cleaned it well. Don't worry."

"Where is it?"

"Taped under my bed. Mother will never find it. Anyway, it made a big difference. I'll give it to you, and you can prepare yourself for the big night."

"I don't want it. I don't want to think of it like that."

"Right. You want to be floating on a cloud with violins playing. Don't be such a child, Kaylee."

"Stop calling me that."

"Stop being it, then," she said. She pouted a moment and then smiled again. "I wasn't sure I was going to do it tonight. I thought I would come close and wait maybe until the next time, but he's good. He didn't force himself on me or anything. We went to his bedroom, and when we were kissing, he brought my hand to his penis. I didn't even know he had taken it out."

"I don't think I want to hear this," I said.

"Sure you do. Stop it. You need to know these things. Just be happy it's me telling you and not some jealous girlfriend or somebody. Anyway, it aroused me quickly, and before I knew it, he was undoing my dress and slipping my panties off. I unhooked my bra. I thought it would ruin things for him to fumble about, you know?"

"Haylee, I can't believe you're telling me this."

"Believe it. He didn't even get undressed for a while, but he was kissing me everywhere, and I mean everywhere, Kaylee. When he went down here, I thought I would pass out. My heart was pounding so hard, and the room seemed to be spinning. Then he got undressed. He had what he needed in the drawer next to his bed."

"How convenient. That means he's had other girls in his room."

"So? I told you he was experienced, didn't I?"

"Didn't it bother you that he was with other girls?"

"Why should it? We weren't engaged or anything. Anyway, he knew I was a virgin, of course."

"How did he know?"

"He knew."

"You told him that?"

"He kept telling me how important it was to relax," she continued, ignoring my question. "Especially down here," she said, holding her hands over her pelvis. "He told me he would be gentle and careful. When he started, I didn't want him to be gentle. I think he was surprised at how good I was," she said proudly. "Oh, and he told me not to worry about any bleeding, because we'd wash and change the sheets."

"How considerate."

"He was impressed that I didn't bleed," she said, smiling. "That's when I told him about Paige's mother's vibrator."

"You told him that, too? I'm getting sick to my stomach," I said. "Let's go to sleep."

"There's more, Kaylee. You should listen. I'm sure you'll be doing it with Matt Tesler."

"I'm not so sure."

"Well, if you don't, maybe I will. He's not bad-looking."

I could feel the blood rise up my neck and into my face. "I want to go to sleep. I'm tired, Haylee."

"Don't you want to hear about the second time? Jimmy was very impressed that I wanted to do it again so soon."

"I'm glad you scored points with him. You can be sure he'll be spreading the news, and we'll both have to live with that."

"You're right. He probably will brag. I don't know why boys can brag about their sex lives, but we can't. It's not fair."

"I'll take it up with the United Nations in the morning," I said, and stood to indicate that she should leave my room.

She stared at me a moment, her eyelids narrowing with suspicion. "You like boys, right? I don't want to learn I have inherited something with you."

"I like boys, Haylee. Don't worry about it."

"Good," she said. "Okay. You sleep on it, and we'll talk about it again. You'll thank me, that's for sure."

"If Mother ever heard about this—"

Her eyes nearly exploded as Haylee's Comet arrived. "Don't you even think about telling her anything!"

"I wouldn't. Of course not. I would suffer just as much as you would. We both know that. I'm simply saying that if Jimmy Jackson brags and other boys talk about you and it gets to someone's parents and then they tell another and another, it could wind its way back to our front door."

She relaxed, looking a little worried now. "That won't happen, and if it does, I'll deny it and say he was just trying to look big. And you'll back me up, right? Right?"

"Yes, Haylee. We always defend each other, remember?"

"As long as you remember," she said. She paused in the doorway on her way out. "The point I was trying to make before you spoiled it, Kaylee, was that I enjoyed it, very much. I feel . . . older, too, like when I got my first period." She thought a moment, smiled, and added, "You don't have to worry about my going after your Matt Tesler. I'm no longer interested in boys who are virgins."

"How do you know he is?"

"I can tell. Once you do it, you can tell," she said. "It's like you got a new pair of eyes, eyes that can see a lot more. Sweet dreams, sister dear," she said, and went to her bedroom.

Her words hung there for a few moments, but they didn't just go away. When I put out the light and lay back on my pillow, I couldn't help thinking about her description of sex between her and Jimmy. I saw myself doing it, but with Matt. Surely it would be different, I thought. Despite how good she said it made her feel, it still seemed more like she was getting something out of the way, more of an initiation than an act of love. That wasn't the way I wanted sex to be for me, and if I came off as more of a prude as a result, so be it.

When I finally did close my eyes, I felt suddenly relieved and even happy.

There was no doubt.

Haylee and I were identical twins, but we were as different as girls from two separate families.

9

Mother was dressed and ready to go shopping even before Haylee and I went down to have breakfast. She had her hair pinned up severely. From the way she was banging pans and slamming drawers, I knew something was bothering her. I hadn't heard our phone ringing, and she was rarely on Daddy's computer for emails, so I didn't think someone had contacted her to tell her something about us or Daddy that would upset her. Haylee and I looked at each other and meekly moved through the kitchen to get our juice. Mother always laid out the vitamins she wanted us to take in two perfect rows beside our juice glasses.

"I'm making scrambled eggs," she announced, in a tone that told us *Don't dare object*. She wasn't even looking at us. She stirred the eggs and milk like a witch driven by rage rushing her brew.

The table was already set, so we sat. Haylee went from fear to suspicion. Did she think I had gone to speak to Mother after she had left my room last night? I shook my head, but she wouldn't stop glaring at me with those eyes of accusation. Mother didn't notice or start interrogating us.

"Don't just sit there like guests. Make your toast," she commanded, and we both jumped up and went to the toaster. Nearly a year ago, she had decided it was all right for us to have coffee at breakfast. While the bread was being toasted, I poured us each a cup. I set Haylee's by her plate. She waited for the toast and brought it on a dish to the table. Mother hadn't said another word. She finished making the eggs and scooped out eight perfectly equal tablespoons for each of us. Then she stepped back to watch us eat.

"Aren't you having any breakfast, Mother?" I asked.

"I'm not hungry this morning. I'll eat something later."

We ate at our usual simultaneous pace. However, Mother's staring was making us both quite nervous. Finally, she sat with a cup of coffee in hand. We hesitated as she lowered and then raised her gaze. Her lips trembled as her thoughts rippled across her face. Even Haylee was frightened now. We both held our breath.

"I had to agree to let you go to dinner tonight

with your father," she announced through clenched teeth. "I didn't tell you last night because I thought it might disturb you and keep you from getting a good night's sleep, as it did me."

"Dinner?" I asked.

"Believe me, I didn't want to allow it, but my attorney said I should. Whatever your father tells you will be lies," she quickly continued. "The best I can say about it is that it will be a good lesson for you. You'll see how a man equivocates and rationalizes his selfish misbehavior. He'll try to turn me into a villain and make himself look like a victim."

"How can he be a victim?" Haylee asked. "He's left us for another family."

"Exactly," Mother said. Then she smiled. "I'm not worried about you. You'll not be easily turned against me."

"Of course not," Haylee said.

Oh, if Mother only knew how Haylee really felt about her, I thought. I quickly agreed, but I added one thought that Mother didn't appreciate. "I wish it had never come to this. I know how in love you both once were."

"Love?" She grimaced as though just saying the word gave her a headache. "Animal passions too often disguise themselves as love," she said. We widened our eyes at her admitting to sexual lust. "The woman is always at a disadvantage. Once you make love to a man, he thinks he owns you. Beware of that, and realize why it's not wise to give yourself away too cheaply or too quickly."

I looked pointedly at Haylee. She started to eat again, faster this time. Mother was staring ahead and didn't notice her reaction.

"Real love is an investment of yourself. You drop every natural defense you possess and replace it too soon with trust and dependence." She paused and looked from Haylee to me. "Love, or the feelings you will come to call love, can be very, very dangerous. Men don't have the same sensibility. They won't even realize it when they do hurt you, and then, when they do, as I told you, they'll find a way to blame you. Tread softly through your adolescent years. It's an emotional minefield. There are no immortal promises, not even the ones you make on your wedding day."

"We can still have fun as long as we're careful, right, Mother?" Haylee ventured. I would have preferred that she not say anything. In the mood Mother was in, any conversation concerning the opposite sex could turn into a swamp.

"Careful?" Her laugh was enveloped in a cold sneer. "That's the most-used self-delusion you'll experience. When people say you can never be too careful, what they really mean is you can never be careful. Period, end of sentence." She rose.

Haylee looked at me to see if I would say something, but I shook my head. I especially didn't want her to talk. This wasn't the time to promote the good effects of a romantic social life, not when Mother was so down on it.

"Finish and clean up," Mother ordered. "I've decided to put on some lipstick and mascara. I won't turn into a ghost of myself. That would be exactly what your father would like to see."

She marched out of the kitchen as if she was going upstairs to take her better self out of the closet. As soon as she was too far away to hear us, Haylee burst out, "She'll never let us go on a date again now."

"Relax," I said. "She'll calm down after this is over."

"It'll never be over." She sat back, pouting.

I began to clear the table and wash the pan. "Empty the coffee pot, and clean it out," I ordered in Mother's voice.

She groaned and began to help. Then we went up to prepare to go shopping. Before I stepped out again, my phone rang. It was Matt.

"Did you pass inspection last night?"

"Barely," I said. Before he could ask, I thought I had better let him know that tonight was impossible. "My mother is upset because we are having dinner with my father tonight. It will be uncomfortable for us, but we have to do it."

"Oh. I'm sorry. Jimmy called me this morning, hoping we'd figure out another double date."

"I'm afraid we're going to have to tread lightly until my mother settles down. Right now, she's so bitter about male-female relationships that the mere mention of another date might cause her to explode."

"Oh?"

"Everything is more complicated for us, although Haylee prefers to ignore it. Matt, I wouldn't blame you for wanting to have nothing to do with us, with me."

"I'd blame myself," he said. It brought a most welcome smile to my face. "We'll figure it out. It's the challenges that make life interesting."

"My stargazing philosopher."

He laughed. "Well, if you want to believe in astrology, the stars will tell us what to do and when."

"Can't be worse than what we're believing in now," I told him.

I promised to call him after our dinner with Daddy, no matter how late that might be. He made a point of telling me that he wasn't going out, implying that he wasn't looking for another girlfriend. I was sure Jimmy wouldn't give Haylee that assurance. When I met her in the hallway, I told her Matt had called and what he had said about Jimmy calling him.

"Damn," she declared. "Why do we have to suffer?"

I nearly laughed. "They're our parents, Haylee.

Of course we have to suffer. It's our family that's fracturing."

"I thought that happened the day we were born," she replied, and pounded her way ahead of me down the stairs.

On the drive to the department store, Haylee pouted. Once again, Mother didn't notice, because she was lost in her own diatribe, lecturing us about dates and romance. She told us things about her early days dating Daddy and claimed that she had always had reservations about him but was blinded by her obsession with the fantasy of a perfect love affair and marriage.

"He was always flirting with other women and telling me it was nothing or blaming it on them. Right from the beginning, he was away from home often. I was so naive then. I had no suspicions, but I'm sure he was having affairs right and left. Contrary to what he told you, he was not that upset with my devoting my life to you. He used it as an excuse to pursue his selfish lust."

I looked back at Haylee. She always preferred to sit in the rear when we went anywhere with Mother. It was easier that way for her to hide her reactions to things Mother said or look distracted by something else, but all this was happening just when she'd thought she had begun a real love life. She couldn't disguise her feelings. She was sinking into a pit of anger and self-pity.

"Lots of men and women stay married and faithful to each other, don't they, Mother?" she challenged.

"As far as you and I know," Mother said, "but open a closet or unlock a drawer in those homes, and you'll find disgusting secrets. It's more like they deliberately ignore the truth and live in blissful ignorance."

The pessimism annoyed Haylee more than it did me. I still believed that once Mother had gotten completely finished with the divorce, she would calm down and not be so dark and gloomy.

Divorce was simply another sort of death, and although the deaths of loved ones diminished people, they went on, resilient and eventually hopeful again. There was really no other choice. I was confident Mother would realize that and would realize how she was depressing us.

I thought of something to say that might change her attitude. "If you stay sad and depressed, Mother, won't Daddy have won?"

She turned and looked at me as though I had just washed and dried a window she could now look through.

"Yes, that's very true, Kaylee." She looked in the rearview mirror. "Is that what you were thinking, too, Haylee?"

"Exactly, Mother. We were talking about it just before we left the house," she lied.

"My girls, my girls," Mother said, nodding. "That settles it. I want to buy you something very pretty to wear to dinner. I want you to look happy and beautiful so he sees what he has lost. We'll do that first, and then I'll look for something new for myself. I've been invited to a party," she revealed, surprising us. "A dinner party at Melissa Clark's home."

"When?" Haylee asked.

"Next Friday," she replied. "I've already made an appointment with my stylist. Actually, I wasn't sure I would go until just this moment, thanks to what you girls were thinking this morning. Of course, I shouldn't just curl up and die. Out of the mouths of babes . . . you're the light at the end of my darkest tunnel."

I looked at Haylee. Her face was lit with excitement, and I knew why. She was already laying the plans for having Jimmy and Matt over when Mother went to her dinner party. She was clearly telling me that we would plan and plot together. After we parked in the lot for the department store and got out of the car, she walked beside me, and when Mother moved far enough ahead, she leaned over to whisper.

"No matter how we feel about him, when we come home from dinner tonight, we will tell her how angry and disgusted Daddy made us."

My clever and conniving sister, I thought. She was always better at deception than I was and always would be. I should have realized it before it was too late, but unfortunately, I was infected with more loving trust than she was.

Mother led us to the more upscale dresses, marching down the aisles determined to spend more money than usual. She paused at the Ralph Lauren displays. We had never shopped here. Before the saleslady could reach us, Mother had already plucked out a black, beaded Leila dress. The tag stated a cost close to three thousand dollars, and she would buy two! I couldn't deny that it was a beautiful dress, sleeveless and with beaded panels along the center front.

The saleslady had just started to greet us when Mother said, "I need two of this in the same size."

"Of course," the saleslady said, as if that was what every mother of every young woman demanded daily. She began to sift through the rack and came up with an identical second dress.

"Try them on," Mother ordered, nodding at the changing rooms. We took the dresses silently and went into the same room. It had a wall mirror.

"Do you believe this?" Haylee asked, and quickly began stripping down.

"No," I said. Mother had the eye for choosing styles and sizes that would fit us perfectly. This dress slipped on like a glove. I zipped up Haylee's, and she zipped up mine. Then we stood in front of the mirror and looked at ourselves.

"I should be going out with older boys, with men," Haylee declared. "Neither of us looks our age."

"I think most men would figure it out pretty quickly."

"You, maybe. Not me," she said defiantly, and walked out.

The saleslady standing beside Mother looked astounded. It must have seemed like one of us had gone into the changing room, looked in the mirror, and then somehow taken her image out of the glass and brought it along. Before we had left the house, we had made sure our hair was brushed the same and we were wearing the same lipstick.

"They'll need new earrings," Mother muttered, mostly to herself.

"Such a perfect fit. For both of them," the saleslady said.

Mother turned and looked at her as if she had just arrived on the planet. "Of course for both of them," she said. "How could it be for one without the other? Never mind," she added, before the poor woman could open her mouth. "Keep the dresses on until we finish at the jewelry counter," she told us. "And you'll need new shoes, too. Do you want to escort us?" she asked the saleslady.

"Of course, madam. Right this way," she said.

The jewelry department had only one pair of the pearl earrings Mother chose immediately for us, so she went with two other pairs at twice the price. After that, and after she had bought the two pairs of shoes she wanted us to have, I calculated that she had spent about seventy-five hundred dollars. We then changed back to the clothes we'd been wearing and carried our boxes as we accompanied Mother on her search for a new dress to wear to the Clarks' dinner party. That also required new shoes for her, and then a necklace that had caught her eye when she was looking for our earrings finished her own shopping.

"I bet this is what most women do when they get a divorce," Haylee whispered as we followed Mother out. "Attack their ex-husband's money. Lucky for us. I'm wearing this dress again with the shoes and earrings first chance I get. Seems like a waste for tonight. We'll only be with Daddy."

"Where are we going for dinner?" I wondered, and stepped up to ask Mother.

"He wanted to take you back to the London House, but I told him you'd be uncomfortable there without me, so I said he should take you to Cheeky's. It's nearly twice as expensive. If it was up to him, he would have taken you to some fast-food joint," she added. "He'll be coming for you at six. I want you to be right on time. I don't want to have to make small talk with him."

"Oh, we'll be ready early," Haylee assured her. "We'd like to get it over with as quickly as we can."

Mother paused to look at her, and I held my breath. If she thought we were just humoring her, it would be worse for us than if we were happy and eager to go out with Daddy.

"I mean, it sounds boring," Haylee quickly added. "Right, Kaylee?"

"We have to do what we have to do," I said.

"Exactly," Mother said, and I gave Haylee a look that told her to shut her mouth.

It was weird at first to see how important our dressing for dinner with Daddy was for Mother. She supervised our hair and our makeup like the producer of some important television show. She changed the shade of our lipstick twice and completed our makeup herself, rattling on about some of the modeling shoots she had done and the little tricks she had learned to highlight her best features.

"Is Daddy going to take pictures of us or something?" Haylee asked.

"He'll take a picture, all right, with his brain," she said. "As will anyone who sees you. The man will realize what he has lost. It will haunt him for the rest of his life."

When everything was completed, she inspected us one more time. Then she led us downstairs to wait in the living room. She wanted us practically as still as statues so we wouldn't mess up our appearance. A few minutes before six, Daddy rang the doorbell, which immediately struck me as so strange—our father ringing the doorbell of what was his own home.

Mother opened the door and stood there for a moment without speaking, as if she was going to block his entrance or had changed her mind and would go against her attorney's advice. Then, instead of stepping aside to let him in, she fixed her gaze on him and called, "Haylee and Kaylee!"

We rose and went to the front door, where Daddy stood waiting in a jacket and tie.

"Wow," he said when he saw us. "You girls look beautiful."

"You probably just noticed," Mother said.

Daddy looked at her, seeming to debate with himself whether to reply, and then stepped back. "Shall we go, ladies?"

I started forward first and paused in front of Mother. Haylee caught up, and Mother embraced us both.

"If you get uncomfortable, call me, and I'll come for you," she whispered.

Daddy had gotten a new car, a black Mercedes sedan.

"A new car!" Haylee couldn't keep from exclaiming.

"Just to pick you two up," Daddy said. "Who wants to sit in front? The other can sit there on the way back."

"We'll both sit in the back both ways," Haylee replied, loudly enough for Mother to hear as she still stood in the doorway.

I glanced back and was sure I saw her smile. Daddy shrugged and opened the rear door. Haylee got in first, and I followed. He closed the door, looked back at Mother, then got in, started the engine, and backed out of the driveway.

"Of course, I knew you guys were beautiful," he said. "You just look years older since I saw you last."

"We are years older," Haylee said. "Especially years older than the other girls in our class."

"Oh, yeah? So tell me more about school. How's it going?"

"We made the honor roll again," I said.

"Why am I not surprised?"

"Despite our family sadness, we went to a party last night," Haylee said.

"Really? She let you go?"

"We didn't sneak out," Haylee replied. "Mother's not an ogre."

I knew what she was doing. She was going to be sharp and smart with Daddy, just to make Mother happy and get her to let us do more, but I couldn't help feeling bad about how she was treating him, despite what he had done.

"What's your new family like?" I asked. I was really just curious and didn't say it to sound mean.

"They're not really my new family. I mean, Cindy's got two young children, a boy, Thomas, who's ten, and a girl, Mercedes, who's eight."

"Was she named after a car?" Haylee asked instantly. "Mercedes?" She let out her characteristic ridiculing laugh.

"No," Daddy replied, smiling. "Cindy's ex-husband is Cuban. They named her after his mother. Mercedes is from the Spanish title of the Virgin Mary, Maria de las Mercedes, which means Mary of Mercies. I didn't know all that before I met Cindy," he added, looking back at us, still with a smile.

"Where did you meet her?" I asked.

"On a job. She works for a company we're going to buy," he said.

"Then she'll work for you," Haylee said.

"I guess. If she continues. So tell me about your party. Where was it?"

"At someone's house," Haylee said. She nudged me. "We watched a movie you might know."

"What movie?"

"What was it, Kaylee?"

"*To Kill a Mockingbird*," I said.

"Great movie. Did you read the book? Is that part of the curriculum?"

"The what?" Haylee asked.

"The course," I said. "What we have to read in literature class. It's one of the optional titles. We have to do book reports and can choose it."

"Even though you saw the film, I'd say read the book."

"We will."

"It's optional," Haylee said. "I might choose something else."

Daddy started to tell us about the books he enjoyed reading in high school and college. For the remainder of the ride to the restaurant, it felt almost like nothing was different. I even could imagine Mother sitting up front with him. When would it really start feeling strange? I wondered.

The answer came to me after we had been seated at our table. As usual, people were gawking at us because of how identical we were and how identically dressed. For as long as I could remember, when we went to formal restaurants, especially places where we sat in plain sight of practically every patron, Mother was there to smile back at people or reply to comments made about us. She was always very proud of us. Not that Daddy wasn't; he was just more subdued about it. He was that way now, and he was also nervous and a bit awkward. It was almost as if he hadn't known us very long.

"So what do you like?" he asked a few moments after we had our menus. He had ordered himself a Scotch and soda, and we had iced teas. Mother was right about the restaurant. It was the most expensive we had been to.

"Do we like shrimp scampi?" Haylee asked me.

"Yes."

"Good." She folded her menu.

I smiled at her and shook my head. She thought she was ordering for me, too. "I'll have the veal osso buco," I said.

"We like that?" Haylee asked.

"We never had it, but I know what it is and always wanted to try it," I said.

"Then I should."

"You don't have to eat the same thing your sister does when you're with me," Daddy told her. "I never saw you as duplicates, even though that was a sin in our house."

And so it's starting, I thought.

"I continually tried to persuade your mother to let you become individuals, your own persons, but she had her theories and research." He smiled, which took me by surprise. "It was like talking to a religious zealot who would keep referring to the Bible. I'm sorry," he said, after the waiter took our orders. "Sorry I gave up."

"Is that the reason you had an affair?" I asked.

He looked from Haylee to me, deciding how much to tell us, how grown-up and ready for such talk we were. "Not entirely, no. A man and a woman have needs, and getting married doesn't change that. What it means is that you're going to satisfy those needs with only one person. That's being faithful, loving."

"Sex," Haylee said, wanting to hear the word and strip away any euphemisms.

Daddy looked like he was going to blush, but he took a deep breath and surprised us both by saying, "Yes, sex. I suspect you both know more about it already than I do."

Haylee laughed. He raised his eyebrows and smiled. I didn't laugh.

"Maybe you two are as old as you look," he commented.

Nothing could have pleased Haylee more. "Of course we are. We know what you mean. Because Mother wouldn't have sex with you when you wanted to, you had an affair and then had to get a divorce, right?"

He looked at me again to see if I was going to add anything, but I didn't say a word. "Well, in a nutshell, yes, but nothing in life is ever that simple, Haylee," he replied, stressing her name.

I raised my eyebrows. "You don't have any trouble telling us apart, do you, Daddy?"

"Not since you were very little. Of course not. Sometimes I spoke too soon, and she'd dump hot coals over my head. As I said, you're two different people who just happen to share physical features in an extraordinary way. They say there's a perfect duplicate for everyone in this world."

"You mean there are two more like us?" Haylee asked.

"That's what they say."

"Mine better not come around here," Haylee declared, and Daddy laughed.

It was the first laugh of the night, and it seemed to crack the sheet of ice between us. Our food came, and Daddy began to talk with more ease about his business, Cindy, and her children. He told us he had put aside all the money we would need for college and said he hoped we would attend two different schools.

"You need the experience of meeting people without your sister hovering in the background. That way, people will see you for who you are faster," he declared. "I know your mother doesn't believe this, but if you come to agree with me, I promise I'll fight for you."

"We have some time to decide," I said. "Until things settle down, arguments will just make things harder for us."

He nodded. "Very true. You're very wise, Kaylee."

Just like any time I received a compliment and Haylee didn't, I looked at her quickly and caught the glint of anger in her eyes. "That's what both of us think," I said. "We've talked about it."

"Oh. Sure. Very good, Haylee. We'll tread softly on the future."

The word *future* must have stirred Haylee's visions of what this coming Friday would be like.

She looked bored with anything else, except to say she enjoyed the choice I had made for dinner. That got Daddy talking about how good a cook Cindy was and how he had already gained five pounds. Before we had our dessert, he grew serious again and talked about the divorce agreement. He wanted to assure us that he would always be there for us, no matter what, and that we could always call him if we needed anything or if anything disturbed us. By *anything*, I knew he meant Mother.

Afterward, on the ride home, he asked us questions about school again and what we envisioned ourselves becoming. More and more, perhaps because of Mother's influence, I was thinking about doing something in psychology, perhaps child psychology. Haylee's ambitions flowed from becoming a movie star to a model to a TV reporter. How she could be so mature when it came to sexual things but sound so much like a child when it came to everything else amazed me. Daddy did his best not to discourage her from anything, but when I told him about my ambitions, he was more attentive and promised he would look into what were the best schools for that field.

Haylee fell into a bit of a sulk when he went on and on about it and practically leaped out of the car when we pulled into the driveway. He got out quickly and kissed us both good night, promising to arrange for another dinner soon.

"You should call well in advance," Haylee told him. "We've got a full calendar of social events."

"Oh, really? Well, that's very good, Haylee."

Mother practically ripped the door off the hinges opening it. Frozen in place, we all looked at her.

"Well, good night again, girls," Daddy said.

Haylee moved away from him quickly so he couldn't kiss her again. He looked at me and then went to his car. I followed Haylee in, and Mother slammed the door.

"I hope we don't have to do that often," Haylee said. "It was very uncomfortable for us to hear all that crap about his new family."

Mother looked astounded but pleased. "Really? How stupid of him."

"I told him to call you way in advance if he wanted to take us to dinner again, because we have a very busy social calendar," she continued. She was on a roll, and I stepped back, in awe of how well she was doing.

"Yes, of course," Mother said.

"I mean, we don't have to roll over and play dead because of what he's doing, do we, Mother?"

"Absolutely not."

"We've talked it over, Kaylee and I. We won't permit our classmates and others to pity us. We intend to be happy, maybe even happier. Just like you," she added, like someone sealing a deal.

"That's very, very wise of you both. Yes, that's what we'll do." She smiled. "My girls," she said, and hugged us both. "We'll all be just fine."

Haylee glanced at me with that look of self-satisfaction, a look that often made me feel sick inside.

It was as if something ugly was being born within my very being, and there was nothing I could do to stop it.

10

I let Haylee take the lead to persuade Mother to let us have a small party at our house while she was at the Clarks' dinner party. I wanted to be with Matt very much, so much, in fact, that I didn't stop Haylee from telling lies about our party plans. Perhaps that was my biggest mistake, because once Haylee saw how easily she could get me to tolerate her little deceptions, it led to bigger and bigger ones and, eventually, the most tragic one.

So in a real way, I had no one to blame more than myself for what she did. I made it possible by being so tolerant.

Haylee went right to work setting the foundation for her deceits about our party. She talked Melanie Rosen and Toby Sue Daniels into lying to their parents about attending a party at our house. Of course, Haylee wanted no one but Jimmy and Matt to come, but she knew Mother would be suspicious of that. She had warned us about getting too serious with one boy too soon. Haylee presented it as a general party for a group of our mutual best friends. I wasn't sure what Haylee was promising them, but both girls were excited and happy to participate in Haylee's ruse. They assured us that they would have dates themselves and be out of their homes so that if Mother ever did check up, she'd be told by their parents that they had gone to our party.

I told Matt the truth and saw that he wasn't comfortable with it.

"Why is it necessary?" he asked me at school on Wednesday, after Haylee had confirmed her plans. "Why couldn't you two just have a party with us?"

For me, it now became a question of how deeply I would go into our lives, into our relationship with our mother, her beliefs about us because we were identical twins, and how bitter she was about her and our father's divorce. I wanted to be as truthful as I could be, but there were alarm bells sounding, too. I could easily frighten him off from having any sort of relationship with me, I thought. No one outside of our home had any idea of Mother's theories about how we should be brought up and how we should conduct ourselves. How much could I tell him?

"Right now, our mother is very sensitive to the idea of either of us having any sort of special boyfriend or relationship. She's very sour about what's happened between her and my father," I offered as a rationale. "So unfortunately, we have to pretend we're not with anyone special."

"Yeah. My aunt Wilma, my mother's older sister, became that way right after her divorce." He smiled. "I'm glad you said you have to *pretend* you're not with anyone special."

"Very hard for me to do," I said, and his smile deepened.

"Friday can't come fast enough."

With mixed feelings, I left him and went to class. I liked him too much not to feel bad about not telling the full truth about our mother and us. Perhaps I was wrong to worry and pay more attention to all that than Haylee did. She was better at ignoring things and absolutely happier because of it. Every once in a while, she would be on me again about being a worrywart.

"Stop looking like you lost your two front teeth. You're moping around too much. You'll make Mother suspicious, and then we'll really have trouble," she said. Then she smiled and changed the topic. "I got a few others who will say they'll be at our house. I'm telling her we have ten now."

"Ten? You're involving too many people, Haylee. Someone's sure to blab. Daddy used to say that two can keep a secret if one is dead."

"Right. And worrying brings wrinkles. You're

going to get gray hair before I do." There was no
stopping her now.

The closer we got to Friday, the more excited
she became. Now it was my turn to issue warnings about how to behave in front of Mother. I
cautioned Haylee not to be too excited about the
party, because that might make Mother suspicious
more than any nervous look on my face would. She
thought about it and agreed. Then she did a very
clever thing—too clever, I thought. She was reaching into a well of darkness that I never knew she
had access to.

She began to pretend that she wasn't sure we
should have the party at all. I couldn't believe it, but
I was thinking that she might have gotten this clever
tactic from our class reading of *Othello*. Right from
the first pages, she was intrigued with Iago, the
character who deceives and destroys Othello and
his wife, Desdemona. He never comes right out and
accuses anyone of anything, but he plants the seeds
of Desdemona's supposed adultery and lets Othello
destroy himself worrying about it.

Haylee began at breakfast Thursday morning.
Mother had gone to her beauty salon and had her
hair trimmed and styled. She really looked more
beautiful than she had in a long time. The medium
to long layers played around her shoulders and
her face. The center part added long, flippy bangs.
She was so happy with her look that she wouldn't

step out of her bedroom without wearing one of her nicer dresses or outfits coordinated with rings, bracelets, and necklaces and, just as we remembered her when we were younger, not without makeup, either.

She told us once that she perfected her appearance not for the people she knew she would see but for the ones who surprised her. They would be more impressed and would talk about how together and organized a person she was even when caught completely unawares. "A beautiful woman is always on a stage," she said, and assured us that we were beautiful.

"We don't know if we should go through with this party," Haylee began. She hadn't told me she would say anything like that, so I was surprised, but I knew not to look it.

"What? Why?" Mother asked quickly. "Did your father hear of it and tell you that?"

"Oh, no," Haylee said quickly. "We wouldn't tell him, either."

"So?"

"It just seems wrong for us to be having fun while you're going through so much. We've decided we can wait."

Mother looked at me and then back at her. Haylee looked so sincere. I thought if I didn't know her, if I were a stranger or someone who hadn't been with us for years, I would believe her, too.

"I won't have it," Mother said firmly. "Whether he knows about it or not, I won't have him turning our home into a funeral parlor, with the both of you sitting around mournfully while your friends enjoy being . . . being young."

"It's all right, Mother," Haylee continued, looking so unselfish it could bring strangers to tears. "Kaylee and I have decided we can just watch something on TV or play some board game while you're out."

"Nonsense," Mother said. "You've invited people. How would it look if you just canceled for no reason? Anyone with half a brain would blame it on the situation your father caused. The waves of pity will drown me out there. I won't have it."

"Well, we didn't think of that," Haylee said, looking very thoughtful. She nodded. "Mother's right, Kaylee. We wouldn't want that, either, right?"

I looked at her and then at Mother and shook my head. I felt as if Haylee had taken my hand and walked me out onto thin ice. Whether I wanted to be or not, I was now part of her dishonesty. Ironically, Mother was right. Whatever one of us did the other would share, whether it was a compliment or a criticism. How could one of us do anything without people looking at the other? "Haylee-Kaylee, Kaylee-Haylee" would be hovering in the air above our heads whether we wanted it or not.

"Then it's settled," Mother declared. "I don't want to hear any more talk about canceling your party."

"Okay, Mother. It's just that . . . well, to be honest, we're not sure we're planning the party right," Haylee continued, now on a real roll. "Everyone orders in pizza. We hate doing what everyone else does, but we're not sure what else we should do."

Mother thought a moment. "Well, let's do something special for sure," she said. "We can make a homemade Italian party for you. We'll do a meat lasagna, that sausage-filled ravioli with marinara sauce, and an eggplant parmesan for those who don't want to eat meat. We'll get it all prepared ahead of time, so all you have to do is warm it up. The two of you can make a very good salad.

"And I know what else," she continued, shocking me with her enthusiasm. "I'll pick up some tiramisu at the Italian deli this afternoon. We have enough soft drinks. It will be the best party any of your classmates ever had at someone's house. I know the two of you and your friends will take care not to make a mess and will clean up before I come home."

"Oh, Mother, that's too much for you to do just when you're trying to get yourself settled again!" Haylee cried, practically in tears. "You have so much on your mind."

"Nonsense. I'm not going to let him disturb one

hair on my head when it comes to making my girls happy," she declared. "As soon as I bring you to school today, I'll start on the party menu."

"You'll be too exhausted to go out yourself, or you'll be so tired you'll have to come home early," Haylee pursued. I couldn't keep up with how quickly she could weave her fraud.

"Absolutely not. In fact, this will give me more energy, and I'll be the last to leave the Clarks'. No one will see me crawl into a hole like some mousy, beaten-down ex-wife," she vowed. "I intend to have a very good time."

When Mother turned her back, Haylee looked at me. I couldn't imagine any actor who played Iago having a more evil, self-satisfied smile.

"If there's only the four of us, what are we supposed to do with all that food?" I asked her the moment we were away from Mother.

"We'll have it recycled."

"What?"

"We'll have either Jimmy or Matt take it to some homeless shelter, Kaylee. What do I care about extra food? We're going to have a good time. Get used to it," she told me. "For the rest of your life."

A part of me thought that maybe she was right. If I didn't listen to her, I could dig myself into a corner of shadows thick with depression and ruin every chance I had for a happy high school life. A year ago, if anyone had told me that I would look to my sister for guidance socially or in anything whatsoever, I would have thought him or her nuts or stupid. Yet here I was, doing just that.

On Friday, I described our menu to Matt. He was amazed and then asked the same question. "Won't you have a lot of leftovers?"

"Haylee's in charge of figuring it all out," I said.

"She's in charge?"

"When it comes to planning anything behind my mother's back, she's in charge."

On our way home after school, Mother described everything she had done. She brought us to the kitchen immediately and showed us all the dishes, instructing us on how to warm up everything and what silverware and dishes to use. She had even set up two folding tables in the dining room to serve as buffet tables. She had cleared away anything she thought might be damaged or broken.

"What are you planning to wear?" she asked us.

Haylee had plotted everything but this and looked at me quickly to reply.

"Nobody gets very dressed up for house parties, Mother, but we're not sure. We want to wear something nice but not too formal," I said, coming to the rescue.

"Yes." She thought a moment and then brightened and said, "There's that black and white lace dress I bought you as one of your birthday presents. It's not very formal, and yet it makes a statement."

I looked at Haylee. I knew she wasn't fond of the dress, because she thought it made her look too young. It had been advertised for "tweens."

"That's a great idea," she nevertheless said quickly. "And we have those shoes you bought us to go with it. Should we wear any special jewelry? We have those diamond bracelets."

"Not for this. My advice is always to lean toward understatement when it comes to fashion. There's a point where ostentation becomes offensive, especially to your girlfriends who don't have good advice about appearance and will only be envious. Now, you'll have to excuse me," she added, smiling. "I need to spend some time planning my appearance."

We watched her walk off.

"We can change after she leaves," Haylee said.

"I don't really mind wearing the dress."

She shrugged. "Maybe you're right. I won't be wearing it all that long anyway," she said with a wry smile.

We knew Mother would want to see us dressed before she left for her dinner party on Friday, so we waited for her in the living room. We were both taken by how beautiful she looked in her new dress. She did a little fashion walk for us the way she used to when we were younger and would clap and laugh.

Then she paused and turned serious. "I have a good feeling about all this now," she said. "With your support, I know we'll come out of it stronger than we were. For a while there, we were three small boats on a rough sea, but we're in control now."

"Thanks to you, Mother," Haylee said.

"Yes," I added quickly. Sometimes I felt like I was holding on to Haylee's tail to keep up—and the devil was sometimes pictured with a tail, I thought.

Mother made sure we had no questions about the food and then hugged us and wished for us to have a wonderful party. "I don't want you to worry about me."

"We'll try not to, but we will," Haylee said.

"Yes," I said.

Mother smiled and kissed us. For a moment, she stood there looking at us. My heart ached with how deeply I had gone into Haylee's pit of deception.

"We'll have so much to gossip about tomorrow," Mother said, and she giggled like a teenage girl.

Haylee was smiling with such self-satisfaction that I felt a little nauseated.

We stood in the doorway and watched her drive off.

"I'll see to the food," I said, knowing that Haylee didn't care and thinking that if I threw myself into the preparations, I would quiet my nagging conscience.

"Good. I'll see to the music. They'll be here soon. Jimmy wanted to pick up Matt, but he insisted on coming on his own. He's not the easiest boy for Jimmy to make friends with."

"I wonder why," I said, and left the answer hanging out there. As with most such things, Haylee ignored it.

Jimmy arrived so soon after Mother had left that I suspected he had been waiting and watching. Haylee hadn't told him anything about the food and was annoyed that he hovered over me admiring it all as I began to set things up.

"Don't disturb the help," she told him. She hooked her arm through his and dragged him into the living room. She turned up the music immediately. It was good that we had no close neighbors.

Ten minutes later, Matt arrived. He immediately began to help me. When we began to bring food into the dining room, Haylee and Jimmy appeared. It looked to me as if they had already been into something, but Haylee would know better than to smoke anything in our house, and I had frightened her by telling her that I had seen Mother measure the amount of liquor in every bottle in the cabinet. I hadn't, but I thought it was a good idea to tell her that.

"Let's eat first," Jimmy said. "I think I'm going to need my strength again tonight."

Haylee was giggling at everything he said and

did. The first chance I got, I pulled her aside and asked her if she had taken anything.

"Did he bring something?"

"Relax," she replied. "I'm in control."

"You're going to mess this up badly," I predicted, and started to dish out food for the boys.

Haylee was quickly over the top with her behavior, sitting on Jimmy's lap and feeding him sloppily.

"This is all delicious," Matt said, trying to ignore them. Haylee had the music so loud throughout the house that he practically had to shout. "I hate to see so much get wasted."

"Maybe I can figure out how to throw out some and freeze some," I said.

"Count me in when it comes to leftovers."

After we ate, the four of us were soon dancing in the living room, and despite the slutty way I thought Haylee was behaving, I was beginning to have a good time. Every once in a while, we would return to the dining room and get something else to eat, but we weren't even making a dent in the amount Mother had prepared.

"My mother worked so hard on all that," I told Matt. "I feel bad about it."

"Maybe you can put some in containers, and I'll take them home and tell my mother your mother made too much. She won't care."

I kissed him. Would I ever find another boy as

considerate? I wondered. Mother never talked very much about any other boyfriend she'd had besides Daddy. I had the impression that dating in high school and even in college was more like training for when you were confronted by the real thing. I knew Haylee thought of it that way. Once, angry at her for how she had belittled my feelings for Matt, I told her she would be in training until she was a member of AARP. Whenever I was able to break through her defenses and strike a sensitive blow like that, she would look at me with eyes so cold that I trembled.

Haylee played some slow music, and the four of us were dancing romantically. I was later sure that it was then, behind our backs, that either Haylee or Jimmy put something in Matt's and my soft drinks. Whatever it was, it made both Matt and me a little groggy and dizzy. I could see how they were both watching us and smiling, whispering and laughing.

"C'mon," Haylee declared. "Let's show them our rooms."

Before I could object, Haylee took Matt's hand and practically dragged him to the stairway. Jimmy took mine, and we were all upstairs quickly. Of course, both boys were surprised to look in the doorways and see how identical the rooms were.

"If you came home drunk, you could end up sleeping in the wrong bed," Jimmy said.

"Oh, there's a big difference. Mine is used more," Haylee said, her comment full of sexual innuendo.

I saw even Matt smiling. He looked drunk.

Haylee and Jimmy were laughing at everything now. She took his hand to pull him into her room, Before she did, she leaned toward me and whispered, "What you need is on your pillow."

I had no idea what she meant until Matt and I went back to my room and we both saw the contraceptive packet on one of my pillows. He froze, a look of astonishment on his face.

"I didn't put that there," I said. Did he believe me?

He shrugged and flopped on the bed. "I feel so weird," he said.

"Me, too."

It was then that the idea that something had been put in our drinks began to worry me more. What if it was something so strong that Mother would be home before it wore off? When the room began to spin, I sprawled out beside Matt. He started laughing, and so did I. Neither of us could help it or stop. We hugged and kissed and laughed, and suddenly, the lights in my room went off. I knew that Haylee had done it.

"It's a party," I heard her say from the doorway. "Start to have fun."

I was annoyed, but as Matt's kisses grew more passionate and his hands moved over my body, that annoyance took a backseat. I was soon returning his kisses with the same passion. His fingers undid the clasp of my dress and slowly unzipped it. I helped him take it off me. My bra followed quickly. His lips nudged and caressed my nipples. He kissed me on the neck, and then our lips met and drew so deeply into each other that I felt like I was floating backward, sinking into a warm cloud.

He rustled out of his clothes until he was in only his underwear, and I was only in my panties. I felt his hardness, and my legs, as if triggered by impulses passed down through centuries, impulses that couldn't be denied, spread to welcome him. When I did that, he quickened every kiss, every caress. He was whispering softly, confessing how I had captured his heart like no other girl could.

Somewhere in the background, I heard Mother's warning. *Beware of promises and compliments made in the heat of passion. It's not the young man's mind speaking; it's his lust.*

But how would I ever know the difference, Mother? I asked. *People in love lust for each other.*

If you stay in control of yourself, you will know, she promised.

Was I losing control?

Matt reached for the contraceptive. I heard it crackling in his fingers.

"Is this what you want?" he asked, in a whisper so soft that it seemed to come from inside me.

Was he now convinced that I had put it there

and my denial was just my hesitation, my innocence and fear? Why hadn't I plucked it off the pillow and made my intentions or lack of them clear? Deep inside, was I happy Haylee had done this? Had it excited me?

"Should I?" he asked again.

I was dancing with yes and no, reeling from the grip of one and then the other. In the back of my mind was the realization that this was what Haylee wanted more than I did, and it was Mother's fault. She had taught us that what one of us did the other must do, or we would become too different and in the end hate each other because of the difference. The yes in me argued that I should do it for Haylee's sake as much as my own.

The no in me was screaming that she was turning me into her. Didn't I always want to be my own person, have my own identity? More important, didn't I want this to be special and to come about only after a commitment of deeper feelings and an investment of trust, just like Mother told us? I liked Matt a lot, but how could all that have come so quickly? This was really only our second date. Yes, we had spent a lot of time talking at school, but that wasn't intimate time.

And what about tomorrow? Could I live with the regret? Could I do what Haylee did and not make it as big a thing as Mother wanted it to be for us?

I wasn't Haylee. I wasn't. This was too soon.

"Not yet," I said.

I could almost feel the disappointment in the air, because some of it was coming from me as well as from him.

He turned away and lay on his back. I felt a wave of cold air come between us.

"It's all right. It's all right," he said. "I just have to calm down a bit."

I put my hand on his chest and pressed my face against his shoulder. We lay there silently. I heard his breathing slow to a regular rhythm and realized he was falling asleep. Whatever it was they had put in our drinks was doing this, I thought angrily. I slipped off the bed and reached for my bra and my dress. Then I went into my bathroom and splashed my face with cold water. I felt tired but not as dizzy as before. Perhaps I hadn't drunk as much as Matt. When I stepped out, I saw that he was on his side now, sleeping. There was no point in waking him. I thought about the food we had left out and decided to go downstairs and put some of it into containers as Matt had suggested. The door to Haylee's room was closed. I wasn't in the mood to talk to her anyway.

While I was taking care of the food, I saw that either Haylee or Jimmy had spilled some marinara sauce on one of the dining-room chair cushions. Mother would be very angry about it, I thought, and hurried to get the stain remover. It took quite a while to get the sauce out of the cushion. After that, I continued cleaning up. We hadn't even touched the tiramisu. Maybe Matt and Jimmy would eat some when they came down. I looked at the clock.

It was almost nine thirty. We still had some time, but I thought I had better get them down here. I hurried up the stairs, intending first to knock on Haylee's bedroom door, but when I reached the landing and started down the hallway, Haylee stepped out of my bedroom.

Totally naked!

She stood there smiling at me. For a moment, I felt as if my feet were nailed to the floor.

"What were you—"

"You're not a virgin anymore," she said, laughed, and sauntered to her bedroom.

I still hadn't moved. What had she done? My heart was pounding. I approached my doorway slowly, almost with baby steps, and paused there looking in. Then I flipped on the lights. Matt was facedown on my bed, also totally naked. I gasped with a moan loud enough to stir him. He turned slowly, his eyes blinking. He rubbed them and gazed at me.

"Hey," he said. "How did you get dressed so fast?"

Beside him on the bed was the empty contraceptive wrapper.

I still had not entered the room.

"What did you do?" I asked, my hands at the base of my throat.

"Do?" He sat up and leaned against the headboard. "What do you mean? You mean my falling asleep? I'm sorry—"

"No!"

My exclamation was so loud and sharp that he seemed to tremble like someone experiencing an earthquake. "What?" he asked, reaching for his underwear and slipping it on. He was grasping at all his clothes.

"My sister," I said.

He shook his head and put on his pants. "Sister?" He looked at the doorway to my bathroom. "You came out of the bathroom . . . naked, and I was surprised, but—"

"It wasn't me," I said.

Now he simply stared at me. His face moved from disbelief to suspicion and then back to disbelief. "You took it out. You put it on me and—"

"I don't want to hear about it," I said, slamming the palms of my hands against my ears.

He hurried to finish dressing. "It can't be," he mumbled. "It can't be."

I turned and went to Haylee's bedroom. The door was closed, but I thrust it open. Jimmy and she were on her bed, both now dressed. They smiled at me.

"How could you do that?"

"I saw you weren't going to do it," Haylee said, "and thought, why waste a good condom?"

Jimmy roared and slapped the side of his leg. "Good one."

"It's just a joke, Kaylee. Don't get hysterical. Now it will be easier for you the next time."

"I'll swear she was in here with me the whole time," Jimmy said, raising his right hand, and they both laughed again.

"If it makes any difference, he kept saying your name, not mine," Haylee said.

"My dad is always saying 'in the dark, all cats are gray,'" Jimmy said. "Meow."

Haylee laughed. Then she stopped and looked soberly at me. "Is everything cleaned up, put away? Oh, don't we still have the tiramisu?"

"Tiramisu? I love it," Jimmy said, starting to get up.

"You put something in our drinks, didn't you?" I looked at Jimmy. "What was it? You brought it."

"Who, *moi*?" Jimmy said. "I wouldn't do that. Maybe you put it in yourself."

"That's my sister. She does stuff and then tries to blame it on me," Haylee said. She rose, too.

"I'm going to tell Mother everything," I declared.

"No, you won't. She'll be just as angry at you, maybe angrier for trying to blame me for something you wanted to do and did."

"We're wasting time," Jimmy said. "There's tiramisu waiting."

They started toward me. I stepped away and went back to my bedroom. Matt was sitting on the side of the bed looking dazed, his hands on his temples.

"They put something in what we drank," I told him.

He looked at me and nodded. "What was it?"

"I don't know."

"That bastard," he said, standing, his hands clenched.

"Don't start a fight here. It will only make things worse."

He shook his head, looked at the bathroom and then back at me. "It was your sister?"

"I don't want to talk about it anymore."

"Where are they?"

"Downstairs, eating dessert as if nothing happened," I said.

"What do you want me to do now?"

"Just go home," I said. "The party's over."

"You're mad at me."

"I don't know what I am," I said.

I picked up the contraceptive wrapper and started out. He followed me down the stairs.

The two of them looked up at us with their mouths full of tiramisu.

"This is delicious," Jimmy said.

"Do you want any?" I asked Matt. He shook his head. He looked ashamed now instead of angry—ashamed and embarrassed.

"I'd better go," he said. He threw an angry glare at Jimmy, who just kept smiling and eating. Then he turned to leave, and I followed him out.

"If you start a fight with him, he'll probably tell everyone what happened," I said at the front door.

"He probably will anyway. He's a jerk and a half." He started to lean toward me to kiss me good night and then stopped. "I'm sorry," he said, and went quickly to his SUV. He didn't look back at me. He seemed eager to get away.

After he left, I went into the kitchen and took out the food I'd been planning to give him and put it with the rest of the wasted food in a big garbage bag.

Haylee came to the kitchen doorway as I worked.

"Jimmy's going to take that trash bag and dump it for us so Mother doesn't accidentally see it or something."

"Do what you want," I said. I put the last of the dishes and silverware into the dishwasher and walked past her and up the stairs.

When I stepped into my room, I stood staring at the rumpled sheets and pillows. How would I sleep in it and not think of what she had done? I sat on the bed, thinking. She had heard me leave and came in and saw the unused condom. If I had settled on the yes instead of the no, this wouldn't have happened. Should I blame myself, too?

I didn't realize I was crying until the first tear dripped off my chin. Instantly, I rose and went to the bathroom to wash my face and prepare for bed. I changed into a pair of pajamas, the exact same pair Haylee had, of course. Suddenly, everything we shared seemed dirty to me. But what could I do about it? Just before I got into bed, she came to my door.

"Jimmy left."

I didn't respond. I got into bed.

"I made sure everything was clean in the dining room and the living room."

I was quiet.

"It was all just fun, Kaylee. It's not as big a deal as you think. Get over it. He'll feel guilty about it anyway, and you'll have him wrapped around your finger for as long as you want."

"I don't want to wrap anyone around my finger, Haylee. That's not my idea of a boyfriend. Besides," I said, now sitting up, "what kind of a boyfriend is Jimmy if he thinks it's funny that you made love with another boy, practically right in front of him?"

"Take a hint. If I cared anything about him really, I wouldn't have done it. He's too immature for me. He was only good for a few laughs," she said. "I'll probably give him his walking papers this week. If you dump Matt, maybe I'll toy with him for a while."

"What?"

"Tomorrow let's just talk up how everyone loved Mother's food. She'll ask fewer questions. Good night, sister dear," she said, and went to her room.

I lay back and stared at the ceiling. My brain felt as if it had turned into a little merry-go-round. I had to close my eyes to keep my head from spinning.

The best thing I could do was fall asleep and get out of this reality.

But I was just as afraid of what I might dream.

11

I didn't want to entirely blame Matt for what had happened. I told myself that whatever Jimmy had put in our drinks had the most to do with it, but of course, in the back of my mind was the question of why Matt still couldn't tell the difference between Haylee and me. Was Mother right about us? That to be happy in this world, we had to embrace our similarities and reject our differences? For most of our lives, she had us convinced that no one could look at one of us without seeing both of us. Could either of us at a moment's notice become the other? It certainly wasn't something I wanted to be true, and I had no doubt Haylee felt the same way.

Matt didn't call me in the morning as I was hoping he would. Twice I started to call him, but I stopped myself both times. I imagined he was still feeling confused and guilty and wasn't ready to talk about it. I did worry that he would go after Jimmy, and I mentioned that to Haylee when she came out of her room in the morning.

"If he sees him somewhere tonight and something terrible happens, it will bring lots of attention to us. Mother will find out everything."

"Don't worry. He won't see him tonight," she said as we were going down to breakfast. "Jimmy's going out with his older brother, who's home on leave. He's twenty and in the navy." Her eyes lit up. "We could probably go with them and have a great time if you'd help me convince Mother. We'll tell her it's another house party or something."

I stared at her, my face clearly saying, *Are you serious?*

"What?" she asked, as if she had no idea why I would be surprised.

"What? You want me to do something with Jimmy after what he did to Matt and me last night? And what you did?"

"You lived. It was just a little fun, Kaylee. You've got to get over it. It didn't mean anything."

"It didn't mean anything? Does having sex mean so little to you now?"

"I meant nobody got hurt."

"Really? I'm nobody?"

"Oh, please. Don't be such a child."

"Find something new to say, Haylee. That's so

worn out that it doesn't even make my eardrums tremble." I started away.

"You'd better not look upset this morning. She'll be all over us, and you'll be in just as much trouble as me," she called after me.

I paused to look back at her and shake my head. Then I continued down to the kitchen, feeling as if my insides had been twisted like rubber bands. She was right, of course. I couldn't show how upset I was, no matter how much I wanted to. As it turned out, it didn't matter. It was difficult, if not impossible, to reveal any unhappiness. Mother was up early making us breakfast and obviously very happy that she had gone to the Clarks' dinner party. We sat at the table, almost stunned at the way she was going on about it. It had been a long time since we had seen her this excited about anything. What surprised us the most was how little she interrogated us about our party. It was as if she had forgotten about it.

Melissa Clark had introduced her to her older brother, Darren, who had been divorced for more than a year. Apparently, he had dominated Mother's attention at the dinner party. What she liked about him, besides his being divorced and therefore sharing the experience, was that he had no children.

"When you get involved with a man who has children from his previous marriage, you're in for a lot of grief," she told us.

She was off and running on one of her long diatribes about the dangers of romance, no matter how old you were. She didn't even pay attention to our reactions. We could have been mannequins for all she seemed to care, but neither of us wanted to interrupt her and start her asking questions about our party. The longer she ignored it, the better we felt.

"Men aren't as complicated as they'd like you to think they are. Most men are very obvious about their intentions. You've just got to be alert and not obvious about how much you're hoping for something to be nice. They take advantage of that. Desperate women do desperate things, things they often regret their whole lives.

"Now, Darren Paul is a relatively easy-to-read man and quite gentle. By the time the evening was over, I must admit that I felt sorrier for him than I did for myself. Not that I have that much to feel sorry about. Sometimes when you have disappointments in life, it turns out to be more of an advantage than you could have dreamed. As long as you learn from your experiences, good ones and bad, you can look forward to being more successful in the future.

"Anyway, to come to the point, I agreed to go to dinner with Darren tonight. I imagine you have some leftovers from the party?"

I looked at Haylee. She was the expert when it came to lies and rationalizations, not only in coming up with them but also in looking so honest as she rattled them off.

"Oh. Everyone went crazy over your food and devoured it all," she said quickly.

"All?"

"There wasn't enough worth saving."

"I always forget how much teenagers can eat. Well, I'm glad of that. And from what I see, you girls took good care of the house. I'll get dinner for you done ahead of time. No worries."

"Maybe you won't have to," Haylee quickly interjected.

"Why not?"

"Melanie Rosen asked if we wanted to go to the movies tonight. Her boyfriend is a senior. He has his own car. They could pick us up, and we can get something to eat at the mall."

Mother looked at me first. I did my best not to look surprised. "Who is Melanie Rosen's boyfriend?"

"Barry Weiner," Haylee said quickly, because she knew I had no idea who Melanie was going with this week. "He's on the basketball team, and he's the baseball team's star pitcher."

"Weiner? I don't know the Weiners." Mother's suspicious eyes returned. They seemed always to rise out of a secret place in her head, the way bubbles rose to the surface of water. "Why would she want you to go along on her date? I've heard of third wheels but not fourth."

I saw Haylee's face tighten. She looked to me for help, but I looked down at my food instead. I wasn't in the mood to help her out of any swamp she stepped in.

"Were you planning on meeting someone you don't want me to know about?" Mother demanded when Haylee took too long to reply. Her fears about our potential misbehavior always haunted her.

"No," Haylee said, but she had already opened the doors to Mother's distrust. I saw Haylee's eyes roll as she scrambled for explanations. "It's not a big date. It's just the movies. Melanie asked us, and Barry said fine. He'd pick us up and take us home."

Mother turned back to me. "What about that nice boy Matt Tesler?" she asked. "I know you both like him. Wasn't he here last night?"

"Yes," I said.

"He has something to do with his family tonight," Haylee blurted. "Otherwise, he would have taken us."

Mother studied her. Haylee did have what Daddy used to call a "poker face." Of course, he said we both did, even though I knew in my heart that he meant only Haylee. My face was more like a goldfish bowl, with all my thoughts swimming in clear view.

"I don't like you going with someone without my meeting him first," Mother said. "Especially someone driving you somewhere. I'm not trying to spoil your fun. You might not yet appreciate what an added burden a divorced woman with children your age has. Whatever good things happen to you will be credited to me, but you can be sure that whatever bad things happen will now be blamed solely on me, especially by your father."

"Mother's right," I said, before Haylee could come up with another idea. I knew what she really wanted was for Melanie and her boyfriend to pick us up and drop us off wherever Jimmy and his brother were. The air was leaking out of her plan. She seemed to wilt in her chair. "You remember how we talked about just this sort of thing, Haylee, and how we felt sorry for Mother having the whole burden on her shoulders."

I smiled as Haylee nodded reluctantly.

"You're the one who actually said it first," I added. It was like sticking pins in a voodoo doll. Her eyes looked as cold and still as marbles.

"That's very thoughtful of you girls. You can invite Melanie and her boyfriend over anytime when I can meet him," Mother said. "I'm a very good judge of people, your father being the sole exception."

Haylee forced another smile, and although the words were bitter lemons in her mouth, she said, "Okay. We'll do that."

Mother smiled again. Then her eyes brightened more with a new idea. "Maybe Mr. Paul and I could drop you off at the movie theater and pick you up afterward," she considered aloud.

"Oh, no, Mother. We don't want you to have to rush your dinner or anything," Haylee said. "It's not that important. Kaylee and I will amuse ourselves."

"Yes. Very thoughtful. It's good that you are not selfish like most teenagers."

Haylee avoided looking at me and ate her breakfast, while Mother continued to describe her evening, the food that was served, and some of the other guests. She gave us bullet-point descriptions of the women she liked and those she thought were phonies. I couldn't help but be intrigued by how she always circled back to Darren Paul, whom we would meet when he came to pick her up for dinner. She started to plan what we should wear to meet him.

"First impressions are like cement most of the time," she advised us. "Naturally, I bragged about you whenever I could, but I don't believe I exaggerated. So I'd like him to spend a little time getting to know you before we go out."

"Sounds serious," Haylee blurted, mostly under her breath but bitterly. Then she looked up quickly and shrugged. "He won't be here long when he comes to pick you up. What difference does it make what we wear?"

"It's the men you don't treat seriously who end

up disappointing you. A few good minutes could be worth a lifetime of happiness or unhappiness. I want him to see how well I've brought you up, really all on my own, and I would like to see how he reacts to meeting you. You can tell a great deal about people from the way their children look and behave and likewise how people react to them."

"We understand. Don't we, Haylee?" I said, smiling from ear to ear.

If looks could kill, I wouldn't just be dead; I'd be tortured to death. She forced a smile and nodded.

"Thank you, girls," Mother said.

After breakfast, Haylee went up to her room to sulk. I began my homework but constantly felt tempted to call Matt. I wanted to tell him that I didn't blame him, but something inside me still kept me from doing so. No matter how much I attributed to Jimmy and Haylee and drugs, I couldn't get myself to believe that he was completely innocent. I imagined him realizing what was happening almost immediately but deciding to enjoy it. And then I thought, what if I wasn't just imagining it? What if it was true? What if he had realized it but pretended he didn't? I kept going back to my belief, my hope, that anyone, even in the dark, even under the influence of some hallucinogen, would know it was Haylee and not me. I envisioned him years from now breaking down and confessing. In any case, whatever he knew and whatever he felt kept him from calling all day.

Late in the afternoon, Mother went first to Haylee's room to choose something for us to wear when Darren Paul arrived. She said that after talking to us this morning about him, she had decided to offer him a cocktail so that he could spend more time with us. "Of course, this isn't a one-way street. I want your impressions of him, too," she said.

And then she said something that made me wonder what her intentions concerning Darren Paul really were.

"The gossips will turn it into breaking news. Good. I want your father to know I'm not going to wither away like some fruit on the vine while he enjoys a new life without us. Someday he'll wake up and drown in regret."

After she went downstairs again, Haylee came to my room. I glanced at her and then continued reading my social studies text.

"Do you believe how Mother is carrying on about this man? It's like she's going on her first date or something."

I didn't answer or look at her.

"Okay, okay, I'm sorry," she said. She sat on my bed. "I was high, too, when I pulled that joke. I didn't mean to spoil your fun."

I still didn't lift my eyes from the page, but I wasn't reading anything.

"You're right about Jimmy, too. What boyfriend would tolerate his girlfriend doing what I did? He's an idiot. I used him, and as I said, I don't intend to be with him much longer. It's just that I don't see many boys I like at our school, including all the seniors. They're all . . . so immature."

"Not all. I really liked Matt," I said. "He is different, more responsible. At least, that was what I had hoped. Now he's probably afraid to look me in the face or look at himself in the mirror."

"He'll get over it, Kaylee. Believe me, he didn't suffer."

"Thanks for that. That really helps."

"I know. I'll apologize to him. I promise."

"I think it would be better if you didn't speak to him at all. If he's really ashamed of himself, he'll only feel worse."

"Okay. Maybe you're right. I'll stay away from him completely, and if Jimmy spreads any stories, I'll deny them. I'll tell anyone who asks that it was you, not me."

"Don't tell anybody anything, Haylee! No one has to know our personal business, especially something like this."

"Right. Yes, that's right. If anyone asks, I'll say it's none of their business. But you've got to help, too."

"Me? What am I supposed to do?"

"Don't act mad at me, or everyone will suspect

something and believe anything Jimmy says, especially after I dump him. We've got to be as close as ever, and then who would think I had done that to you and you would still be as close to me? Right?"

"So you want me to pretend we're close?"

"No, not pretend. I want you to forgive me and be my sister. I want you to mean it. I mean it when I say I'm sorry."

"Right," I said. I couldn't help smiling to myself. She would always figure out all the angles. "I'm tired of thinking about it."

"Me, too. We'll just have a fun night together tonight while Mother goes on her hot date," she said, rising. She walked over to me and hugged me. "I really didn't mean to hurt you. Sorry, sorry, sorry," she said, before giving me a peck on the cheek, and leaving.

For the first time, I began to wonder if Haylee was the more vulnerable of us after all. She went after friends, whether they were girlfriends or boyfriends, with more desperation than I did. She had more of a need to be popular. She would hate to hear me say it, but I now believed that I was the one with more self-confidence. Mother dreamed of having two daughters who would never suffer from sibling rivalry, but Haylee was and probably would always be afraid that people would like me more than they liked her. She flaunted the attention boys gave her. She emphasized anything she could do better than I could. She was a more aggressive athlete and often let me know it. Now she was stressing how much more sophisticated she was. After all, she knew more about sex and drugs.

Maybe my feelings toward her should be more in line with pity than anger, I thought. It brought a smile to my face thinking how angry she would be if she knew I had even considered it.

I returned to the homework. As usual, I would have it done before she would, and she would copy most, if not all, of it. It was only the essays we had to write for English that she had to do on her own, but I usually read her work and repaired the grammar and syntax. I still studied with her for exams, and although she wasn't keeping up with my grades, she was close enough to keep Mother from making it an issue.

Just after six, she returned to my room, wearing the dress Mother had chosen for us.

"I feel like someone's Barbie doll. She's going to treat us like two storefront displays for the rest of our lives," she said, as I went to put on my dress. "She'll press buttons to make us smile simultaneously and will want us to say the same things at the same time, too. 'Pleased to meet you.' Maybe we should make it sound like a question. 'Pleased to meet *you*?' Think she'll put us in the pantry if we do that?"

"Don't toy with her about this, Haylee. It obviously means a lot to her. She's been in such a dark fog since she discovered what Daddy was doing. If she's happier, we'll be happier," I pointed out.

"You're right. You're always right," she said, grimacing for a moment and then smiling again. "Luckily for me, I have you as my twin sister. We each provide what the other needs, right?"

"Haylee-Kaylee," I said, my voice dripping with sarcasm that she either ignored or didn't hear.

"Kaylee-Haylee," she replied, as if it was something automatically triggered, maybe in both of us.

Despite everything, how could I hate her? Mother was probably right about that. It would be like hating myself or at least a big part of myself. We all went through valleys and over hills. Who else could really be my best friend or hers, even though she might not realize it as much as I did?

"Okay, let's get down to the stage," I said.

Mother was waiting in the living room. She looked more nervous than I had seen her lately. "How do I look?" she asked us.

She stood up and did a slow turn, like someone modeling the dress in an expensive boutique. Her hair and makeup were as perfect as ever, and she was wearing a dress that always brought her compliments. She had first worn it two years ago at a dinner celebrating her and Daddy's anniversary. It was a black silk-blend, sheer-insert, fitted Victoria Beckham.

Somehow, despite her depression and rage, Mother held on to her willowy figure. She wasn't an exercise enthusiast but kept herself so busy around the house that she probably took more steps and burned more calories than women who ran a mile daily.

"You look beautiful, Mother," I said.

Haylee came in on "beautiful."

She was also wearing her rose gold Swarovski watch, which had been her anniversary present that night two years ago. I think she saw the way I was staring at it.

"I'm not going to toss out the beautiful things your father bought me. I earned everything, believe me. That would be cutting off your nose to spite your face." She held her wrist up, displaying the watch. "Consider it premature alimony," she said, and laughed. "It will impress Mr. Paul."

Haylee looked stunned. Neither of us had seen Mother this high on anyone, especially another man.

"What does he do?" I asked.

"Oh. He'll especially appreciate this watch. He owns three jewelry stores in Pennsylvania. Two are in Philadelphia, and one is in Pittsburgh. He's working on fourth and fifth locations. You'll like this, too. He plays piano. His mother made him take lessons when he was a child and continue when he was a teenager. He kept it up. Maybe he'll play something for us."

"He sounds very nice. Why did he get divorced?" Haylee asked.

Mother widened her smile. "Why do you think?"

We both shook our heads.

"His wife cheated on him. See how much we have in common?"

As if on cue, the doorbell sounded. We really were on a stage, I thought. Everything we and the people around us did seemed to be following a script.

Darren Paul had a bouquet of red roses in his hands. He was taller than Daddy and had a light brown, red-tinted, well-trimmed beard. He was stouter also, and I didn't think he was nearly as attractive as Daddy, but then again, not many men were. He was smartly dressed in a dark gray suit and a light blue tie. His hair was thicker and longer than I had expected.

"Hi," he said. "This is a nice location. I always thought about buying something in this area. Oh, for you," he said, holding out the flowers.

"Oh, how beautiful!" Mother cried, as if she had never seen red roses or been given any flowers. Matt's had been just as beautiful. "Thank you," she said, taking them from him. "We'll put them in water right away. Girls," she called, and we stepped forward. "I'd like you to meet Mr. Paul."

"Oh, they should call me Darren," he said. He had a voice much deeper than Daddy's and a smile that looked tentative. Daddy was always sure of himself when he met someone new. I imagined I would always compare men with Daddy, especially any men Mother dated.

"I'm Haylee," Haylee said quickly. "This is my sister, Kaylee."

"Pleased to meet you," we both recited in perfect unison, and he looked at Mother to see if this was some sort of rehearsed, clever little amusement. She kept her proud smile.

"Yes, pleased to meet you guys. When your mother said you were identical, she meant identical. But in your case, it's identical beauty," he quickly added.

"Thank you," we recited.

He widened his eyes. I was sure he was wondering if we would say everything together like a chorus.

"Kaylee, would you put these in a vase for us and bring them into the living room? I thought we'd have a cocktail before leaving," she told Darren.

I took the flowers.

"Perfect," he said, and followed Mother and Haylee into the living room, complimenting Mother on the house. She immediately went into how it had all fallen on her shoulders, the decorating and the furniture purchases, especially all that was bought for us.

When I brought the vase in, Haylee was sitting

on the settee across from Mother and Darren. He must have waited for me before asking any questions, because the moment I entered, he said, "I hear you're both very good students. Any idea what you want to go for?"

"Go for?" Haylee said.

"What career to pursue," I said. "No. We both have varied interests right now, and there's time."

"Very wise," he said, nodding.

Mother smiled.

"Mother tells us you're in the jewelry business. Is that what you always wanted to do?" I asked.

"I thought I was going to be governor," he said. "No. My father started the business, and I expanded it after he passed away."

"Why didn't you expand it when he was still alive?" Haylee asked.

He laughed. "Dad was somewhat reluctant to make changes or take chances," he said. He looked at Mother. "These two are bright and not shy."

"They're far more mature than other girls their age," she said. "And most important, they're dependable."

"I can see why you're very proud," Darren said, and sipped his drink. "It's not easy when there are two working at it, from what I see."

"No, it wasn't easy on my own." Mother made it sound as if Daddy had died years and years ago.

"How long were you married?" Haylee asked.

"Nearly ten years," he said, and then took a longer sip on his drink, as if the answer drove him to it.

"How come you don't have any children?" Haylee quickly followed, sounding like a prosecutor in a courtroom.

I thought Mother would be angry at her pointed question, but she still looked pleased.

"It didn't work out for us," he replied. "And as it turns out, that was a good thing."

"Mother says you play the piano," I said, rushing to change the subject.

"I tinker a bit."

"We'd love to hear you play," I said.

"Oh, well, you have to lower your expectations."

"That's easy. We have none," Haylee said.

"In that case, I'll do it," he said, rising and going to the piano.

Mother looked even more pleased, her eyes dazzling. We rose, too, and the three of us gathered around the piano.

"I'm not up on modern songs," he warned. "But this is a favorite through time."

I had heard the song, but I didn't know the title. Haylee looked uninterested, but when she saw my face, she brightened quickly. Suddenly, Mother sang a line, in French, and Darren sang another. When he finished, they laughed.

"I've heard it," I said. "But I don't know the title."

"It's 'La vie en rose' by Edith Piaf," Mother said. "You've heard it because it was your father's and my wedding song. Actually, I chose it. Your father wasn't into wedding songs. That should have given me a hint."

"It's always been one of my favorites," Darren said. He finished his drink and rose.

"Everything is ready for you to warm up for dinner," Mother told us. She took Darren's glass and brought hers and his to the kitchen. We followed them.

"All set, then?" Darren asked her.

"Yes," Mother said.

"Enjoy your evening," I said.

"Have a nice time," Haylee added.

"It's been great meeting you, girls," Darren said. "Next time, you'll play something for me."

"Yes, they will," Mother said.

We watched them leave.

"Next time?" Haylee said. "He sounds like they should start planning a wedding."

"Let's eat," I said. I didn't want to talk about it. I was still trying to accept the fact that Daddy was basically out of our lives, and, as they say, this was another nail in the coffin.

Haylee shrugged. It was obviously not bothering her as much, or she was better than I was at hiding it. At least, that was what I thought until a little while later, when we sat to eat our dinner, and she suddenly said, "I know I don't act like it most of the time, maybe more because it would upset Mother, but I do miss Daddy."

"Why shouldn't we?"

"It's so strange seeing her with another man," Haylee said.

"Maybe it's mostly for her ego. She feels she's been dumped, remember, even though she'd never say it."

"You're right. I never thought of it like that. I've got to stop hanging around with infant minds," she said. "What they have is contagious."

I laughed. I was really laughing at her, but she thought I was laughing at her clever remark. Would she ever notice the difference?

"What should we do tonight?" she asked. "I really don't want to play any board games. You always win. I just said it to please Mother."

"Let's practice piano," I said. "We'll work on Mozart's *Figaro* duet just the way we used to and surprise Mother and Darren when he comes again."

"If he comes. Maybe she'll have a boring time, or maybe she'll meet someone else."

"Whatever. Let's do it for Mother, then."

"Okay," she said. "And then we'll just make

some popcorn and watch a dumb movie, the dumber the better."

"Haylee-Kaylee," I said, shaking my head.

"Kaylee-Haylee," she replied.

We cleaned up after ourselves and went to the pianos. Of course, we were quite rusty, not having practiced for a while, but Haylee surprised me by staying with it until I thought we had done enough.

"A few more practice sessions," I said.

"Okay. Time for a movie?"

"Pick out what you want. I'll look into the popcorn."

I never would have expected it, but we had one of our best nights together in a long time. When Mother came home, she found us both on the sofa, the TV still on, both of us asleep next to each other.

When I woke, Haylee woke, and we sat up quickly, because Mother was standing right in front of us and smiling.

"We didn't hear you come in," I said.

"I've been standing here for almost ten minutes. I didn't want to wake you. You looked like you did when you were infants. My girls."

"Did you have a good time?" Haylee asked, wiping her eyes.

"Good enough," Mother replied. "I learned something from you."

"What?" Haylee asked, astounded that Mother could learn anything from us.

"Have no expectations," she said. "Then you have nothing to lower in order to be pleased."

For a moment, we said nothing, and then we both laughed. Mother laughed, too.

And for the first time in a long time, we were all laughing together.

12

At breakfast on Sunday, Mother told us that she had invited Darren Paul to come to dinner at our house Friday night. This little romance she had begun had instantaneously stirred up the gossip she was hoping for. The silence we were so used to now in our house was shattered. She seemed to be on the phone all day having conversations with women she had hardly spoken to during the last year or so. She appeared to relish the attention. Haylee and I quickly realized that as long as she was so occupied with her own romantic adventures, she wouldn't hover so closely over our social lives, whatever they might be.

I was skeptical when Haylee told me she was through with Jimmy Jackson, but she didn't call him all weekend. He didn't call her, either, which made her angrier. She wanted to be the one to do all the disrespecting and dumping.

"He's taking me for granted," she told me on Sunday night. "He's in for a surprise."

He sauntered over to us almost as soon as we entered the school building Monday morning.

"Hey, girls, what's happening?" he asked with a smug grin on his face.

Neither of us replied, but he tagged along.

"Hey, what's the rush?" he said as we quickened our steps toward our homeroom.

"Sensitive stomachs," Haylee said. "Bad odors make us sick."

"Huh? Oh, I get it. Sorry you missed me Saturday night," he told Haylee just as we joined the other girls in front of our homeroom.

She turned on him. "Don't flatter yourself. I found our old jack-in-the-box, and that gave me the same laughs and thrills you could."

"Ha ha. I have a thrill for you," he said, and tried to put his arm around her.

"Take a bath before you approach someone," she said, moving away from him.

He turned crimson. He looked at the other girls, who were amused and amazed. "Big deal, twin," he muttered. "You're about as hot as yesterday's hamburger."

"Which is probably still in your pocket," Haylee retorted. None of the girls laughed or smiled at that. Everyone held her breath, waiting for his response.

"I'm not wasting my time talking to you," he said, and walked off, as if her rejecting him was as meaningless to him as tossing away a gum wrapper.

She then went on to lecture the girls about wasting their time with immature boys. Suddenly, she sounded like the prude in our family.

"You have to have more respect for yourself," she said. "You don't ever want to be labeled. Don't act desperate," she continued. "Once they think they have you, they'll treat you badly. Never commit entirely to any boy—at least, any boy here."

If I closed my eyes, I could think I was hearing Mother talking. Because of how easily Haylee had driven off Jimmy, the girls surrounding her looked very impressed. Even Melanie was awestruck, and I knew she considered herself the leader of our pack.

"What did he do to deserve the brush-off?" she asked.

Haylee glanced at me and then turned back to all of them and said, "He opened his mouth—and not while we were kissing, either."

There was a moment of silence and then loud laughter. Haylee smiled at me and nodded in the direction of our homeroom.

Matt was standing near the doorway. He wore the look of a frightened puppy, glancing at me and then shifting his eyes down quickly. I stepped forward and paused in front of him.

"I'm sorry I didn't call you over the weekend," he said. "I started to a few times and stopped, because I wasn't sure how to begin and how you would react."

"I felt the same way. I guess it was good that we both had time to think about it."

He watched the others around us and then shifted left a few steps so we'd be beyond their hearing range. "Look. You have to understand what happened. I was dozing off because of what they put in our drinks, and then I looked up and saw who I thought was you coming out of the bathroom, your bathroom. What was I to think? It was dark and—"

"You told me all that. When exactly did you realize it wasn't me, Matt?"

"Not until it was almost over. I had my eyes closed, and you two sound so much alike, and . . . you wear the same perfume—"

The bell rang.

"It's hard for me to accept. Maybe we should stop talking about it," I said. "See you later." I didn't mean to sound skeptical or indifferent, but I supposed that was how it sounded to him. After all, he wasn't giving me anything new.

"Sure. Later," he said bitterly, and walked off quickly.

I turned and saw that Haylee had been watching us and waiting for me.

"What did he say?" she asked as we entered the classroom.

"He blamed it on our perfume," I replied.

She laughed, and we took our seats. Despite how strong we both appeared to our friends because of how easily we were tossing away boyfriends, I knew she was on shaky ground just as much as I was. Something deeply significant had happened this past weekend. I believed that now, during every day for at least these high school years, it would seem that our lives were constantly changing. We would continually be asking ourselves who we were, what we were becoming. Although that might be true for everyone our age moving from adolescence to young adulthood, it was especially so for Haylee and me. Perhaps what had happened this weekend was a real wake-up call. We had to work harder at being individuals, even if some of the things we did displeased Mother. Neither Haylee nor I felt like a little girl anymore, and so much of what Mother had designed and hoped for us was framed in a little girls' world. I felt I had to do more about it than Haylee did, that I would have to help my sister find herself in a more sensible way. I could hope that she realized that some of what she had thought important was not. Time would soon tell.

Jimmy Jackson was not as indifferent to her dismissal of him as he had pretended in the hallway. He didn't like being made a fool of in front of our classmates. Some had already spread the story about how casually Haylee had brushed him off. As we suspected he would, he began to tell stories about us and ridiculed Matt. Haylee was better at countering it and turning it back on him, telling girls that Jimmy was inadequate as a lover and was just trying to cover up for it by making up lies about us.

That afternoon, Matt and Jimmy did get into a fight. Mr. Allen, the physical education teacher, broke it up before it got too serious, and like two lions who knew they would only tear each other apart, they chose to avoid each other for the remainder of the day. Jimmy lost interest in it all and drifted back to his old friends and girlfriends.

Matt and I continued to circle each other all that day and the next, trying to find ways to mend the tear in our budding relationship. Haylee stayed away from him as she had promised, and if he began to approach me while we were together, she would quickly walk off. It didn't really matter. Every time I looked at him, I saw the guilt in his face. Every word he spoke had a tentative sound to it, as if he thought I wouldn't believe anything he said now. Some of that surely came from me, from the way I looked at him and responded to him.

He didn't call Monday night or Tuesday night. Although we talked to each other a little in school during the remainder of the week, we sounded more like two people who knew very little about each other. He spent most of his free time with the few friends he had and slowly began to drift back into that private world he had once occupied. To keep from thinking about it, I dove deeper into our schoolwork. Haylee surprised me by following my lead. Her conversation now was peppered with references to herself, how much she had learned, especially about our maturity in comparison with our classmates and even the girls in classes ahead of us.

If I had been wiser, I would have noticed some warning signs and perhaps paid more attention to her, but I thought my sister was simply going through another phase. Right now, she was acting the role of the sophisticate. During lunch hour every day, she was holding court, repeating Mother's diatribes against men, sometimes word for word, and ridiculing every other girl's romance with a high school boy. Before the week ended, however, I began to see that the girls she thought were feeding off her as if she was the queen bee began to drift away. Some sat with other girls and boys, and those who remained were constantly changing the subject. Even Melanie Rosen and Toby Sue Daniels, who had been the closest thing to best friends for her, retreated. The girls who remained with us were girls who probably wouldn't have a high school romance anyway. I had always thought that one of them, Denise James, was gay. She was shadowing Haylee more now and repeating some of her phrases as if they were biblical.

"I think Denise is falling in love with you because of what you're saying these days about men, Haylee," I told her. "You're giving her hope."

"Hope?"

"I don't think she ever liked boys or will ever like men. Be careful."

She started to laugh and then stopped, looked back at Denise in the hallway, and said, "Let her fall in love with me. I'll break her heart as easily as I'd break Jimmy Jackson's."

My sister's on a roll, I thought. *There's no stopping her now.* It amused me for a while and kept me from thinking about Matt. Our contact with each other was falling back into only occasional glances and nods. The air between us felt as if a funeral procession had just passed through. I guessed the more I blamed Matt, the less I had to blame Haylee.

I looked for other things to capture my attention. We began to help Mother plan her dinner for Darren Paul. She had three recipe books out on the table on Wednesday and Thursday night and read from them as if they were bedtime stories, putting extra emphasis on certain ingredients or spices.

"There's much to be said about the way to a man's heart being through his stomach," she told us. "All of these women I know who have maids preparing their dinners every night have such thin relationships with their husbands. When they go into their dining rooms, it's the same as going into a restaurant. Half of them don't know how to scramble eggs. They become just another knick-knack in the home. Whenever I see them out with their husbands, they look more like escorts than wives."

"But you always cooked and baked for Daddy," Haylee pointed out. "It didn't work for you two."

I wondered if Mother was going to be angry that Haylee had said that or if she was thinking about it deeply herself.

"That," she said after another moment, "is how you can tell how self-centered he is. He wanted everything to be solely for him, or at least first for him and then the rest of us. Be sure," she said, waving her finger at us, "that the man you fall in love with worships you, and I mean worships everything you believe and do and not just your pretty face and body. That's the difference between a mature man and a boy. Just because a male reaches thirty or forty doesn't mean he's not still a boy," she declared, and slammed her recipe book closed like a preacher shutting a Bible after a fire-and-brimstone sermon.

"Lemon roasted chicken with arugula salad and dilled orzo," she declared. "For dessert, marble angel-food cake with strawberry topping. You girls are in charge of making the dessert. End of story," she said, and stood up.

"Wow," Haylee said when we went up to our rooms. "Mother is really going for the jugular with this guy. Maybe she hears wedding bells."

"Does she really want that, or is she out to prove something to her girlfriends and Daddy?" I said.

Haylee shrugged. "What's the difference in the end?" she said, and went to her room.

Depends on what you think of as the end, I thought.

That night, we found out that Toby Sue Daniels was having a party on Saturday, but we weren't invited. Haylee thought the main reason was that Jimmy Jackson was invited, but Sarah Morgan, who was never invited to anything, told me she had overheard Toby Sue tell some other girls that Haylee was too negative about boys now, and she knew she couldn't invite me without inviting her. Haylee's reaction should have worried me more. Her indifference about it was so uncharacteristic.

"We wouldn't have much to say to them anyway," she told me. "Especially the boys."

She also surprised me by wanting to practice our piano duet every day so we could play for Darren Paul and make Mother happy. Haylee didn't put up any argument or even look upset at the thought of us wearing the same dress. Mother stood by, watching and listening to us play, a broad smile on her face. With the dinner she was making and the way we were contributing, she was happier than I had seen her for some time.

On Friday, Darren arrived with two bottles of wine and another bouquet, this time bigger and with mixed roses.

"I wasn't sure of the menu, so I brought a white and a red," he said.

"Like a good Boy Scout," Mother said. "Always prepared."

Haylee laughed. Darren looked like he wasn't sure it was a compliment, but Mother didn't add anything more.

She handed the wine and flowers to us. Haylee and I had set the table with our best dishes and silverware, water and wine glasses, and linen napkins. We put the bouquet Darren had brought in the middle. When they had their cocktails, Mother permitted us to have a taste of the martinis she had mixed for herself and Darren, and for the first few minutes, we sat and listened to him talk about his jewelry-store expansion. I was surprised at how interested Mother appeared to be. She was never this interested in Daddy's business details.

Both Haylee and I were polite, but after a while, we were quite bored, because he was going into his business and accounting details as if they were the most exciting things in his life. Either he was nervous, or he just liked the sound of his own voice.

Both of us were happy when Mother finally interrupted to tell him we had prepared a piano duet just for him.

We went to the pianos. As if he hadn't noticed it before, he commented on the fact that there were two pianos.

"Unusual," he said. "I mean, I'm sure they could have alternated lesson days, right?"

"Of course not," Mother said a little sharply. "Whatever they've done in their lives, they've done together."

"But two pianos . . ." he said, almost stuttering.

"There is two of everything they own," she said.

"Everything?"

"Down to their socks," Mother declared proudly.

He looked at us as if seeing us for the first time, his gaze moving from Haylee to me and back to Haylee.

"Do they always dress alike, too?"

"Generally, yes," she said. "My girls are unique."

"That's for sure."

"If you should ever think of bringing them something, be sure it's the exact same thing for each," she added.

He looked at her with a slight smile frozen on his lips, like someone who was waiting for a joke's punch line.

"Girls," Mother said, nodding toward the pianos.

We sat and began the duet. When we finished, Darren and Mother clapped.

"Very impressive," he said. "They seemed to be equally proficient."

"Of course they are," Mother said.

"You make it sound as if that's true for everything, but I'm sure each of you has something special," he said to us.

I looked quickly at Mother. Her eyes seemed to harden. "What's special about them is that they are identical," Mother said, pronouncing each word clearly through clenched teeth. "They have the same talents and interests and do equally well in school. They even have the same friends."

He nodded and cemented his lips. He wasn't going to say another word about it. Mother broke the deep silence by declaring that it was time for dinner. He tried very hard to win back her favor by complimenting everything, down to the way the napkins were folded.

"They do that," Mother said when we served the salad. "Each one did two."

He nodded and looked at us. "Division of labor, huh?" he asked us, smiling.

"Two halves make a whole," Mother said. "Together they are my perfect daughter."

"Haylee-Kaylee," Haylee said.

"Kaylee-Haylee," I said.

Darren actually looked frightened for a moment. He nodded and offered to pour the first glass of wine.

"Oh, no, Darren," Mother said. "Haylee will pour the first glass, and Kaylee will pour the second. We've always done it that way ever since they were capable of doing it," she explained.

Haylee rose and poured the first glass. When she sat, Mother lifted her glass first to make a toast.

"To my girls," she said. "My raison d'etre."

"To Mother," we responded in unison. "Our raison d'etre."

We drank.

Darren Paul sipped his wine and then coughed into his napkin. "Sorry," he said.

"Shall we eat?" Mother said, sounding a little annoyed.

He did eat, but he looked as if he was having his last meal before his execution. Nevertheless, he raved about the food as much as Daddy would.

Mother told him we had made the cake, and afterward, Darren and Mother went into the living room to have an after-dinner cordial. We cleaned up. While we worked, we tried to listen to their conversation. They didn't seem to be talking that much. When we entered, it seemed as if all the air had gone out of the room.

"I was just explaining to Darren how your father often made things difficult for us, especially when I was homeschooling you."

We looked at him. Mother elaborated on some other things Daddy had done to make it harder for her to raise identical twins correctly. He listened, nodding and looking at us—to see if we were unhappy about it, I supposed. We wore our usual noncommittal faces, which I was sure he thought were almost ceramic. Afterward, he piled compliment after compliment on us all, but when he walked out and the door closed, it had a permanent sound.

I wondered if he would ever call Mother again. He had suggested that he was going to be very busy during the next few months with his business expansion. Mother didn't seem terribly upset about it and rarely mentioned him during the days that followed. One night, after we had asked about him, she said, "It was just as I told you. You can tell about someone from the way he reacts to your children, and—although you girls have been quite discreet for my benefit—how your children react to him. I saw that you weren't very impressed. You don't realize how lucky I am to have you help me navigate the waters of dating after so long. I'll not make another mistake," she pledged.

I thought the experience might discourage Mother from having a social life again, but she had other dates. Girlfriends were always trying to find her a new husband. We met most of the men at dinners at our house or when they picked her up, but none of them had any staying power. Meanwhile, the divorce was consummated, and our distant relationship with Daddy was carved in cement.

Whether all of this affected our own social life didn't seem to matter. We weren't doing much. Haylee refused to get serious with any high school boy, even though many did try—mostly seniors, too. She didn't even try to get me to go on double dates.

Like her, I avoided getting into a new relationship. She worried that it was her fault, but I assured her that I wasn't pining over Matt anymore. Before the school year ended, Matt and I did have another serious conversation, but it was going to be our last—and not because I was still disturbed about what had happened. He surprised me with his news.

"My father has taken a new position in a hospital in New York City," he said. "We're moving. Our home is up for sale, and my mother's been interviewing for bank positions in New York."

He didn't sound very upset about it. If anything, he sounded relieved.

When I asked him if he was upset, he thought a moment and said, "We're just luggage. We'll probably treat our own children the same way."

I took that to mean that he *was* upset. He made a vague promise to stay in touch through emails, but it was as if he had left months ago and I was speaking to his shadow. I told Haylee, and she asked me if I was disappointed.

"I guess I am when I think deeply about him," I confessed. "I still think he's someone special and probably will be for someone else."

"So you still hate me?"

"No," I said. "I can't hate you."

"Because Mother wouldn't permit it?" she said.

I laughed.

"You know she's never going to find another man. As soon as they see how weird we are, they all run for the hills. And we are weird," she insisted. "That's why I'm afraid to start a romance with any other boy in our school. I'll never have a real boyfriend until we're separated, and neither will you."

"That's silly," I said.

"No, it's not. And after we find our boyfriends, our lovers, our husbands, it will be better if we don't live too close to each other," she declared. She sounded as if she had been thinking hard about this for some time.

Maybe she was right, I thought.

As if she had decided that she should prepare herself for us separating, she spent more and more time alone in her room, often on her computer. We were still doing homework and studying for tests together from time to time as the last school quarter approached its end. We also played the piano almost daily, which pleased Mother. Just as we had done for Darren Paul, we performed for any other men she invited to our house. That usually led to comments similar to the ones she had made to Darren, and those comments either shocked or disturbed her dates enough to keep them from coming back.

Although it was very subtle at first, we both sensed that Mother was becoming more distracted with her own effort to find satisfaction in her new situation and identity as a divorcée, but one who wouldn't look depressed or defeated. When Haylee began wearing different clothes from me, doing her hair differently, and even spending time with other girls without me, Mother didn't pounce the way she would have in the past. Neither of us was unhappy about it.

However, I began to sense more of a distance between Haylee and myself. It was never easy for us to keep secrets from each other. Whether there was any scientific proof for it or not, I believed we possessed mental telepathy between us. Perhaps it had come from how we had tried to have the same feelings about things so Mother would be pleased. Whatever, I sensed something different was happening. It was as if she had constructed a little wall around a part of herself, her thoughts and feelings. I would often sense her drifting away from whatever conversation we were having with others in school and even with Mother at home. She looked like she was anticipating something, waiting for something.

If I asked her if she was all right, she would quickly reply, "Yes, sure. Why not?"

I didn't want to say that she seemed upset, because that wasn't exactly it. I knew when Haylee was upset, and she showed no signs of that. I wouldn't even say she was troubled or worried. She was simply distant, like someone who had left her body and was wandering about somewhere else.

Finally, one night after dinner, after we had watched some television with Mother and listened to her go on about something she had heard about Daddy and his "new bed pillow," how they were already having trouble, we started up to our rooms. Haylee was more eager to get to hers. She said good night, but I stood in my doorway and watched her go into her room. Then I followed. She turned, surprised.

"What?" she asked.

"You tell me," I said.

"What?"

"Have you been seeing Jimmy secretly?"

"Are you kidding? Never. I don't even waste a thought on him."

"Then what is it, Haylee? And don't say 'nothing.' You know when something is on my mind, and you know I can tell the same thing about you. Well?"

She was silent a moment, considering. "I think I'm in love with someone," she said.

"What?" I smiled. "How can that be? You haven't gone on a date or hung out with anyone for weeks and weeks."

"There are other ways."

"What other ways?"

She shifted to her right so I could see the computer.

I could feel my eyes widen. "You met someone on the Internet?"

"Yes. We've been talking and telling each other things for quite a while. I sent him pictures. Only of myself," she emphasized.

"Does he go to our school or one nearby?"

"No, he's older."

"How much older?"

"Older."

"Haylee, I asked how much," I said, insisting on an answer.

"He's in his mid-twenties. Maybe a little older."

"You mean he's out of college?"

"He never attended college. He's a telephone repair man. His father died almost fifteen years ago. His mother died just recently, and he has no brothers or sisters. He's very good-looking," she added, "and very sweet and sensitive. We've been reading a book together."

"How?"

"We read a chapter or two and then talk about it."

"What book?"

"*Pnin* by Vladimir Nabokov. Mrs. Kasofsky did me a special favor and ordered it for the library, but I'm the only one she's given it to, and maybe I will be the only one. She likes us to read."

"She's a librarian. Of course she likes us to read. How did you come to choose it?"

"He told me about the book, and I got it," she said, opening her desk drawer to show it to me. "He's very good at analyzing the characters."

"How can you fall in love with someone from reading a book together?"

"There's more. We share a lot of likes and dislikes. We're going to meet soon. If you tell Mother about any of this, I swear I'll never talk to you again for the rest of your life."

"I won't tell, but I'm not sure you should meet a man that old whom you've only met on the Internet, Haylee, and especially one so much older."

"Don't start mothering me, Kaylee. I'm an adult, far more adult than anyone else in our class—in our school, for that matter. It's not your chronological age that matters; it's your mental and emotional age. There's a character in *Pnin* who makes that clear."

"So that's why he wants you to read it? He wants you to think like the character?"

"It's interesting. It's interesting to talk to someone mature."

"How long have you been doing this?"

"Long enough to know him well."

"But what if he's lying about things?"

"I can tell by the way he answers questions about himself. He's told me about his weaknesses as well as his strengths, told me things that frighten him, that annoy him, told me things he didn't like about his parents, too. When someone is that open, you can trust him."

"Well, I don't know," I said.

"Well, I do. Just forget about it now. It's not your business. This is something involving just me for a change."

"I can't help worrying about it," I said.

"Worry all you want. Just keep your mouth shut. Understood?"

I nodded.

"Thank you," she said. "When I'm ready, when we're ready, I'll introduce you to him."

"But you haven't even met him yet yourself."

"That's why I said 'when I'm ready.' This means a lot to me, Kaylee."

"Okay, okay."

"I'll let you see a picture of him," she said, and turned to her computer.

I approached slowly when she brought the picture up. "He looks older than mid-twenties," I said.

"It's the lighting. He had someone take it with a cell-phone camera. You have to admit he's very good-looking and has a sensitive face, don't you?" She turned to look at me. "Don't you?" she demanded.

I didn't like his eyes. They were beady, and who nowadays parted his hair in the middle? "Yes," I said.

"As sensitive-looking as Matt?" she asked with a little tease in her voice. "Someday you might forgive him."

"There'll never be a someday. Matt's leaving," I said, and told her about his father finding another job.

"Just as well," she said, quickly changing her mood. "Spilt milk." She smiled and looked at the computer again. "That's why someone stable, mature, is so hard to find." She went silent, just staring at the man.

"What's his name?"

"Anthony."

"Anthony what?"

She turned and looked up at me, smiling. "Oh, no," she said. "I'm not telling you his full name and then have you go do some search on the Internet and start trouble. You know what you need to know for now. Good night, sister dear. I like privacy when Anthony and I talk."

"You're not talking. He hasn't called you, right? Or Skyped you or something?"

"I told him not to. This is fine," she said. "For now. 'Night," she said.

I glanced once more at the picture on the screen and then left. I heard her close the door behind me.

For the first time in a long time, I went to sleep with fear hovering around me.

Perhaps it had always been there in my room, waiting for me to turn off the lights and think about my sister, who flitted about fire like a moth, intrigued enough to get too close and get its wings singed by the flames.

Would the fire she brought to herself spread to me?

13

Of all the secrets we'd ever had, this was the hardest to keep. Every night, when Haylee retreated to her room, I worried that she was getting deeper into this strange Internet relationship. Sometimes, late at night, I would wake up with a suspicion and quietly step out of my room and see the glow of her computer screen leak out from under her door. When I mentioned this to her the first time, she said, "He contacts me on and off all night. He's really a very lonely man. I help him go back to sleep."

"What about you?"

"Oh, I feel good about it and fall right back to pleasant dreams," she said.

Now I actually hoped that Mother would walk in on Haylee while she was conversing with him. I almost broke my promise and suggested that Mother do that, but the fear of how hard Haylee would take it and what it would do to our relationship kept me back. As the school year was drawing to an end, I did think that we were closer than ever as sisters and even friends, despite her secret Internet relationship and how it hung there between us like a scream frozen in the air.

Haylee and I did more together besides practicing piano and homework. What little social life we had we clung to together. We were no longer hanging out with different friends from each other in school, as most of Haylee's friends had come to resent her lecturing them and ridiculing what they considered to be fun and exciting, something she had considered that way, too. On the other hand, Haylee seemed to be more tolerant of my friends, even Sarah Morgan.

Sometimes I would wonder why my sister was trying so hard to please me. Was it simply to keep me quiet about what she was doing on her computer? She did her homework better and seriously studied for our finals. I didn't want her even to think that I harbored any suspicion of her having ulterior motives. I was afraid to ask her if she had planned her rendezvous with Anthony. I didn't wake up and go out into the hallway to check. It was easier for me to ignore that she was still having Internet conversations with a man who definitely looked older than she said he was.

As if she knew that it would be better for me

if we didn't talk about him, she didn't mention him again for some time. So much time had gone by since she had spoken about him, in fact, that I wondered if it had all ended. Perhaps his dallying with a girl as young as Haylee had lost its novelty for him. If he had brushed her off and she was too embarrassed to tell me, my bringing it up would only pour salt on the wound.

But then one night, she called me into her room before we got ready to go to sleep. She closed the door softly after I entered. Mother was still downstairs, on the phone again with one of her friends, gossiping about the divorcée dating scene. She sounded younger on these phone calls, her conversation lightened with giggles and laughter.

"Anthony and I have decided that it is finally time for us to meet," Haylee said excitedly. "We have planned on where and when. It will be our first real date."

"You really are continuing with this, Haylee?"

"Why shouldn't I? Just to show you what he's like," she continued, "I was pushing to meet much sooner, but he kept holding off, telling me he wanted me to be absolutely sure I wanted this. Predators don't give victims second and third chances. They pounce at the first opportunity."

"Maybe he's just very clever, Haylee. He's drawing you in deeper and deeper by deliberately not rushing you."

She shook her head at me. "Thanks. I was hoping you would be excited for me. I guess I expected too much."

"I'm just saying—"

"No, you're not just saying," she snapped back at me. "You won't let me be happy, will you?" Her eyes brightened with a new suspicion. "You haven't found anyone to replace Matt. Are you jealous? Is that it?"

"No. Of course not. I'm just concerned."

"Well, you know I need you now to help with Mother," she said.

She was right. Despite how Mother had loosened her grip on us, she was still quite involved with everything we did, especially if it was during the evening. She insisted on first meeting whoever would drive us anywhere and, if not, then taking us there herself and picking us up. And we always had to have a specific destination and purpose. Just hanging out at a mall, like our friends often did, was forbidden. She told us it was the easiest way to get into trouble.

"You must always have a purpose for whatever you do," she explained. "Loitering, no matter how innocent it might seem, usually leads to something you later regret. There's truth in some old sayings, like 'Idle hands are the devil's workshop.'"

Now I asked Haylee, "How can I help?"

"I actually got this idea from her. Remember when she was first going with Darren Paul and she volunteered to have him take us to a movie theater when they went to dinner and then pick us up?"

"Yes."

"So that's it. We'll ask her to take us to a movie near where Anthony and I plan to rendezvous. We'll both go into the movie theater when she drops us off. You'll stay, of course, and watch the film. That way, if she asks questions about the movie, we'll have the right answers. Okay?"

"I don't know," I said. "This is still making me nervous."

She looked away, as though she had to count to ten before looking back at me.

"You won't even tell me his full name, Haylee," I added.

"I'll tell you that night. I promise."

"When is this supposed to happen?"

"Next Saturday night," she said.

It was Sunday now. I would have almost a week to toss and turn over it.

"Well? Are you going to help me or not? I think you'd have to agree that I've changed, become more mature, and I regret what I did with Jimmy that night, right? Right?" she hammered.

"Yes, Haylee, right, right."

Could it all have been happening for the reason

I feared, just to get me to cooperate with her Internet romance? What choice did I have now? I had let it go on this long without telling Mother.

"Okay, then. We'll wait until Tuesday to mention it. I'll read up on the film that's there, and we'll talk about it in front of her, so she'll believe we're excited about seeing it. You'd better be just as enthusiastic."

My sister Haylee, I thought, still the conniver, the planner, cleverly constructing her deceit. I would never be as good at it, and maybe in this world that was a weakness after all.

"What's the movie?"

"I don't know. I haven't looked yet. It's going to be at the Riverside."

"The Riverside? That's almost fifteen miles away, Haylee. We've never been to that theater."

"It has to be that one."

"Why? Can't he meet you somewhere closer? We don't know that area."

"Stop asking so many questions," she snapped. "There are reasons. We've been talking about it for weeks. You'll have to trust me about it. You do this for me, and I'll owe you big-time."

"I don't need you to owe me, Haylee."

"Whatever," she said. "Will you do it? Or will you keep asking questions until I go on social security?"

"Very funny. Maybe I should go with you for this first meeting with him," I suggested.

She pulled back as if I had thrown hot soup in her face and grimaced. "Go with me? Meet him together so he can compare us?"

"No."

"You never stop competing, do you?" she said. "Despite all Mother has done to prevent it, you're always competing."

"It has nothing to do with competition, Haylee. I just thought you might feel safer if I was there with you. If it was the other way around, I'd want you there."

"Well, it's not the other way around, and I don't have any of those fears. I feel safe. Don't you think I know when I know someone well enough to trust him? Are you the only one who can tell what's important about people?"

"Of course not."

"So?"

"Okay, okay," I said. "You'll go yourself, but you'd better tell me his full name."

"I said I would."

I thought a moment and then sat on her bed, hoping we could have one of the close sister-sister talks we used to have. Maybe I could still get her to change her mind.

"Tell me more about him. Why doesn't he have a girlfriend at his age?" I asked, stressing "age." "Has he been married? Does he have children?"

"No, he's never been married, and of course he

has no children. He's had girlfriends on and off, but he says most of the girls he's met turned out to be immature, self-absorbed airheads. He was devoted to his parents. When his father became seriously arthritic, he had to do more to take care of them and their property. He gave up a lot in his own social life to do it. That should tell you a lot about him."

"Maybe he's too introverted for a social life. That's a big reason for people who live on the Internet."

She stared at me.

I shrugged. "It's true."

"Maybe he is," she said, "and maybe I bring him out of it. Maybe I'm the first girl who has. What's wrong with that? Well?"

"Nothing."

"Matt was like that when you first met him, wasn't he? He wouldn't even join a sports team. Did I tell you to avoid him because he was so unsocial?"

"No, but we know how that turned out."

She shook her head.

"Okay, okay," I said. "Where did he grow up?"

"Here in Pennsylvania. He wants to travel more now, but he's still keeping up the family property and hasn't decided whether to sell it or not. He's someone who cares about memories. He's not flighty." She smiled. "In the beginning, it was hard to get him to joke and not be serious, but I finally got him to lighten up."

"It doesn't bother him that you're in high school?"

"He couldn't believe it when I told him my age. He said he's met many girls our age but none as centered as I am. I gave Mother credit for that," she said. "He was surprised she had done so well, considering how we were practically fatherless."

"Are you expecting to introduce him to her one day?" I asked, wondering just how much of a dreamer she was. If she did, it would be like setting off a nuclear warhead in front of Mother for sure.

"We'll see. The way you do something like this is to take baby steps, Kaylee. It's just as I advise girls in our class. Don't overly commit to anyone too soon. See? I know what I'm doing. But," she added, "I know I'm going to want to commit to him. I have this deep feeling for him. He makes me feel better about myself, too."

I nodded. I couldn't change her mind. Maybe it was better to just let her work through it, make discoveries herself, and eventually tell me I had been right. I heard a beep on her computer.

"That's Anthony," she said. "Do you mind?"

I looked at the screen and then at her and got up. "Be sure, Haylee. Please. That's all I ask."

"I will," she said. She gave me a quick hug and kissed my cheek.

I smiled.

"'Night, Kaylee-Haylee. And thanks."

"'Night, Haylee-Kaylee."

I left her room. She closed the door softly behind me.

When I entered my room, I realized I had been holding my breath and fighting with myself not to just run down the stairs and unload it all in Mother's lap. If something happened, she would blame me. Envisioning that nightmare actually made me tremble. I had a very hard time falling asleep. Once or twice, I sat up and thought that maybe the way to handle this was to go to Daddy. He could keep a secret. I'd go along with it and have him follow Haylee and then confront this Anthony whoever and bring it to a quick end.

But of course, she would know I had done that. The choice was simple: take the risk and let her dabble in this fantasy romance, finally realizing how foolish it was, or lose her as a sister forever. There was no doubt about that.

I fell back on my pillow and looked up at the dark ceiling, hoping that sleep would take me out of this quandary. It was almost morning when it finally did. The contrast between myself and Haylee at breakfast was very sharp. I could barely keep my eyes open and moved like a turtle. She was full of energy, seeming happier than ever, bouncing about the kitchen, doing this and that for Mother.

"Aren't you feeling well?" Mother asked me.

Haylee turned to me quickly, her eyes raging with fear and warning.

"I spent too much time studying," I said. "I'll be fine."

"And you?" she asked, turning to Haylee. "Did you study enough?"

"Oh, yes, Mother."

"I'm looking forward to you having very good grades. Everyone expects children of recent divorces to do poorly in school, but we're going to show them different, aren't we?"

"We are," Haylee said. "In fact, we plan to do better than last quarter, don't we, Kaylee?"

I looked up at Mother. I knew Haylee was barely doing as well as she had done last quarter. "Yes," I said.

Mother looked pleased.

Haylee gave me another dirty look full of warnings, and then we finished breakfast and got ready to be driven to school.

"You can't look like that, morning or afternoon or night," Haylee lectured when we went upstairs to get ready. "If Mother thinks you're worrying about something, she'll drill us like a CIA interrogator, and I don't have confidence that you'll hold up your side of it."

"I can't help what I can't help," I said.

"Well, try harder, especially at Tuesday's dinner," she ordered.

I calmed myself by convincing myself that she would back out on her own when it came right down to doing it. She was putting up this brave front just for me, and before Saturday, she would tell me something had happened between her and this Anthony whoever and that whatever had happened had ended it. But on the contrary, she came into my room every night to tell me how excited she was and how excited he was. On Friday, she revealed some more details.

"The reason we're meeting where we're meeting is that it's very close to his home," she said.

"His home? You're going to a strange man's house?"

"He's not a strange man! How many times do I have to tell you that? We've been talking to each other for weeks and weeks. I know far more about him than I do about boys I've known for years. He's very open and honest about himself. The truth is that I haven't been half as honest and revealing with him as I should be."

"What does that mean?"

"It means, like I said, I'm taking baby steps. So don't worry."

"Where is his house?"

"I don't know exactly. It's more like a farm."

"Haylee, this is so crazy, but okay, okay," I said quickly, seeing the expression on her face start to change into rage. "If you're still this confident on Saturday, we'll follow your plan."

"Good," she said. She smiled. "And thank you, Kaylee. I mean it."

"Right," I said, not knowing how I would get through the day.

I had been hoping that when Mother heard about the theater, she would tell us to go somewhere closer, and that might scare off or at least discourage Anthony, but Haylee's luck was riding a high wave. Mother had a new date with Laura Demarco's brother, Simon Adams, who had lost his wife in a terrible car accident a year and a half ago. Apparently, he was finally ready to date, and Mother was to be his first since the tragedy. Laura had introduced them, and he had asked Mother to dinner. As it turned out, the restaurant he had chosen was only five miles from the movie theater to which Haylee had insisted we go.

When Mother first told us about her dinner date, I was hoping that would mean she would either tell Haylee we had to go the following weekend and that Anthony would be upset or get cold feet and that would be that, but instead, Mother thought it was all serendipity, "as if planned by the angel who protected us."

Haylee chose one of our sexiest outfits to wear

to the movies, a black sweetheart-neckline romper outfit. It made us look more busty and left little to the imagination about our rear ends, because it was tighter on us now than it had been when Mother first bought it. I thought that would send a signal and Mother would start her usual cross-examination, so I didn't object, but she almost didn't notice at all. She was engrossed in what she was going to wear herself on this very special date, a date she said carried more responsibility.

"Simon is very vulnerable and sensitive now," she told us. "I have to be more of a therapist than a date. I've got to dress a little more conservatively than usual. When you meet him, be extra friendly."

"We will," Haylee promised.

"Yes," I said.

I waited to see if she would add anything, squint at what we were wearing, and send us back upstairs to change into something more appropriate for a night at the movies, but she seemed to look right through us. She didn't even notice the extra makeup Haylee had put on and insisted I copy, the mascara and the glossy lipstick. I did it all willingly, expecting to send signals.

Oh, Mother, I cried inside myself, *can't you see what's happening? Can't you look at us the way you used to when we were younger and see every one of our thoughts? Are you so blinded by your own little romances?*

It was discouraging. If Mother wasn't so involved with her own life, she surely would have picked up on what Haylee was doing or at least sensed that it wasn't something she'd like her to do. As Haylee successfully slipped past Mother's usual scrutiny, I realized there was nothing more that I could do to stop it.

We were both surprised when Simon Adams arrived to take Mother to dinner and us to the movies. He was a good two or three inches shorter than she was and not very good-looking. His nose was too big, and his eyes were a dull brown, with drooping eyelids that made him appear sleepy. He wore a dark gray jacket and a black tie, but he looked like he could use a haircut. His dark brown hair was a little unruly at the sides and fell lazily over his forehead. He knew about us being identical twins and pleased Mother by immediately saying that he had never seen a pair of twins so indistinguishable.

Before we left, Haylee leaned close to me to whisper, "This is Mother's charity date, for sure. He looks like one of Snow White's Seven Dwarfs."

"Charity date?"

"She wants to help him get back into the world and will prove to her friends and especially Daddy that she is strong enough to do it. She wants to make the point that if she was suffering, she wouldn't be able to help someone else."

I looked at her askance. "How do you know all this?"

"You just don't know her as well as I do, Kaylee. You just don't," she said.

Maybe she was right. She was the one capable of fooling her all the time, especially now.

Simon Adams was polite and did seem more like someone indebted to Mother than someone romancing her, and all during the ride to the movie theater, she talked to him the way someone would talk to a child, comparing her divorce with his tragedy to justify her advice.

"To me, Mason Fitzgerald is the same as dead. I wouldn't have resented receiving sympathy cards the day the divorce was finalized. He's as good as dead to my girls," she emphasized.

Simon nodded after everything she said, never challenging or questioning anything. Haylee kept poking me and smiling. The only good thing about it was that it was keeping me from thinking about what she and I were about to do. A cold chill passed through me when Simon pulled up to the movie theater. For a few seconds, I nearly cried out and confessed. *Mother, we're lying. We're not really going to the movies. Haylee's going to sneak off and meet a man much older whom she met on the Internet!*

The words flew through my brain and smashed against a wall of hesitation and fear, crumbling before they could get anywhere near my tongue.

Haylee opened the door quickly.

"We'll be right here waiting for you," Mother said. "Don't go wandering about if we're a little late. I'm not familiar with this area."

"We won't," Haylee said. "Thank you, Mr. Adams."

"You're more than welcome," he said. "Enjoy the movie. I've been thinking about seeing it, too."

"Maybe Mother will want to see it. We'll tell you how it is," she said.

Mother turned quickly to look at her, and I hoped she was angry at Haylee for saying that, but she surprised me. She smiled.

"C'mon, Kaylee," Haylee said. "We don't want to miss the start of the film."

She got out. I didn't move. *Stop her!* I heard myself screaming inside my head.

"Kaylee!" she cried from the sidewalk.

"Thank you, Mr. Adams," I said, and got out of the car.

Haylee grabbed my hand, as though she was afraid I might change my mind. Mother smiled at us. Haylee turned and, still holding my hand, started for the ticket booth. Mother, as Haylee had anticipated, did not let Mr. Adams drive off until she saw us enter the movie theater.

"It's a little early yet," Haylee said as soon as we had entered. "Let's find seats in the back. You want some popcorn?"

"No." I was too nervous even to chew gum.

"I do," she said, and stopped at the counter to buy a bucket of popcorn and some soda.

"Aren't you nervous about this?" I asked her as we entered theater number one.

"No," she said. "I'm tired of telling you that I'm not afraid and want to see him very much, so stop asking."

We sat in the aisle seat and the next seat in the very last row. The movie trailers had started. Haylee began eating her popcorn. I felt numb. She looked at her watch and ate some more popcorn. She offered it to me, but I shook my head. I was watching the screen, but I wasn't hearing or seeing anything. I kept waiting for her to hand me the popcorn and get up to go. The fact that she was waiting so long gave me new hope. Maybe, just maybe, she was changing her mind, or, even more possible, this rendezvous was never really arranged, but she didn't want to tell me yet. In her mind, she might still think I was somehow envious. My hope began to build, and then—

"Oooh," Haylee suddenly moaned. She shoved the bucket of popcorn at me and crouched, holding her stomach.

"What?"

"Oh, no," she said. She got up and hurried out of the theater. I followed her into the women's lavatory. She went right to a stall.

"What is it?"

I heard her start to throw up.

"Haylee?" I tried opening the stall door, but she had locked it. "Let me in."

She groaned, heaved, and moaned. After another minute, she unlocked the stall door. She was sitting on the closed toilet seat, holding her head as she bent over and rocked.

"What happened? What's wrong?"

"Something upset my stomach. Maybe it's the flu. Mindy Lorner came down with it today, just like that. One minute, she was talking to me on the phone, and then suddenly, she said, 'I've got to go to the bathroom and throw up.' She didn't even hang up. You're probably going to get it soon, too. You were talking to her on Friday when I was."

"I'll call Mother," I said.

"No! Not yet," she said. "I'll get through it, but you have to do something for me."

"What?"

"You have to go meet Anthony and tell him what happened."

"What?"

"Please. You have to."

"Can't you just email him or call him?"

"No. He'll think I've been playing with him, and he'll never contact me again. He'll believe you if you go there. Just tell him and come back," she said. "I'll be fine until you do. We don't want to ruin Mother's night, too, anyway, right?"

"I don't know, Haylee. You're sick. He's not the most important thing right now."

"He is to me. You can do this for me, can't you? Please. I'll be all right. I'm close to the bathroom. Kaylee!" She screamed at my hesitation. "I'm sick. Do this for me!"

The whole thing was making my head spin. "How did you get sick so fast?"

"I just told you. It's the flu," she said, took deep gasps, and lowered her head. "Are you going or not? Are you going to make me do it? I'll be throwing up in the street."

"Where do I have to go?"

"Go left out of the movie theater and then two blocks to a coffee shop on the corner of Barnes and Hyman Way. The shop isn't open, but he'll be standing in front of it. He'll be wearing a red cap. Just go. Tell him what's happened, and come back. If I can't stand it anymore, we'll call Mother, but I'd like to try to give her time to have her dinner date."

"What if something more happens to you while I'm gone?"

"Nothing more will happen. I'm not dying. I'm just sick to my stomach. Go!" she said, and closed the stall door.

I stood there for a moment.

"Barnes and Hyman Way," she said behind the closed door. "Left and two blocks. Red cap." She groaned.

"This is crazy, Haylee."

"You're making me feel sicker," she said. "Well?"

"You didn't tell me his full name like you promised you would."

"Oh, what's the difference now?"

"It matters to me," I said.

"His name is Anthony Cooper. Just tell him, and come right back. Hurry."

"Okay. I still don't like this, but I'll do it."

"If I'm not in my seat when you get back, I'm in here. Go. The faster you get it over with, the better it will be. For both of us."

I turned, hesitated at the door, and then left and walked out of the theater, pausing at the ticket booth to tell the woman working there that I had to go somewhere but would then return. She shrugged, clearly indicating that she couldn't care less. I turned to the left and started walking quickly.

The evening had gotten cooler. I was sorry now that I had agreed to wear this outfit. The sky was mostly overcast, and the streets were not well lit. I hugged myself and hurried along. My intention was to say everything in practically one breath and then turn and run back to the movie theater. I wondered why this Anthony would have chosen this address to meet Haylee. Why couldn't he have simply come to the movie theater at a set time? Maybe she had never told him our plan, I thought, so he didn't know about the movie theater. She had said she wasn't as forthcoming about herself as he had been about himself. He might not know how tightly Mother kept her eyes on our every move. Haylee probably had him believing she could do whatever she wished. If he knew the truth, he would have ended it for sure. Well, now he would, so maybe this would turn out to be the best thing.

There was little traffic on these streets, and houses were gradually fewer and fewer as I went along. Some of the houses looked run-down and deserted, windows dark, lawns overgrown or spotted with dead grass. I was hoping it would be busier when I reached the corner where the coffee shop was. When I started to approach it, I realized it wasn't just closed up for the day; it was out of business. The sign in front was hanging from one side, and the words on the front window were faded.

I didn't see anyone standing there. Maybe he had decided not to show. Perhaps he had realized what he was getting himself into and finally was frightened. He probably worried that this rendezvous was a trap set by the police, that Mother had found out about his Internet seduction of Haylee and had reported it. There was lots of that going on. If that was his decision, it was more than fine with me. I could turn around and hurry back to tell Haylee that he was a no-show and she should consider it all over.

I crossed the street and slowly approached the closed-down coffee shop. A car came along, slowed down, and then kept going. It looked like two men with a woman in the rear. It disappeared around a corner, and the street was quiet again. I was surprised at how little traffic there was. I was getting more frightened standing here. *I'll count to ten*, I thought, *and then I'll turn and run back*.

"One . . ."

"Hi, Kaylee," I heard, and spun around to see him standing there, red cap and all. He had his hands in his pockets. "I was afraid you weren't coming."

Why did he call me Kaylee, not Haylee?

The streetlight was very dim here, but I could see him clearly enough when he stepped out of the shadows. He wasn't much taller than us, but his shoulders looked wider than they did in his Internet picture. His hair looked thinner, too. I thought there was even a little gray in it, and it suddenly occurred to me that he had posted a picture of himself when he was younger. He was even older than I had first thought. Haylee would have been disappointed. He was far from good-looking in person. Too bad she was too sick to come. This would surely have brought it to an end.

"You mean Haylee. She's not coming," I said. "I'm sorry. I am her sister, Kaylee. Haylee has taken ill, maybe a stomach flu. I came to tell you she won't be here."

He laughed and stepped closer. "You never stop with the jokes. That's what I like about you. You have a sense of humor that runs on nuclear energy or something."

I didn't like his voice. He spoke in a loud whisper, raspy, like someone who had just had the front of his neck in someone else's tight grip. He didn't have a beard or a mustache, but he looked like he hadn't shaved for days. The granite-like stubble was all over his neck and Adam's apple. He was wearing a jean jacket, a black T-shirt, and a pair of creased black pants with dirty white running shoes and no socks.

I took a step back. I paused and thought. It couldn't be that she had used my name and not her own and not even told him that she had a twin, an identical twin, could it?

"You know about Haylee and me being identical twins, right?"

He threw his head back and laughed harder. "This is great," he said. "I knew you would come up with something special for our first real meet. My van's parked right there." He nodded to his right.

It was in the shadows, but I thought it was dark brown and looked a little beat-up.

"I was going to bring you flowers or somethin',

but then I thought I should just have something special for you at the house."

I stared at him. He wasn't believing me. He refused to believe that I wasn't Haylee. This was very confusing. My heart was starting to pound under my breast like some jungle drum transmitting warnings. I stepped farther back and shook my head.

"This is not a funny story. This is true. I am Kaylee, but I'm not the one who's been talking with you over the Internet. That's Haylee. She's back at the movie theater. Our mother dropped us off there. Haylee got sick in the theater before she could leave and wanted me to tell you in person that she can't be here. Our mother is coming to pick us up after the movie, but if Haylee gets sicker, we'll call her to come earlier. I'm sorry," I said. "That's the truth. I've got to get back to her now."

I started to walk around him, but he reached out and seized my left arm.

"You are a very entertaining young woman," he said. "We're going to the farm now, just as we planned. I've cleaned things up for you."

"No," I said, tugging my arm away. "I told you. I'm not the one who was supposed to meet you. That's Haylee. I am Kaylee, but you have us confused."

"Enough," he said, losing his smile, his voice more raspy, almost inaudible. "You carry things too far sometimes. I meant to tell you that. Let's go."

"I've got to get back to my sister. If you touch me again, I'll tell the police."

My voice was shaking now, trembling along with the rest of me. When I looked around, I saw how deserted the street was. There were no houses with lights on, no stores, and, right now, no traffic. Where were we?

I started to walk away.

"Stop it, Kaylee," he called after me.

I walked faster, my legs trembling so hard that I thought I might trip before I reached the curb.

I never did.

He was behind me quickly, and I felt a tremendous shock to the back of my neck.

Then everything went black.

14

I thought I was in a pitch-dark room and then realized there was a hood over my head and my face. I was seated in a chair, a rocking chair, and there was a chain attached to a bracelet fastened around my left ankle. The hood smelled of grease and gasoline. It made me cough, and then I was in the middle of a scream when the hood was pulled off and I was looking at Haylee's Anthony.

He stood under the dull light of a hanging black metal fixture shaped like an upside-down bowl. His shoulders were hunched up, and he was smiling so hard that his lips lost color and resembled rubber bands ready to snap. Now he was wearing light blue pajamas and a pair of black slippers. He was cradling a cat with eyes that looked tinted yellow. It gazed at me with interest and was so still that I thought it might be a stuffed toy cat.

"Hello there," Anthony said. "I'm sorry about how I got you here, but that didn't really hurt, did it? It was more like anesthesia."

"Where am I? Why have you done this to me?"

"Oh, where are my manners? This is Mr. Moccasin," Anthony said. "See his paws, the white lines? They look like moccasins, don't they? Mr. Moccasin, meet Kaylee."

I didn't think I could breathe, much less speak. I realized I was no longer wearing my own clothes, including my bra and panties. I was wearing a thick, faded pink flannel nightgown. I gazed around. It looked like I was in a basement. The only two windows were boarded up on the outside. The walls were paneled in a light wood, and in front of me was an old, heavy-cushioned brown sofa, a small coffee table, and a bookcase on the wall behind the sofa. Besides books, there were little figurines and toys on the shelves, model planes, and model cars. Next to the shelves were drawings pinned to the walls. They looked like the drawings a child would make of mountains and trees. In all of them, there was a cat.

The concrete floor was partially covered with thick, tightly woven area rugs. To my right was a metal sink, a counter with a linoleum surface, and a small two-door refrigerator. Beside that was an oven and a range with a teapot and a pan. There was a cabinet above this, and beside it was a closet without any doors. The shelves were stocked with boxes of cereal, rice, cans of soup, and other things, and on the counter was a bread box.

I turned slightly to look at the rest of the basement. Just behind me was an area meant to be a bedroom. There was a double bed with a metal headboard, two large light blue pillows, and a light blue comforter. There were two wooden side tables and a dark wood dresser with half a dozen drawers. There was also another area rug. A second similar hanging fixture lit that area. On my left was a table with four chairs, and on that wall was a framed poster that read "Home is where the heart is." The words in script were inside the outline of a heart, like what you'd find on greeting cards.

On my immediate left in front of me was a small room with a toilet, a bathtub, and a sink. There was no door. It, too, had an area rug, but this one looked softer.

"I know it's not much," Anthony said, watching me. "But I have many good memories. I moved down here when I was only twelve. I told some of my friends at school, and they were jealous that I had my own place. I couldn't sneak anyone in, though. Anyone who came here had to go through the house and get past my mother and father, but you know a lot about all that. I did show you some pictures, but it's different when you actually see it, right?"

He put the cat down, and it walked slowly around his legs, rubbing its body against him but keeping its gaze on me.

"He'll get to know you, and then he'll be your buddy, too," Anthony said. "Cats are naturally suspicious and afraid. That's why we have that expression, *scaredy-cat*. Right? Thanks to Mr. Moccasin, there's never been a mouse or a rat down here."

I moved my leg and looked at where the chain ran back to the wall. It was attached to an embedded metal clamp. I quickly saw that the chain had enough length for me to reach anywhere, including the bathroom. I was a prisoner.

I was swallowing back my utter hysteria, but I felt as if a hole were forming in my chest. I realized I needed to take deep breaths to keep from fainting.

"You hungry?" he asked. "I can make us some tea, and we can have homemade biscuits with jam. I made the biscuits myself, and not from some ready mix. My mother taught me how to cook and bake when I first moved down here. She said, 'You've got to learn how to be independent, Junior.' She always called me Junior because my father's name was Anthony, too. She could have called me Tony. Dad didn't want anyone to call him Tony, but my mother thought it would make my father angry if she called me that. 'Junior,' she said, 'you're going to be on your own sooner or later in this life. We're not going to be around forever.'

"They were both much older than most parents when they had me. My mom was forty-one, and my dad was fifty-two. My mother was surprised she got pregnant. She thought it was change of life and didn't realize I was inside her until the sixth month." He smiled. "I started knocking on the door. But you know all that. Anyway, I've been making my own food for years. It's not easy going to restaurants when you're alone, you know. People look at you, and you can see it on their faces, the question: 'Why is he alone? Where's his girlfriend, or even a boyfriend?' It's always easier to eat at home. But I told you all that. I just like telling you things face-to-face now. It's better this way, right?"

"You're going to get into very big trouble for this," I said, gasping after every word. "My sister will tell my mother, and they'll have the police here soon. I was supposed to go right back to the movie theater and get her because she got sick."

"Still talking about a sister, and a twin to boot," he said, smiling. "How come you never mentioned her before? You can make up stories faster than . . . than Scheherazade. You know her, the *One Thousand and One Nights*. It's on the bookshelf there. I've got lots for you to read. I promise. You'll never be bored down here, even though there's no television. My mother wouldn't let me have a television, and I haven't bothered hooking one up. I've got lots of good board games and magazines. You'll take care of this place, too, clean it daily. It gets dusty somehow. After tonight, you'll wash all the dishes and keep the kitchen as spotless as I do, okay? You said that would be okay because you were so used to doing it at home. There's a vacuum cleaner in the corner there," he said, nodding to my left. "And in the bathroom, in the cabinet, you'll find dust cloths and cleaning fluids, polish. The bathroom has to be extra clean. This is a germ-free place, and we don't want that to change, right? Oh," he added, moving toward the cabinet over the counter, "I got a dozen bottles of that vitamin you said your mother gives you every morning. So," he said, pausing to rub his palms, "I'll fix us some tea, okay?"

He went to the stove. The cat suddenly ran past me.

"I'm sorry about the chains," he said as he filled the teapot with water. "I don't expect you'll have to have them forever, of course. Someday in the not-so-distant future, you'll never want to leave." He turned and smiled at me. "I know. I could tell from all you told me about yourself. I told you what I missed and needed, and you told me much of the same. We were meant to be, huh? The Internet is the new Cupid. There are companies that advertise matchmaking. We just bypassed them."

He opened the stove and took out a platter of biscuits.

"These are perfect. Look at that," he said, holding them up for me to see. "I know you're not much of a cook, but no worries. I'm a great cook. Before they died, I used to cook dinner for my parents, and I always made them lunch before I left for work. On weekends, I'd do a breakfast to die for, things like French toast, pancakes, poached eggs. You name it, I did it, and I'll do it for you."

He put the biscuits on the counter and waggled his right forefinger at me.

"You're a bit spoiled, I know. You admitted it. I don't think you should have taken advantage of your mother like that," he added with a scowl. "Mothers are precious. Until . . . they're not," he said, and laughed. "What do you prefer? Strawberry, orange, or grape jam?"

He looked at me and waited.

I slowly rose. "Where are my clothes?"

"Those? They're going to that bin for poor people. I'm surprised your mother let you wear something like that. You told me she was once a fashion model."

"Why are you doing this?"

"I'm hungry," he said. "I didn't eat much tonight. I was so excited about meeting you."

"Why are you keeping me here?"

"Why? Because we should be together. You said that many times, Kaylee."

"No, I never did. That was my sister, Haylee. I'm not Haylee!"

He shook his head. "We're not going to get along if you keep that up," he said.

"This is kidnapping. You can go to jail for a long time for doing this."

He thought for a moment and then shook his head. "No. Think of it more as convincing. *Kidnapping* is not the right way to put it. That sounds like I'm doing it for ransom or something."

The teapot whistled.

"You like milk in your tea or honey? Or both?"

"I don't want any tea. I want my clothes, and I want you to unchain me."

"Why are you acting like this? I've done nothing you didn't expect."

"Nothing I didn't expect? How can you say that?"

He shrugged. "We agreed we should live together. You said your mother would stop us from even just seeing each other and that you wanted me to come up with a way to make it possible. Voilà!" he said, holding out his arms. "It's all right. You have nothing to fear. I don't intend to hurt you in any way. I'm going to make you happy, not sad. Oh, for a little while, you might be sad, but that goes away. Believe me, I know.

"I'll tell you a secret. There are lots of secrets I've never told you, but we'll have plenty of time for them. But here's one. Sometimes, when my mother thought I was being nasty or disrespectful, she would lock me in down here. One time, she did that for almost ten days. She cried about it afterward, and I didn't hate her for it. I got over it. So don't worry. You'll get over it," he said, putting biscuits on a tray.

"Listen to me, please. I do have a twin sister. I'm not the one who was on the Internet with you. I am Kaylee Fitzgerald, and my sister is Haylee Fitzgerald. Our address is Seventeen Wildwood Drive in Ridgeway. It's about fifteen miles from here. If you go there tomorrow, you'll see my sister. I'll make sure either she steps out with me or we look out a window together. Okay? Please! Okay?"

He ignored me and continued preparing two cups of tea and fixing a biscuit with jelly.

"Let's sit at the table," he said, nodding toward it. He carried the tea and biscuits there on the tray and sat. "C'mon. It will be the first time we've sat and eaten something together. Very special. Everything we do for the first time together will be very special."

"I want my clothes back!" I cried.

"I have clothes for you, lots of clothes. I kept all my mother's things, and most of them will fit with some adjustments. My mother taught me how to do all that, too. She said, 'Junior, these skills will come in handy while you're still a bachelor.' I have a sewing machine. 'Course, she thought I was going to marry a woman just like her. You're far from just like her, from what you've told me. C'mon, the tea's getting cold."

"I want you to take off this chain," I said. He was speaking so softly that I thought I could get him to do it if I demanded it. "Now!"

He held the teacup and stared at me. "You're not behaving at all like we planned, Kaylee. We planned this for a long time. You were the one who wanted to do it sooner, so I don't know why you're acting like this. Were you lying to me all that time? That would be very bad. Lying is a kind of rot, my mother would say. The more you lie, the more your brain rots."

"I'm not the one who was on the Internet with you! That was my sister, Haylee!" I screamed. I stood up and shouted for help at the top of my voice.

He calmly drank his tea. "No one can hear that," he said. "The closest neighbor is a mile away. We're on my family farm, not that we did much farming. We had a little vegetable garden and always had chickens for the eggs. When I was much younger, we had a milk cow, but it got to be too much for my father, so he sold it. Once it was a real farm, though. My great-grandfather and my grandfather ran it. We grew corn here. Everybody's dead. I'm the last of the Cabots. Until, of course, we have children. We'll keep going until we have a boy, right? You agreed."

I sat again, covered my face with my hands, and began to sob.

"Hey. Is this one of your performances? You told me how good you are at fooling people. C'mon, stop it now, and have some tea and a biscuit. What do you think about our first breakfast being French toast? I'll bring down clothes for you in the morning.

"Oh," he continued, "there's a brand-new toothbrush in there and toothpaste, lots of soap and shampoo, plenty of clean towels and washcloths, too. You sure you won't have any tea and biscuits?"

I kept my hands over my face but then stopped sobbing and looked at my wrist. He had taken my watch, so I had no idea how much time had gone by since I'd first met him on the corner, but surely by now Haylee had realized something was wrong. Maybe the movie wasn't over and Mother and Simon Adams hadn't come to pick us up yet. What I feared was that Haylee would believe I wanted to stay with Anthony, that I liked talking to him or something, and she wouldn't panic about my not returning. She would probably be more angry than afraid for me. And I had no idea if she had gotten sicker and was spending all this time in the bathroom.

She couldn't have told him she was me. He just had the two names confused. They were too similar. That had happened many times in our lives.

"Well," Anthony said, "I've got to get to bed. I'm getting up especially early just to make you breakfast before I go to work. I don't always work on Saturdays, but the schedule just fell that way this weekend. I promise, I won't work next weekend. When I'm home, I'll spend all my time with you."

I watched him carry the tea and biscuits back to the counter. He washed his cup and wrapped the biscuits that remained as carefully as if they were precious jewelry. He placed them in the bread box and then, after washing down the counter, turned back to me.

"See how nicely I keep everything, how clean and organized? You have to do the same, Kaylee. Or you might lose some privileges."

"What privileges?" I screamed. "You have me chained to a wall. You've abducted me. Someone surely saw you."

"No, I was careful about that. They could turn that corner into a cemetery these days. And I really wish you would stop saying words like *kidnapped* and *abducted*. We're not starting out on the right foot, as my father used to say. He said it about everything. It was as if you had a definite wrong foot and should be hopping all the time to avoid using it. Your mother ever say that to you? Now that you're here, I'm looking forward to hearing lots more about your mother. I understood why you hated her comparing you with her all the time. Parents sometimes won't let their children be their own person. My father was more like that to me than my mother, but she would often do and say similar things. You know, when you think about all we have to tell each other about ourselves, it will easily take years."

He smiled.

"But neither of us is going anywhere soon," he added.

I felt trapped in a nightmare. No matter how hard I shook myself, I couldn't wake up. When he walked toward me, I cringed.

The cat reappeared and sniffed around the floor beneath the counter.

"Mr. Moccasin will find any crumbs, only I don't drop any. My mother would have killed me. She was one of those people who believe cleanliness is next to godliness. She'd be down here every night inspecting. I had to change my bedsheets twice a week and do my own laundry. Actually, I was doing it when I was eight. She would say, 'Junior, good habits die hard, so form them first.' Wise old lady, my mother. That's why I want you to form good habits here first."

"Please," I said. "Let me go. I won't tell anyone what you did. I'll just go home. Please."

"Just go home? This is your home, Kaylee. That was the plan."

"I'm not the one you were talking to all the time. You have me mixed up with my sister, Haylee. I swear."

His face seemed to transform into cold, dark marble, the shadows closing around him. "I didn't mind this in the beginning," he said in a firm, hard voice. "I can play games as well as anyone, but you're carrying it too far and too long. I want you to stop it."

After a long moment, he smiled again, and his whole body seemed to soften. He stepped out of the shadows.

"Let's not make our first night together an unhappy one, Kaylee. We've been looking forward to this for so long."

I shook my head. "You were talking to my sister, Haylee. I swear," I said, sucking back my tears but finding it harder to breathe.

"You're as pretty in person as you are in pictures, Kaylee. When I was undressing you, I thought you were the most beautiful young woman I'd ever seen. You look like that Venus statue. I was very careful when I touched you. I didn't even want to leave fingerprints. That's how gentle I was and always will be."

I felt my throat close up, and my chest felt so heavy I thought I would smother my own heart. All I could do was sob.

He stood there watching me and then reached out and grasped my hair. I screamed in pain.

"There's only one thing to do with you when you're like this. That's put you to bed. Stand up," he ordered. "Stand!"

I rose, trembling. He seized my upper left arm and turned me toward the bed. He pulled back the comforter and plumped the pillow.

"Get in," he said. "Go on."

I shook my head, but he seized my arm again, and I got onto the bed. He pressed on my shoulders so I would lie back, and then he pulled the comforter up to my shoulders and tucked it under me.

"Comfy?" he asked. "It's a brand-new mattress, just for you, and for me, of course. But not tonight. Tonight I want you just to enjoy our hideaway by yourself. It is a hideaway. In here, we can hide away from all that's unpleasant in the world. We don't have to watch the news together or read the papers. This will be our world. We'll create our own news. Later on, when you're ready, we'll go out, and we'll enjoy the farm. We'll have picnics and go on hikes and do everything you dreamed we would, but we have to have our . . . what should I call it . . . what did you call it? Yes, I remember, our honeymoon. This will be our honeymoon."

The cat leaped onto the bed

"Oh, look, Mr. Moccasin likes you. He's going to sleep beside you. That's something. He doesn't particularly like anyone else. He won't let anyone but me pet him or hold him, but I bet he will let you soon."

He reached up and pulled the cord on the light above us, and half the basement went dark. Then he leaned over and kissed me on the cheek.

"Sleep tight, and don't let the bedbugs bite. I'm joking," he added quickly. "There are no bedbugs, not in this farmhouse. When you wake up, I'll be right here making your French toast. You did say it was one of your favorites, Kaylee. I have home-grown maple syrup for us and farm-fresh eggs to use. You told me what coffee you like, and I have it. Oh, and there's fresh fruit, too. We'll eat healthy."

He petted Mr. Moccasin, looked at me, and smiled.

"I don't remember ever being happier than I am at this moment. Thank you, Kaylee, for bringing us together," he said.

He walked to the doorway, reaching up to pull the cord of the second light on his way. It dropped darkness all around me. There was the tiniest sliver of light coming through a board over one of the windows. I heard the door close and his footsteps on a stairway. After that, I could hear him walking above me. It was the only sound, except for the pounding of my heart resonating in my ears. And then I heard his cat start to purr.

I sat up and reached down to the ankle bracelet.

I couldn't find where it was fastened. It was impossible to slip it off. I tried and tried, until it was too painful, and then I began to sob again. The cat came closer, and I felt its head against my right hand. I had the mad idea that it was trying to comfort me. I slipped off the bed and in the darkness made my way to the door through which he had gone. It wasn't locked. That gave me a surge of hope. I opened it slowly. The light seeping under the door above the stairway lit it enough. I started for the first step, moving slowly so that the chain wouldn't make too much noise, but I was able to get only to the middle of the stairway before I ran out of chain. When it tightened, a wave of panic deep and wide came over me. I sat on a step and gasped. My gasps turned into sobs. If I could only see a clock, I would know how much longer it would be before Haylee would realize I was not coming back and tell Mother.

What would she tell Mother? I wondered as I envisioned that moment. She would have to tell her all about her Internet romance. Mother would be furious, but she would put all that aside and concentrate on getting me back. They would go right to the police, and Haylee would tell them everything she knew about Anthony. It might take a while, but they'd find me tonight, I thought. I must stay calm.

After a few more deep breaths, I picked up the chain so it wouldn't rattle on the steps and went back into the basement. I thought it best to close the door again so he wouldn't know I had tried to get out this way. Then I moved slowly back to the bed. I didn't see Mr. Moccasin on the bed. I sat on it and then just lay back without pulling the comforter over me.

Moments later, the door was thrown open. Anthony reached up for the light cord. He stood there, holding Mr. Moccasin. I had not seen the cat go out with me, and I must have locked him between the basement and the upstairs.

"Why did you let Mr. Moccasin out, Kaylee? He's here for you."

I didn't answer.

"You weren't trying to leave, were you? I was about to go to sleep." He put the cat down. "When I heard Mr. Moccasin crying at the door, I realized I had made a terrible mistake. I shouldn't have left you alone in a new place. I don't know what's wrong with me, not realizing that. I'm sorry. Of course I'll sleep with you. You'll find that I'm a little shy. That comes from living alone so long, but I promise, I'll get over it. I know you're not shy."

He reached up and pulled the light cord again. Silhouetted by the tiny bead of light through the boarded window, he walked toward the bed slowly. I cringed. He fixed the comforter again and got into the bed beside me. I felt him reach for my hand.

"Feeling better?" he asked.

"What time is it?" I asked, hoping he would just tell me, hoping he wouldn't realize why I was asking.

"Oh, it's late," he said. "Way past my bedtime."

"How late?"

"It's close to midnight, Kaylee," he said.

"No!" I cried. That was two hours past when the movie ended.

"Oh, don't worry. I'll be fine," he said. "I have an easy day tomorrow. Just think about French toast." He brought my hand to his lips and kissed it. "I can't believe we really made it happen," he said.

I wanted to pass out, but I couldn't close my eyes or slow my heart from pounding. He drew closer to me and kissed my cheek.

"I'll go slowly," he said. "I promise. It's when you rush things in this world that you make mistakes, even in love." He leaned back on his pillow. "Good night again," he said. "Don't worry now. I'm here. Nothing will ever harm you."

The cat was on the bed again. It settled in between us and almost immediately began purring.

"Hear him? Mr. Moccasin is here with us. All the world is good."

I lay there with my eyes open, listening, praying for the sound of the police pounding on his front door. To keep myself from screaming, I imagined Haylee crying and saying she was sorry she had started all this and how it was all her fault.

It's all right, Haylee, I thought, confident that she heard me, that our telepathy was working and that it would bring her to me. We'd hug and kiss and vow never to be cross with each other ever again. *I forgive you, Haylee.* Oh, how happy she would be, almost as happy as I was. I would even help her with Mother. *She didn't mean to cause all this turmoil, Mother,* I would tell her. *She was experimenting, but she's sorry. Please don't be angry at her, because you will be angry at me, too, for not warning you. You remember? Everything one of us does the other does, too. Every pain I feel, Haylee feels, and vice versa.* We would both be crying by now. Mother would be shaking her head, and then she would hug us both to her just the way she used to hug us, and all would be forgiven.

My vision of this was so vivid I could feel myself smiling and my body calming. I could feel myself rising off the bed and floating safely above all this. It was only a matter of time.

Just a little longer, and the darkness would be peeled away to reveal smiling, grateful faces. We would all be safe again, wouldn't we? I was convincing myself of this when something occurred to me. It rang like an alarm in my head. Haylee had told me that his name was Anthony Cooper, but he had said his family name was Cabot. Did she just say any name that came into her head to get me to go, or did he tell her the wrong name deliberately? Why would he tell her the wrong name if he thought she really wanted to be with him?

It didn't matter, I told myself, and relaxed again. He had been on the Internet with her. She would only have to show the police, and they would track him. They could do that. If they could find hackers, they could find him. Haylee would give them all that was needed. She couldn't do it fast enough. She was actually just as frightened at this moment as I was. Almost all our lives, we were happy together and sad together at the same time. We shared everything. This would be no different.

In fact, I thought I could hear her whispering now, just the way she and I used to whisper when we were little girls, sharing a room and a bed, and Mother had turned off the lights after saying good night. It was so important that we comforted each other, especially when we were in the darkness.

"Kaylee-Haylee," my sister would say.

"Haylee-Kaylee," I would reply.

And we would both fearlessly embrace sleep at almost the exact same moment and see each other in our dreams.

Now turn the page for a sneak peek at

BROKEN
GLASS

Book Two in the Mirror Sisters series

By V.C. Andrews®

Available Spring 2017 from Pocket Books

Prologue

My mother's dinner date, Simon Adams, stepped out of his car right after Mother started screaming at me. She had practically leaped out of his car before he came to a stop when she saw me standing there alone. I had waited as long as I could to walk out so that I would be one of the last to leave the theater. No matter what my twin sister, Kaylee, thought or what anyone else might think, I couldn't be exactly sure what would happen after she had left to, as she believed, meet my Internet lover and make my excuses. I had a pretty good idea, though. Otherwise, I wouldn't have sent her.

The movie theater we had gone to as part of my plan was one of the few that weren't in a mall these days. Most of the stores on the street in this neighborhood were already closed by the time the movie ended. People scattered quickly to their cars in the nearby parking lot or on the street, as if they were worried that it was a dangerous area. Maybe it was. I had no idea what it was like. We had never gone to a movie or shopped here.

"What are you saying? What are you saying?"

Mother shouted after I began to explain Kaylee's absence. "What do you mean, she's not back? Back from where?"

I started to cry, always a good touch. Mother hated to see either of us cry, always expecting that the other twin would soon start, too.

"Where is she?" she demanded, stamping her foot.

"I don't know," I said. I kept my head down.

Only hours ago, Mother had seen Kaylee and me go into this movie theater, and now, when they drove up, she saw only me come out and stand there looking frantically in both directions. I was sure that my face was full of enough concern and panic to impress her. I had planned how I should look and sound. When you think ahead to what a scene will be like, it's like rehearsing for a play. Mother wasn't doing or saying anything I hadn't expected when she heard what I had said. I could have written her dialogue, too.

I glanced behind me and saw the cashier, a woman in her sixties, and an usher who was no more than twenty, gaping at us. We were probably better drama than the movie now playing. Some other people walking near the theater paused on the sidewalk to look our way.

"How could you not know where your sister is? Maybe she's still in the theater. Is she in the bathroom?"

"She's not in the movie theater bathroom."

"You checked?"

"I didn't have to, Mother." I took a deep breath. "Kaylee left to meet a man very soon after we got here, but she was supposed to return before the movie ended," I blurted, and continued to cry.

"What? What man?"

"What's going on?" Simon asked, hurrying up to us. He looked at the theater entrance. "Where's the other one?"

The other one? He wasn't sure which twin I was. I nearly stopped crying and started laughing.

Mother looked at him, annoyed, but ignored him. I couldn't blame her. He wasn't exactly what anyone would describe as a strong-looking, take-charge man. He had lost his wife just more than a year ago in a traffic accident, and either the tragedy had made him meek and helpless or he had always been that way. I had referred to him as Mother's "charity date," because she had told us she was his first date since his wife's death and she was going to take extra care with him. I had told Kaylee that it seemed more like emotional and psychological therapy than a romantic evening. Mother had gone out with at least half a dozen men since her and our father's divorce, but none of them were good enough for her to continue dating. I doubted Simon would be.

"What's the matter? What's going on? Where is she?" Simon asked again.

"I'm trying to find out. She says Kaylee left the theater to meet a man," Mother told him.

"A man? Who? What man? Did you know about this?" He grimaced, making it seem like this was her fault.

"Of course not! That's what Haylee was about to explain." She grabbed my shoulders and shook me. "Talk, and stop crying," she said.

I took a deep breath, wiped away my tears, and began with "I'm sorry, Mother. I should have told you, but Kaylee would have hated me."

"What are you saying? What should you have told me? Hated you for what?"

"Kaylee was carrying on an Internet relationship with some older man. I told her she could get into big trouble, that men like that are dangerous, but she insisted he was all right. According to her, they were talking almost every night for the last month or so on her computer, and she liked him very much."

Mother stared at me in disbelief. She shook her head as if my words were shower water caught in her ears. Every part of her face seemed to be in motion as she reluctantly digested what I was saying.

"She met someone on the Internet? These things can be bad," Simon said. "So where is she?" he asked me, stepping forward, suddenly more aggressive and manly. "As you can see, your mother and I are very concerned."

He was showing off for Mother, I thought, and smiled to myself. He was still pathetic.

"Talk," Mother ordered. "Quickly."

"She said she and this man finally decided to meet, but she knew you would never approve of it, so she came up with this idea to pretend we were excited about the movie," I said, the words rushing out of my mouth like water bursting through a dam.

"Pretend?"

"It was her plan. After you took us here, she left the theater to meet him somewhere. She promised to be back way before the movie ended. Right up to the time she left, I tried to talk her out of it, but she wouldn't listen."

Mother looked up and down the street. "Which way did she go? What else do you know?"

"That's all I know. I went along with it because she said she would hate me forever if I didn't. I couldn't have her hate me. I couldn't. We're too much a part of each other. I've been so worried." I started to cry again.

"We'd better call the police," Simon said. Mother didn't respond. She stood there almost frozen in place now. I was afraid to look at her. Sometimes I thought she could read my thoughts. "I'll call the police," he said.

He took out his cell phone and stepped back toward the car.

"How could you let her do this? How could you keep it a secret from me? Didn't we talk about when either of you should come to me to tell me about the other getting involved with someone dangerous?"

I nodded but kept my head lowered. "She made me promise," I said. "I couldn't betray her."

"Her? What about betraying me?"

I raised my head. "I told her that, Mother, but she said we needed to believe in each other if we were to be forever special sisters. I was afraid of breaking her heart."

"This is so unlike her," Mother mumbled.

I looked up at her quickly. "It's unlike me, too."

"Yes," she said, nodding. "Yes."

Simon returned. "They're on their way," he said. "You don't even know which direction she took?"

"She just told me they were meeting at a place he had decided on because it was close enough for her to go to his house and get back before the movie ended," I replied, wiping the tears from my cheeks.

"To his house?" Mother said, the words taking a strong grip on her worst fears. "She went to his house, to a strange man's house?"

"That was the plan she told me they had made."

"Does he live alone? How old is he? How did she meet him on the Internet?"

"I don't know any of that. She wouldn't tell me that much," I said.

"Men who do this sort of thing know how to find vulnerable young girls," Simon said, nodding like some sort of expert on teenage girls. I looked at him with an expression that shouted, *Shut up. You're making it all worse*. I guess I was effective. He backed up a step.

"How long has this been going on?" Mother asked.

"Maybe six weeks, maybe seven."

"And you both kept this a secret from me that long?" she asked, her face now a portrait of disbelief. She looked like a little girl who had just learned that Santa Claus was not real, something I'd never believed. Most of life was a fairy tale. Who needed to add a fat man with a beard?

"You were . . ." I looked at Simon. "Busy with your own problems. At least, that was what Kaylee thought, and I did, too. She convinced me that you'd only start worrying so much about us that you would be unhappy again, and we were both upset at how horribly Daddy had treated you. She said that would all be my fault if I told."

"This is so unlike them," Mother told Simon. "They've never done anything even remotely like this."

"Do you know his name?" Simon asked.

"She told me a name, but I'm not sure it's his real name."

"What does that mean?" Mother demanded.

"He could have made up a name," Simon said, "or your sister could have made one up. Right?" he asked, as if I was now the expert.

"Maybe," I said. I turned back to Mother. "He might be right. I don't know if she wanted to tell me his real name, so she could have made it up just to shut me up because I kept asking her."

"What name did she tell you?" Simon demanded.

"Bob Brukowski," I said. "It never sounded real to me."

"I can't believe this," Mother said, shaking her head. "This is not happening. It's not happening." She put her hands over her ears, as if she could simply block out reality and return to our perfect world by closing and opening her eyes.

"It's a problem all over the country now," Simon said. "Young girls being exploited through computers."

She pulled her hands from her ears as if they had been glued to them and made two fists. "It's not a problem for me! Or it shouldn't be," Mother said. The veins in her neck looked like they might burst. Her eyes were bulging, and her nostrils widened.

He pressed his thin lips together and nodded. A police patrol car pulled up to the curb, and two officers got out quickly. Simon turned and hurried to them, happy, I thought, to get away from her. He explained what was happening, and the officers came over to us.

"Mrs. Fitzgerald," the taller one said, "I'm Officer Donald, and this is Officer Monday." He took out a small notepad. "What's your daughter's name and age?"

"Her name is Kaylee Blossom Fitzgerald, and she's sixteen. This is her sister, Haylee. They are identical twins, so you don't need a photograph to recognize her," Mother said. "Or you can take one of Haylee with your cell phone. There's not an iota of difference between them, down to how many freckles they each have. They wear their hair the same way, and they are dressed in the same outfit, the same color tonight. They sound the same, too."

Both policemen looked at me, astounded. The shorter one almost smiled at how ridiculous Mother sounded.

"Haylee," Officer Donald said, "why don't you tell us everything that went on between your sister and this man. Don't leave out anything because you think it's too small a detail or not important, okay?"

"Okay."

"Why don't you sit in our car?" he said, stepping to the side so I could do that.

When I started for it, Mother began to follow, but Officer Monday asked her to wait. I knew why. They thought I wouldn't say things in front of my mother. Simon took her hand. When I looked back at them, their roles appeared reversed. She suddenly looked like his charity date. How ironic, I thought. He was the one using psychology on her. It brought a smile to my face that I wiped away instantly as I got into the patrol car. The two officers got in and turned to me.

"So," Officer Donald began, "tell us how this all started and everything you know about the man. We understand your sister told you his name?"

"She told me a name, but as I told my mother, I

don't know if that's his real name. It was Bob Bru-kowski."

"Did he send her a picture of himself over the Internet?" Officer Monday asked.

"I guess he did, but I never saw anything on her computer. I know only what she told me about him. Maybe she thought if she showed me his picture, I'd tell her he was too old for her or some-thing."

"So tonight you just know she was meeting this Bob Brukowski somewhere in this neighborhood, and the man was definitely older, and he was going to take her to his house?"

"Yes. She made a big deal about him being an older man and not a high school student. She was bragging about how much a mature man was at-tracted to her. I kept warning her, but she wouldn't listen."

"So what happened tonight?" Officer Monday asked. "How was this all set up?

"She had a plan," I began, and started to de-scribe it. As I spoke, the belief that Kaylee really would never be back grew stronger and stronger. I half wished that I had been there hiding in the shadows and watching, like the director of a movie, when Kaylee had met him.

"Does your sister have a cell phone?" Officer Donald asked.

"Yes, we both do, but we didn't take our cell phones tonight." I shrugged. "I guess I should have made sure we did. I was just so nervous about it all that I forgot."

"I've got a teenage sister," Officer Monday said. "Like all her friends, she won't even go to the bathroom without her cell phone."

"We were too involved in my sister's plan. We didn't think," I said more emphatically, and threw in a few well-placed sobs.

I knew now that it was over, that it was happening. I should have felt more remorse, but a little voice inside me asked, *If your twin sister is gone, are you still a twin? Won't people stop mixing you up? Won't you become your own person finally?*

I had to be careful not to let the policemen see my smile. They wouldn't understand.

No one who didn't know us and how our mother had brought us up would understand.

Even with all the warnings and the bad stories out there, whose mother wouldn't have a hard time believing her daughter would do something like this? Everybody thinks they're raising angels. I saw that from the way my friends' parents talked about them. How could their daughter be doing something as terrible as carrying on a romance over the Internet with an older man? And right under their noses? This was all especially true for our mother.

Simon Adams was right. Examples of this were

constantly on the news. But our mother was always very confident that we wouldn't do anything that was so forbidden or stupid. In her eyes, we were such goody-goodies. I hated it when she bragged about us and people looked at us as if we were right out of a fairy tale about two identical princesses, Cinderella clones without so much as a blemish on our behavior or complexions.

When we were little, both of us used to believe that we hadn't been born. We had descended from a cloud of angels and just floated into the delivery room. The stork really did bring us.

Mother had no idea how many things we had done recently that she wouldn't approve of, mainly things I had done and that my dear abused sister would have to go along with or at least keep secret. Kaylee would have been suspected less. After all, no matter what Mother told other people or even what she told us, I knew in my heart that she favored Kaylee, despite her effort not to show any bias.

However, I had no doubt that her favoring Kaylee gave her nightmares. What if I could tell that she did favor one of us over the other? How horrible for her. All our lives, she had made an effort to treat us equally and to think of us as halves of the same perfect image of a daughter she had created. The smallest thing that could make one of us different from the other was vigorously avoided. She was adamant about not loving one of us more than the other.

No one suffered more under this rule than Daddy, who sometimes accidentally and sometimes deliberately tried to treat us as individuals. I pretended to be as upset about that as Mother wanted us to be, but in my secret chest of feelings and thoughts, shut away from Mother's eyes, I was pleased, even when he did something for Kaylee that I might envy. At least, in his thinking, there was a difference, and we weren't simply duplicates or clones, as some of Mother's friends occasionally referred to us. It always annoyed me that she didn't mind when people said that. I did. Who wanted to be a clone?

I was tired of hearing how we were monozygotic twins developed from a single egg-and-sperm combination that splits a few days after conception, that our DNA originated from the same source. I didn't even have my own DNA like most everyone else. I'd had to share everything with Kaylee from the moment I was conceived. Mother often told people that we even took up and used equal space in her womb and that everything that had come from her to nourish us was consumed in "perfectly equal amounts." I never knew how she could know that, but she would say, "How else would they be so identical at birth?"

According to Mother's logic and beliefs, how could I ever even exist without Kaylee? Our hearts beat with the same rhythm. We took the same number of breaths each day. If one of us sneezed, the other soon would, and that was true for every yawn, every ache, and every shiver. We were the mirror sisters; we lived in each other's reflected image.

Well, maybe not now; maybe finally not now. I could walk away, and Kaylee would be stuck in the glass looking out. "Come back, come help me!" she would cry.

"Help yourself," I would say. "I did. That's why you're trapped in the mirror."

Another patrol car arrived on the scene, and before we went home, we all drove around, Mother in one car and me in the other, searching for any sign of Kaylee. Sometimes the police would stop to ask a pedestrian if they had seen a girl who looked like me, and I would have to make myself more visible. On one stop, I actually stepped out of the vehicle.

"She's wearing the same clothes," they told potential witnesses. They all shook their heads and apologized for not having seen Kaylee. One elderly man looked as if he might have something to tell them. He was studying me so closely. My heart stopped in anticipation, but after another moment, he shook his head and told us his eyesight wasn't what it used to be.

It seemed like we drove for hours. At one point, we passed the closed-down coffee shop, and I held my breath again. Was Kaylee still there, maybe lying on the side of the road? How would I react to that? It was deserted. There was no one on the sidewalks, no one in the street, and no one sitting in any vehicle. Even the shadows looked lonely.

Simon was left behind to wait at the movie theater in case Kaylee showed up there. When we returned and saw him alone looking confused and helpless, Mother grew more frantic. She wanted more police, more cars, and insisted that they knock on every door within a mile of the movie theater.

"He wanted Kaylee to meet him nearby," she said. "He has to live somewhere in this neighborhood."

They tried to reason with her, but she spun around on Officer Donald, the first policeman who had arrived at the movie theater, and screamed, "Do something! Don't you understand? My daughter's been kidnapped, or she would have been back by now. She's being held somewhere against her will or taken so far away we'll never find her. Every minute that passes is terrible!"

"You've got to stay calm, Mrs. Fitzgerald," he told her, and looked to me to do something to help her, but I just lowered my head and looked as powerless as they felt.

A policewoman arrived, probably called in by one of the other cops to help handle Mother. To be truthful, even I was shocked at how she was behaving. Kaylee and I had seen her upset many times, of course. She used to pound on herself so hard when she screamed that she would have black-and-blue marks, but she was lashing out now and throwing her arms about so wildly that I thought they would fly off her body. She began screaming at me again for keeping Kaylee's secret.

"Don't you understand that you've been kidnapped, too?" she cried.

Everyone looked at her oddly then. I had to explain what she meant, how she believed that nothing ever happened to either of us without it happening to the other. Of course, it still made no sense to the police. It was then that I told Officer Donald about Daddy and how Mother's insisting on both of us being treated exactly the same had led to their divorce.

"It became too much for my father," I said.

They looked sympathetic. They didn't have to say it. I could see it in their faces. It would have been too much for them, too, maybe for anyone.

Officer Monday returned to the patrol car to see about getting in touch with Daddy.

At one point, Mother broke away and started running up the street, insisting that the search go on and that we shouldn't wait for additional assistance. We were wasting precious time. She had started toward someone's front door when they rushed up to her. She was pulling her own hair and had to be forcibly restrained. The policewoman, Officer Denker, asked me for the name of our doctor.

"She has to be calmed down. She could hurt herself," she told me.

I gave her Dr. Bloom's name. Simon Adams

stood off to the side now, looking too stunned to speak. I laughed to myself, imagining that he was thinking, *What did I get myself into?* I was surprised when Officer Monday came over to tell me they had located my father and that he was going to meet us at our house. I had thought for sure he was on some business trip miles and miles away.

We hadn't had much contact with Daddy after the divorce had been finalized. Mother seemed to keep up with the news about him and his girlfriend. Apparently, from the last we were told, that romance had ended, and Daddy was living in an apartment by himself. We were supposed to go to dinner with him a week from now. Almost daily, Mother warned us that he would try to play on our sympathies.

"Poor him," she said. "He's alone again. But he's always been alone. He prefers it, no matter what he tells you. He's too selfish to be with anyone," she assured us. "Don't waste a tear on him."

Mother had practically passed out by this time, emotionally exhausted. Officer Denker was with her in the rear of one of the patrol cars, commiserating. I had heard her tell Mother that she, too, had a teenage daughter. Mother looked at her and shook her head. Kaylee wasn't simply a teenage daughter. Didn't she understand? Kaylee and I were special.

Naturally, all the police activity in front of the movie theater had drawn a crowd. Anyone who showed up was questioned, but as I had expected and hoped, no one knew anything. Two plain-clothes detectives arrived, and I had to tell my story again. A Lieutenant Cowan asked the questions. He was older than Detective Simpson, who I didn't think was much older than a college student. He was by far better-looking, with sort of rusty light brown hair and greenish-brown eyes. Every time I answered one of Lieutenant Cowan's questions, I looked at Detective Simpson to see his reaction. I even smiled at him once.

"We'll need your sister's computer," Lieutenant Cowan said. "Your dad's on his way, and your family doctor is coming to your home for your mother, so why don't you ride back with us and keep telling us all you know, all you remember?"

"I'd better ask my mother," I said, looking at the patrol car she was in.

"Better to just come along," Lieutenant Cowan said. "She's calmed a bit. They'll start for your house."

I shrugged and followed them to their car. Before I got in, I looked at Simon Adams. He appeared to be totally lost now and not sure if he should remain waiting.

"My mother's date doesn't know anything," I told Detective Simpson. "Maybe you should tell him to go home. My father's coming," I added, implying that this might be a problem.

He looked at Simon and then at Lieutenant Cowan, who nodded.

"Get his name, address, and contact numbers," he told him.

I got into the backseat.

The patrol car taking my mother started to leave. When it pulled in front of us, I saw her spin around in the backseat and press her face to the rear window, looking as if she was clawing at it with her hands while she screamed. I looked down quickly, mostly embarrassed by her. Everyone would see how pathetic she was, but the good news was that most would feel sorry for me, I thought. Not only had I probably lost my sister, my other half, but my mother wouldn't be the same.

They'd be right about that. Mother was going to need me. She'd need me twice as much as she ever had, especially with Daddy not living with us. I'd have to be more like Kaylee sometimes, but that was all right, because I could go right back to being myself. Without Kaylee there, I could do many new things, and everything I wore would seem to be mine alone. There would be no one imitating me, duplicating me.